The Lonely Lord
by
Audrey Harrison
Published by Audrey Harrison

© Copyright 2019 Audrey Harrison

*

This book was proof read by Joan Kelley. Read more about Joan at the end of this story, but if you need her, you may reach her at oh1kelley@gmail.com.

1

This book is dedicated to Kerry Ollerton

Kerry, I wish you could have understood and accepted how much everyone thought of you, because to us you were very special. Hope you are at peace now, you funny, lovely girl.

Prologue

Bath 1816

I am alone. Completely alone. Strange really when a ballroom full of people surround me, but the reality is that I've always been alone. I've never actually felt as if I belonged to anyone. Perhaps there is one person who cares, but that's probably more to do with familial obligation than any real fondness for me, so I've never actually opened myself to him completely. What would be the point when his affection is not really mine?

It hurts. Sometimes at least. Most of the time I can ignore the emptiness that swirls inside me, but occasionally it hits me when I least expect it. It is like a dark mass pressing on my insides and nothing shakes it off. I've learned to function whilst trying to ignore it, but it is always there — this feeling of being different from everyone else, being separate, a watcher of what is happening in the world, rather than someone who takes part in life.

I don't know how to be a part of society. Not finding it easy to express what or how I'm feeling, I usually utter the wrong words and alienate myself further. How do people communicate with ease? Make others laugh? Stir sympathy? I just blunder my way through. It is sometimes easier to remain aloof. I often wonder if I am a misfit in society, or if I am truly devoid of any emotion beyond feeling adrift. I don't honestly know the answer.

I wonder if all these people have a clue how any of us really feel. Do they ever stop to think, perhaps behind that smile, those meaningless words we all utter, that there might be hurt or pain or loneliness? Probably not. I idly wonder why as the dance continues in its long-ways set. This ball is a prime example of my life: meeting people, but not really touching them in any meaningful way. In most ballrooms, all anyone is interested in is how can their friends and acquaintances benefit them? If the answer is naught, then they look beyond them in the hope of seeing a better option in their wake. Even I have been considered as a possibility by some of the scheming mamas who frequent the chaperone seats. Very soon, though, they move onto an easier target, someone who does not blunder or insult almost every time they speak.

No one has ever been close enough to really get to know me. Perhaps I have nothing of value to offer, and I'm the last person to realise it.

I have sometimes wondered what it would be like to be connected to someone. To care unconditionally and wholly for that one person. Is it fulfilling, or does it bring pain of its own? If I wanted to care about another person, I would have to release the tight hold I have on my inner self. That would risk the emptiness I feel taking over and destroying me completely, and I cannot let that happen. I am tense inside, but at least there is some sort of control.

I doubt I will ever have the courage to find out if there is anything to feel other than emptiness, so, I'll never find out if there is an alternative state to mine. If that is the case, my constant thoughts are little more than wasted energy. I know this, but sometimes the musings intrude in a way that I cannot so easily dismiss.

A sigh escapes. I will have to force myself to rally soon. I need to join this noise, this chatter, and pretend I'm one of them. To pretend I'm a member of the ton, the top of Society. In some respects I am already at the top; my ancestry is of the highest calibre, but that is part of the

6

problem. I am expected to marry before my next birthday; my father's will dictates it.

Do I want to? No.

Do I have a choice? No.

Do I pity the person eventually persuaded to attach themselves to me? Yes. Utterly.

Chapter 1

Bath 1816

Anthony Russell, Earl of Lever, entered the large townhouse on Great Pulteney Street. He'd worked his thoroughbred, Belle, to her limits, cantering over some of the seven hills that surrounded the limestone spa town. He'd needed the fast physical exercise to free him of the after-effects of the previous evening. It had been yet another tedious foray into Bath society. He wasn't sure how much more of it he could take. The thought of remaining for goodness knew how many more days darkened his brow even more than normal as he entered the marble-tiled hallway of his rented home. After he was helped out of his greatcoat, he nodded to his footman once he was free of the heavy garment. The servant stepped back to almost disappear into the fabric of the building, as good staff were wont to do.

Striding into the large square dining room on the ground floor of the many-floored townhouse, Anthony acknowledged his grandfather who was seated at the round table in the centre of the room, finishing off a large plate of eggs, ham, and steak.

"Aren't you supposed to be eating something purging?" Anthony asked, helping himself to coffee from the long side table that was filled with numerous delights of breakfast fayre to tempt the two gentlemen of the house.

"The problem with food that does you good is that it tastes like sawdust or worse," Gabriel Bannerman, Anthony's maternal grandfather responded. He was a gentleman of more than sixty years, handsome and

9

distinguished looking, his features still firm, albeit showing signs of age. Salt and pepper streaks gave a hint of the dark mop of hair he'd had in his youth. He had the unlooked-for distinction of being Anthony's only full-blooded surviving relative on both his maternal and paternal sides of the family. Although Gabriel's grandson did have a stepfamily from his father's second marriage, neither of them dwelt on those relations if they could help it.

"As you have only looked at it before dismissing it, I'm surprised you can say what it tastes like with any authority," Anthony said, noticing an untouched mound of unappetising-looking Bath Oliver biscuits on one of the plates.

"They look like they taste vile," Gabriel countered.

Anthony seated himself opposite his grandfather. "If you no longer have faith in the healing qualities of Bath, does it mean you're ready to leave this God-forsaken place?"

"Are you not worried it would be of detriment to my health if we left?" Gabriel responded, a twinkle in his grey eyes. His grandson took after him in eye colour, but Anthony's very often looked like dark turbulent seas, whereas Gabriel's appeared paler and constantly sparkled with merriment.

"As you are unconcerned about your health, why should I try to convince you otherwise? It would likely result in your boxing my ears if I were foolish enough to attempt it," Anthony said with a shrug.

Gabriel chuckled. "I knew there was a reason why you are my favourite grandson."

"I'm your only grandson," Anthony pointed out.

"Be thankful you are not my least favourite then!" Gabriel became serious. "Are there no ladies to tempt you in this fine town?"

"This town is well beyond its best," Anthony responded. "As are most of the ladies residing in it."

"You have to marry before you reach thirty, or the main portion of your father's will is lost to you and goes to that brat of a brother of yours," Gabriel was open in his dislike of the late-Earl's second family. He'd married a silly, young chit and had produced two equally silly sons. Most presumed that the death of his daughter and jealousy over her replacement made Gabriel caustic towards Anthony's stepfamily, but anyone knowing his stepmother and half-brothers could understand his dislike.

"I'm fully aware of that fact, but there is time yet."

"Four months is hardly any time at all!" Gabriel expostulated fiercely.

"As I can hardly slow down the passage of time, it will have to be enough," Anthony responded, crossing his ankles, showing off his high-quality boots to their best, and putting the cup of coffee to his lips. This was a conversation they had several times each day, and it added to the tediousness of his situation.

"I suspect, as there is no one who has ever made you smile let alone light-hearted and besotted, I feel time is against you in finding a suitable lady who will set your heart alight," Gabriel said.

"Thankfully, those traits were not specified in the will. I need to find a wife; turning into a love-struck fool were not the words father used or one of the conditions he placed on me," Anthony pointed out.

"No. The least said about your father's terminology, the better," Gabriel said grimly. "Although to be fair to him, he probably knew that, without being pushed, you'd never marry," he acceded.

"He should have just given the money to Giles, if that was his intention," Anthony said. "As it is, Fanny is hoping I will not marry, so her son will have the biggest portion of the wealth, even though he won't have the title. You know what a fuss my stepmother makes when she does not get exactly what she wants. Perhaps it is easier to just give in to her wishes than bow to my father's terms. It is not as if he will ever know the outcome."

"I disliked your father, especially his brutish, idiotish ideas. He must have known it would split the family. You have to stand up to that foolish woman and marry before your birthday. Don't roll over and let Giles access money he isn't entitled to."

"Without funds, the title is worthless and without someone with money at the head of the family, the estates will fall quickly into disrepair. With Giles unable to inherit the entailed estate, just the unentailed money would go to him. Separating the wealth in such a way would be disastrous. My stepmother did her best to try to bankrupt father whilst he was alive. I have no objection to my brothers as such, but I refuse to let three hundred years of history be wasted because I cannot find a wife in a timely fashion. So as much as it galls me, I am looking to marry," Anthony admitted to his grandfather for the first time.

"I'm glad you are seeing sense, but by Gad! You sound a real cold fish!" Gabriel exclaimed.

"A suitable lady who is willing to attach herself to me will suffice enough to meet the ridiculous restrictions of the will. I am asking for nothing more," Anthony said with a slight shrug.

"With such a limited list of requirements, it must be easy to choose someone for a life-partner. I am surprised you are

12

still unwed. There must be a large number of eligible young women for you to consider."

"You would think so, wouldn't you? Unfortunately, the task seems beyond me," Anthony said with a grimace, for the first time allowing that finding a wife wasn't the easy task he was making it out to be. "I have yet to meet someone whom I could bear to face every day for the remainder of our lives."

"That's because deep down you are a romantic fool," Gabriel said with a grin at his grandson.

Anthony let out a derisive laugh. Any form of amusement was a rare sound where Anthony was concerned, and a laugh full of humour was even more scarce. "With comments like that, we should be looking at your mind, not your body, for what ails you. You are clearly deluded."

"It happens to the best of us," Gabriel prophesied.

"What? Losing our minds? Is there something in my family history I should be aware of?" Anthony taunted.

"Get away with you, you coxcomb! You know exactly to what I'm referring. I have a good mind to box your ears after all, impudent pup! Even the most heartless of people can fall in love when they least expect it. You might not be as immune as you think," Gabriel scolded.

Anthony smiled slightly. "I doubt that. When you stop being a romantic old fool, I will stop tormenting you."

"I never had you down as a liar. We both know full well you will plague me until my dying day!"

"Only if you're lucky," Anthony said. He was fond of his grandfather, despite them being strangers for the first part of his life. He thought his grandfather liked him, but there were often doubts that made Anthony question his relation's true feelings towards himself. Theirs wasn't a fawning relationship, but one of banter and teasing. It was

13

the closest thing to a loving family Anthony had ever experienced, and although sometimes he was suspicious of it, it was precious to him.

For Gabriel's part, he could never express his true feelings to his grandson. Without a doubt it would result in a withdrawal on Anthony's side. The boy had never received love from those around him, his mother dying when the child was still being wet-nursed by a tenant on the estate. When he'd returned to his family home, he was brought up in a cold, formal environment. Gabriel had not had any contact with Anthony until he was fifteen. Despairing at the clashes between the young man and his stepmother, the late Earl had contacted Gabriel, asking for his help.

A lesser person would have refused to come into their lives after such a long exclusion, but Gabriel had taken it as an opportunity he'd only been able to dream of: finally meeting his only grandson. With care and intuition, Gabriel had built a relationship with the aloof, detached child and had the reward of seeing a little thawing of his nature towards himself. Not enough that Gabriel didn't lament the difference his daughter would have made to the boy if she'd lived, but he'd learned a long time ago that repining over what was lost was of comfort to no one.

"Time for the parade around the Pump Room, I feel. I quite like taking the waters," Gabriel said, rising from his seat, his plate empty.

He could have gone to Brighton to take the sea air when his doctor advised a change of diet and scenery, but he had wanted Anthony to shine. In a location where the best of the *ton* would be staying, Anthony's idiosyncrasies would not show him in a favourable light, but in the town where women vastly outnumbered men, Gabriel was certain there would be more opportunities to find a good wife. It wasn't

14

only the previous Earl's will that made Gabriel hope to see his grandson settled. Anthony was reasonably rich without the extra legacy, maybe not to live as he could now, but he would by no means be destitute. Gabriel's motivation had more to do with the fact that he couldn't stand the thought of his grandson being left alone in the world without someone to love him when Gabriel eventually died.

Anthony groaned, putting down his coffee cup. "Lead me to my daily penance."

Gabriel chuckled. "You think every entertainment is a penance!"

"In this town especially," Anthony said, before joining his grandfather on the walk to the Pump Room.

*

Although Bath was in decline as a resort that the wealthy normally attended, there were still many people frequenting the place. The highest in society might have moved on to Brighton, but the new upcoming middle classes were quick to take their places. So, although not bustling with the finest titles in society, it was still a busy city.

No one with a title and fortune would necessarily seek out anyone from the growing middle classes — the ones who'd made their fortunes through trade and enterprise — but Gabriel was of the opinion that Anthony needed someone who was as far away from his father's ilk as he could find. He cursed his son-in-law to the devil almost every moment of every day for the damage he'd done to his own son.

Gabriel's family were well-to-do but not titled aristocracy, so there had been quite a commotion when his daughter, Eliza, had attracted the young Earl of Lever. It was only after the wedding that Gabriel had realised a controlling, vicious man lay underneath the polite exterior.

15

Understanding that his new father-in-law wouldn't stand for the ill-treatment of his daughter, even when married, the Earl had immediately cut-off contact and forbidden his wife to see her family ever again.

Gabriel and his wife had been banished from his daughter's marital home, and it had broken their hearts. It had been the last time he'd seen his darling Eliza, only reading of the birth of her son and then subsequently her death in the newspaper years later.

He'd been astonished when he had received notification that he was invited to the estate of the Earl of Lever for an extended stay, having accepted that he would never see his grandson. He'd grasped the unlooked-for opportunity and built a relationship with his only living relative, being a widower by the time the invitation was issued. He was thankful for every day of the last fourteen years he'd spent with Anthony, but now it was time to look to a future in which he wouldn't be in his grandson's life, and he was determined that the young man would not be left alone and unloved.

Entering into the busy Pump Room, Gabriel retrieved a glass of the warm, foul-smelling water and seated himself on a chair at the edge of the large space but one that was in clear view of the entrance.

"You're nothing but a nosey beak," Anthony muttered, standing grimly next to his relative, his hands behind his back, a firm frown marring his features.

"Society watching is one of the undervalued pastimes I enjoy. It gives an insight into people's lives that they wouldn't allow you to see when in conversation with you. It is fascinating to watch what an individual can inadvertently reveal about themselves."

"I'm not interested enough in anyone to waste my time on such a venture," Anthony admitted.

"You are missing out, my boy."

They were soon approached by some acquaintances of Gabriel. They'd been in Bath for barely four weeks. In that time Gabriel had gathered around him a large set of friends. Anthony had made no new acquaintances, as such, other than those his grandfather had made. The master of ceremonies had suggested he introduce some young ladies in order to expand Anthony's acquaintance when it was clear the eligible young man was not going to ask to be introduced to anyone himself. The master of ceremonies had acted mainly because of the words Gabriel had spoken quietly to the man as a result of Anthony not exerting himself. It still didn't result in anything beyond having the occasional dance, and even then it was usually as a result of his grandfather's instigation and cajoling.

Soon the men were chattering and laughing uproariously at some tale Gabriel was imparting. Anthony couldn't help but shake his head in wonderment; his grandfather knew how to keep an audience entertained. It came naturally to him. Anthony wondered, not for the first time, if they did indeed share any history, or if some mistake had been made about the family connection. Anthony didn't resemble his maternal side, apart from his dark hair and clear grey eyes, which weren't unique to their family. His facial features were very much of the aristocratic line he came from, sharp and angular. He was considered attractive, having an athletic build and being tall and muscular, but he would never be one of the main ringleaders of his peer group. His abrupt personality and awkwardness in many situations caused most in society to give him a wide berth. Anthony presumed his nature, as far as he knew, he took after his father's side. Cold and unfeeling, which even though he was rich and titled, was not an endearing quality.

The group eventually dispersed from around Gabriel, and the older man sat back with a contented sigh.

"Had enough adoration from your gaggle of gentlemen?" Anthony asked.

"There's nothing like a good laugh to set you up for the day," Gabriel admitted. "You should try it sometime."

Anthony rolled his eyes. "I admit, I almost smiled at the story about the grouse shoot."

Gabriel laughed. "I will get a chuckle out of you one of these days!"

Anthony grimaced at the comment, but was prevented from making a retort by the approach of a woman.

She was of middling height and still of a slim build although she was an older lady. Her features were such that she looked as if in her younger days she would have been considered a beauty. She was followed by a younger woman, who was hanging back a little. The elder person was wearing a slight frown when looking at Anthony's grandfather.

"Gabriel? It is you, isn't it?" the elder stranger asked.

Gabriel had been looking at Anthony and hadn't noticed the approach of the pair but turned when his name was called. He took only a moment before he stood quickly, holding out his hands in welcome.

"Patience Hancock! As I live and breathe! How the devil are you? I have not seen you in these last twenty years or more," Gabriel exclaimed.

Patience laughed at the welcome. "It is more than forty years, Gabriel."

"I am only thirty-one; it can't have been that long!" Gabriel responded with a smile.

18

"Still deluded, I see," Patience said fondly. "You are looking well."

"And so are you. You haven't changed a bit, Patience, still as beautiful as ever."

"I see your penchant for flummery has not yet left you," Patience responded, but she squeezed Gabriel's hands, which had grasped her own once he'd recognised her. She was an elegant woman, her figure not having spread as the years had passed. Her hair was completely grey, mostly hidden under a cotton-frilled cap, but her warm brown eyes danced with pleasure at seeing her old friend.

Gabriel turned to Anthony. "Let me introduce you to the woman who rejected me and broke my heart in the process. Patience, this is my grandson, Anthony Russell, the Earl of Lever. Anthony this is Mrs Patience Hancock, the love of my life."

"Ignore him, my Lord. His wife was the love of his life. I was a fleeting infatuation. I am pleased to make your acquaintance. Please allow me to introduce you to my granddaughter, Mrs Julia Price."

The younger woman moved forward when being introduced and curtsied. She was an attractive woman, not beautiful but pleasing, with pale skin and rich chestnut hair. She was of middling height with a slim figure; her eyes were a warm brown and smiled at the pair. "It's very nice to meet you both."

"What are you doing here, Patience?" Gabriel asked.

"My great-grandson, Julia's boy, is taking the waters. He has been unwell these last few months, and so we decided a trip here might be of benefit," Patience explained.

"I'm sorry to hear that," Gabriel sympathised. "I hope he will rally soon."

"I am sure he will. Grandmother was being over-cautious," Julia said with a fond smile at her grandparent.

"Can't be too careful where the child is concerned. My Miles is one of the two most important people to me. Whatever medical care he needs, he will have. He is the most delightful child, a perfect grandchild," Patience said firmly.

"A few weeks in the outdoors will return him to health. He does not need the dubious merits of the baths or the waters," Julia continued.

"Where is the boy now?" Gabriel asked.

"Gone with his nanny to obtain tickets to watch the balloon flight on Friday."

"Are you all going?" Gabriel asked.

"Oh yes! Miles is insisting on it," Patience said.

"In that case, let's make a party of it," Gabriel said. "We can bring a picnic and get a prime spot."

"What a good idea," Patience smiled with approval.

"Anthony will buy our tickets and arrange the food for us all," Gabriel said, glancing at his grandson and almost laughing at the look of astonishment on Anthony's face. "His carriage will collect you on Friday. What is your address?"

"We're staying in Henrietta Street," Patience answered.

"We can walk. It is hardly any distance and would inconvenience his Lordship," Julia said quickly. Having noticed the expressions flitting across Anthony's face, she was under no illusion that he didn't want to be a member of their party. It wasn't a surprise really; he hardly knew them and a Lord in his prime was hardly likely to want to attach himself to two women and a child whom he didn't know.

"Not at all! Anthony will oblige; won't you, boy?" Gabriel insisted, enjoying Anthony's consternation.

"Of course. It would be my pleasure," Anthony said grimly, leaving none of them in doubt that it would be anything but.

Chapter 2

Friday morning dawned without the downpour that Anthony had hoped for. Gabriel was ready in plenty of time for the trip, forgoing the usual morning expedition to the Pump Rooms.

"Who is this woman really?" Anthony asked as they climbed into the coach. Boxes had been attached to the back, containing food and drink capable of feeding many more than the five it was intended for.

"I was not funning. She broke my heart," Gabriel explained.

"But I thought you said you loved your wife."

"So formal, Anthony. That was your grandmother you're so coldly referring to. She might not have known you, but she would have loved you if she had," Gabriel said at Anthony's words. He received a nod of acknowledgement from his grandson. It was usually the closest thing Anthony ever did to apologising. "I did love dear Lizzy and will until I take my last breath, but the affection I felt for Patience was there before I met your grandmother," Gabriel explained. "In fact, if I had not been running from the pain of losing Patience, I would never have met my darling Lizzy and you wouldn't exist. You have a lot to thank her for."

Anthony raised his eyebrows, but said nothing.

"Patience chose her husband over me. We were both smitten, but she said Hancock was the more steadfast of us," Gabriel said.

"So much for your stories of deep and overwhelming love that women need to feel before they will commit. Steadfast

22

is not a quality you've ever mentioned before," Anthony couldn't help mocking.

"I was completely besotted with her, and because of that, I acted rashly. On many occasions I was naught but a jealous fop. She did not see what was driving my behaviour, and we parted acrimoniously when she accepted Hancock's offer over mine," Gabriel said wistfully. "When I met your grandmother, I'd learned a hard lesson. I was to be even more in love with her, but I acted more sensibly, letting her see I was worthy of her. I kept the smitten fool at bay until we were married."

"The poor woman," Anthony said.

"Don't mock what you did not see," Gabriel said, his tone sharper than usual. "I loved that woman until her illness took her away from me. I don't fear my own passing because I know she will be waiting for me. My commitment goes beyond the 'til death do us part' vow. For me, even her departure from this life was not enough to separate us from each other. I carry her around with me each and every day and will do until I breathe my last."

Anthony paused. The words had been said with a passion he rarely saw in Gabriel. The man was usually all laughter and funning, never serious. He realised he'd upset him with his dismissive words. Although not one to bother with his actions or words upsetting anyone, he never wanted to intentionally upset his grandfather.

"I'm sorry," Anthony said sincerely, for once actually voicing an apology. "I know not everyone has my poor outlook on people and life in general."

"No. It would have been different if your mother had lived," Gabriel admitted. "Although your father would have probably beaten her spirit out of her the way he did with you."

23

"You are presuming a lot," Anthony said returning to his usual stiffness. "I am my father's son. I was brought up correctly as was right for my situation in life. There were no beatings involved."

"Sometimes a beating does not take the physical form you would suspect," Gabriel said quietly. He reached out and squeezed his grandson's arm, feeling it stiffen under the affectionate touch. That he was so unused to physical contact saddened Gabriel. "Let us put this melancholy aside. We are to have a good day with pleasant people."

Anthony didn't respond.

*

The carriage drew up outside number ten Henrietta Street. The three they were to collect were already standing on the pavement. The young boy waiting with the two women was hardly able to keep still in his excitement. Julia crouched down to whisper something in her son's ear when the carriage stopped and received a solemn nod of acknowledgement. The child received a peck on the cheek and a ruffle of his hair as Julia stood straight once more.

Anthony observed the action with a growing sense of foreboding. It was clear that the mother, as well as the grandmother, indulged the child, if he correctly interpreted the actions and words that had been said previously and what he'd just observed. It didn't bode well for the day for one who had little interest or experience with children.

The three were helped into the carriage, and Miles started to speak as soon as he'd entered the vehicle. "Thank you, my Lord, for allowing us to accompany you. Are you as excited as I am to see the balloons?"

Julia couldn't hide the grimace that flitted across her features. "That was an extra sentence you added on to our practiced greeting, Miles."

The young boy grinned at his mother before turning expectantly to their host.

Anthony looked at the child as if he'd never seen anything like him before. "I'm not particular about seeing balloons for entertainment. I am here to accompany my grandfather."

The cold tone didn't seem to faze the child. Instead, he turned to Gabriel. "Do you like balloons, Mr Bannerman?"

"I certainly do!" Gabriel responded. The differing tones of the two male occupants of the carriage couldn't have been more pronounced. "I hope you will explain fully about what is happening when they start. I don't want to miss a moment."

"Mama has been reading me books describing the workings of the balloons. It is all to do with catching the right winds as well as the fire. It must be terrifying to be so close to the flame," Miles babbled enthusiastically.

He had found an ally in Gabriel who kept asking questions the boy could answer until they approached the gates of Sydney Gardens. Thankfully, for Anthony's sanity, the journey was only a matter of minutes, most residents having chosen to walk to the event or using the more common method of Bath transport, the sedan chair. The footmen unloaded the food and followed the group when they'd all alighted from the carriage. On an area of grassland not too distant from the currently grounded balloon, the party settled on their chosen spot.

Anthony had seated himself away from Miles and Gabriel, who were already best friends, both chatting ten to the dozen.

Julia watched her son and the old man with a smile playing on her lips. She saw Anthony looking at the scene and presumed it amused him as much as it did her.

25

"Your grandfather is a natural with children," she said.

"Some would say it's because he still acts the child," Anthony responded.

The words caused the smile to broaden on Julia's lips. "As he seems to be having the best of times, I can only envy his outlook on life," she replied. She was ignoring the unwelcoming air surrounding the Earl, deciding to be pleasant whether or not he was in return.

Anthony shook his head. "He spends most of his time at some frivolous activity or other."

"At his age, I suppose he has earned the right to live life as he chooses."

"We all have obligations. Age does not reduce them," Anthony said coolly. He was being decidedly rude; even he knew she was only being polite, but he couldn't talk to others in a natural way. On the rare occasions he'd tried, it had seemed forced somehow. He wondered once more if he was actually related to easy-going Gabriel.

Julia inwardly groaned. She cursed her seating position, especially when there was no real opportunity to move without appearing bad-mannered. "Are you in Bath for the waters?" she asked, trying for a more general topic.

"My grandfather is, yes. He decided he would choose Bath over Brighton," Anthony responded.

"That is a shame for you."

Anthony looked surprised, not expecting a comment of pity. "Why for me?" he asked, his curiosity stirred.

"The last place a young man with a title and fortune would wish to be is in an unfashionable resort like Bath," Julia pointed out. "You must feel hounded by the hordes of women following your every movement."

"I doubt that would ever be an issue for me," Anthony admitted, his honesty always at the forefront of his speech, even when it was to his own detriment.

Julia stretched out her legs in front of her, the folds of her Pomona-green dress folding around her slim frame, her outdoor boots peeking out from the bottom of her dress, and with a teasing look towards Anthony, she continued. "Your words leave me to conclude one of two things, my Lord. Either you welcome a multitude of women and are quite a rake under that stiff exterior, or there is some dark affliction that puts off every woman you meet, so the throng will stay away from you."

Anthony looked in astonishment at the impertinence of the woman sitting next to him. He couldn't believe she'd had the audacity to speak to him in such a way.

Julia flushed at Anthony's expression of indignation. "Grandmama! I've done it again. It seems my words have gone too far for his Lordship, and he is now shocked beyond speech!" she choked out, but there was the hint of a laugh beneath her words.

"Already Julia? Tsk. Your open nature will get you into trouble one of these days," Patience responded.

"It already has," Anthony said stiffly.

Julia laughed unaffectedly at the words and Anthony's demeanour. "I am sorry, my Lord. I truly am, but I've learned that I must get my fun wherever I can. I was only teasing and meant no harm. I am sure you are one of the finest specimens around."

Gabriel intervened. He had been watching the interaction taking place and could have scolded his grandson for being a brutish oaf. "Your boy is a fine young man. He is a credit to you and your husband."

27

"Thank you," Julia said, but her tone and expression changed slightly. After being relaxed whilst she'd been teasing Anthony, her posture became as rigid as his.

"Is your husband with you in Bath?" Gabriel persisted.

"No. I am a widow these last two years," Julia admitted.

"I am sorry, child. There's nothing quite like the loss of a spouse is there?" Gabriel asked kindly.

"Not in that wastrel's case!" Patience responded hotly.

"Grandmama!" Julia hissed, flushing once more, but this time there was no laughter involved.

"It's the truth," Patience insisted.

"He is the father of my son and deserves some respect on account of that," Julia said.

"Come, Patience, Miles, let us see how close we can get to the balloon before it starts to take off, shall we?" Gabriel offered, quick to intervene in an uncomfortable situation, whilst at the same time giving his grandson a pointed look.

A silence descended on the pair left on the picnic rugs as the three vociferous ones in the party walked away, the two adults on either side of the child, holding his hand as he skipped along beside them.

It was minutes before Anthony broke the somewhat uncomfortable stillness. It seemed as if all the crowds of people had become louder since the pair had descended into silence. "If it's any consolation, I could curse my grandfather to the devil at least a dozen times a day," Anthony said, more out of honesty than any wish to console.

Julia smiled, but it didn't make her eyes twinkle as it had when she had been teasing him. "She is right, but I don't wish to be constantly reminded of my folly. And I don't wish my son to be continually hearing that his father wasn't a good man. It matters to no one now. Miles should have happy memories of his Papa."

28

"Your son seems a chirpy chap, so you have something to be happy about, I suppose," Anthony said ineloquently. It had taken much for him to deliver such words, which for him, were positively gushing.

It seemed Julia was also surprised at the words with the half-confused, half-amused look she shot Anthony. "I can never regret my marriage, for without it I would not have Miles. It was worth the pain for that alone." She revealed as little about her marriage as she could. The memories weren't good ones, but for some reason, she had the feeling that Anthony was a person who wouldn't ridicule or ask inappropriate questions. She had no idea where the certainty came from, but it was an instinct she decided to trust.

"My grandfather talks about the pain of being in love. I suspect you are talking about a different sort of pain. It all seems too difficult to me," Anthony admitted. He would never normally have spoken so openly, but she'd looked a little lost and unhappy when her grandmother had spoken, and he was aware of how that felt. Unused as he was to feeling empathy towards another, he had understood at least some of her discomfort and was responding to it—a unique situation for him.

"I've seen love matches, and they have not seemed anything but a happy union, but I am not a person who can speak about it with authority," Julia admitted. "One thing is for sure though: This is far too serious a conversation whilst out on a sunny day and a picnic!"

Anthony smiled slightly. "I suppose it is a little odd."

Julia watched the crowd gathered around the balloon, all eager to see the wonderous event take place. "I wonder what it would be like to be able to fly away, not having a care in the world and never look back?"

29

Even Anthony could not be unaffected by the wistfulness in Julia's voice. "I don't think we can ever leave our pasts behind."

"As a gentleman, aren't you supposed to indulge me on my whimsical flights of fancy?" Julia asked with a huff.

"I would not know where to start," Anthony admitted.

Julia laughed. "Trust me to choose the most straight-laced gentleman to sit by."

"I am sorry you're burdened so," Anthony said stiffly.

The smile fell from Julia's lips. She wasn't usually such an insufferable companion that she seemed to be in this instance, but she couldn't work out how to reach such a difficult character to make their forced time together pleasanter. "I am sorry. You must wish me a hundred miles from here."

"I wish myself twice that distance," Anthony responded.

Julia blinked at the insult given to her. She knew he was there under sufferance, but hadn't expected him to be quite so brutal. The last two years she'd striven to be someone who was light-hearted, pleasing, forcing herself to learn to smile once more, but Anthony's harshness had reminded her of a time in her life that was much darker. She would never willingly put herself in a situation where she would be punished again. "I see," she said stiffly. "I shall leave you be, my Lord. Your company is as welcome to me as clearly mine is to you." She stood and walked towards the balloon to join the others. Her posture was stiff, and if insulted had a walk, she portrayed it perfectly.

Anthony had opened his mouth as if to speak at her words, but he'd closed his lips without offering apologetic platitudes, which she wouldn't believe and he wouldn't mean, even if he could find the appropriate vocabulary. He

30

watched her retreating form, glad he was once more alone and yet strangely sorry that the teasing had stopped.

Chapter 3

Julia managed to shake off the sting of Anthony's words by concentrating on Miles' excitement and remaining in the crowds of people gathered around the balloon. She was filled with as much wonder as her son as the balloon rose into the air, inelegantly at first, before the winds took it upwards in a more graceful climb. The ropes that had tethered the rounded giant were released by the men on the ground with obvious relief, as it had been akin to holding back a straining beast as it fought for freedom. The brightly coloured material strained as the gas filled it and it rose above the heads of the onlookers. The men in the basket looked down at the crowds, relieved and exhilarated at their ascent. Julia's party all watched with wide eyes and wonderment as the now graceful equipage rose high above the treetops to much cheering and waving.

Miles was beside himself with excitement, and Gabriel was in his element along with the boy. They were both exclaiming and pointing, watching and commenting on every second of the balloon's progress.

Julia smiled at her grandmother. "Miles seems to have made a new friend."

"Gabriel was always full of life. The years don't seem to have changed him," Patience admitted. "His grandson seems more reserved, but as a gentleman of fortune and status, I suppose that is not uncommon or unsurprising. Especially, in a town where he is probably one of the highest-ranking personages there is."

"And he's rude!" Julia said.

"The titled often are," Patience soothed.

"That is no excuse for bad behaviour," Julia said.

"Let's go and have some food," Gabriel interrupted the ladies. "So much excitement has made Miles and me hungry."

"Miles is always famished," Julia admitted.

"He's a growing boy," Gabriel said in defence of his new friend.

"Would you not like to go for a walk through the gardens before we have something to eat?" Julia asked Miles, trying to delay their return to Anthony.

"My grandson has brought a feast. I promise you will not be disappointed," Gabriel said persuasively.

"I think Julia is a little reluctant to return to such a charming host," Patience said with a smile, knowing full well the reason for her granddaughter's reluctance and receiving a glare for revealing it.

Gabriel groaned. "Has the buffoon made a poor impression so soon? I was hoping you would have today before you discovered his propensity for insulting anyone and everyone."

"At least I know it was not just my charms he has taken offence at," Julia said, a little reassured.

"Unfortunately, not," Gabriel said, being honest about his grandson, more so than he would to anyone else.

The group walked back towards Anthony, who seemed completely out of place alone on the picnic rug on the grass. Others had also brought picnics and were having a jolly time of it. There was food and drink being consumed with much merriment, whereas Anthony was seated on the ground, his back ramrod straight, his expression clearly showing his opinion of the day. His clothing was exquisite, standing out above those who surrounded him, being of the finest materials, fit, and design. He attracted a few curious glances,

33

he was a lone attractive man, after all, but he remained unapproached though; no one was brave enough to consider seriously finding out more about the person who wore such an unwelcoming scowl.

Gabriel fell a little behind Julia and Miles and offered Patience his arm. "I apologise in advance for my grandson. While you are in Bath, I'm going to be following you like the infatuated pup I was all those years ago, and as a result, you will see much of Anthony."

"What ails him?"

"A poor upbringing," Gabriel admitted. "I curse his father to the devil."

"As I curse my son-in-law. One shouldn't speak ill of the dead, but I also don't believe in turning sinners into saints just because they have passed on," Patience said.

"No. Nor I. It grieves me that I was not there as Anthony was growing, perhaps I could have had some influence, but I was kept away."

"Families can be difficult. It broke my heart to see what Bruce did to Julia, but I could do nothing. If I had spoken out about the little I saw and the rest I suspected, he'd have cast me off, and I needed to remain near her. My daughter died when Julia was ten. When she married, I was determined Julia wouldn't lose me as well as her mother, even though it pained me to be around that man," Patience admitted.

"Our children should not die before us, but it is too often the case. I miss my Eliza every day, though I've not seen her for over thirty years now. Lizzy never got over the loss of Eliza, even though we were not part of her life. It almost killed me to watch my wife's pain, whilst at the same time going through my own," Gabriel responded. "I am so glad to be reacquainted with you, Patience. It is the best thing to have happened in a long time." Gabriel's funning had

34

disappeared completely as he spoke the words, admitting a little of what he felt.

The woman smiled and patted Gabriel's arm with her free hand. "And I'm glad to have you in my life again. Although I was right when I chose Hancock over you, it was still a sad day when you left my circle of friends."

"I was a fool then."

"We were all young and foolish," Patience admitted. "Now, enough maudlin reminiscences. Let us enjoy ourselves."

"Yes. Let's show the young 'uns how to live life! What say you, Miles? What scrapes can we get into while you are staying in Bath?" Gabriel asked as they all reached Anthony.

Miles was a slight boy, pale and thin at seven years old, but he had the same colouring as his mother. He would be a handsome young man when he grew, but his fragile appearance made him seem delicate. Gabriel hoped that Julia was right that although the child had been ill he would soon recover. He was such a happy, eager soul, Gabriel couldn't bear to think of him ailing, or worse.

While smiling at Gabriel's words, Miles' eyes lit up. "I would like to get lost in the labyrinth," he said. "And go on a horse ride."

"Now, Miles, we have spoken about horse riding," Julia warned.

"But I want to be as good as Papa was! So I need to ride every day!" Miles appealed to his mother, his eyes filling with moisture.

Julia flushed slightly. She couldn't continue to scold Miles when to do so would reveal their straightened circumstances.

Anthony saw the discomfort on Julia's face, and although it was out of character, he spoke to Miles to distract his threatened bout of tears. "You like horses?"

"Oh, yes!" the child responded, the tears immediately forgotten. "Papa had some bang-up horse flesh in his stable. My favourite was a dappled-grey. Mama said we could not afford to keep them when the creditors insisted on us paying Papa's bills."

"Miles!" Julia hissed, mortified that her son was speaking so freely. It wouldn't have been so bad apart from the way Anthony already looked at them. He'd certainly want to distance himself further now that he could guess at their straightened circumstances.

For the second time in as many minutes, Anthony responded to someone else's distress. "I have a horse who's sixteen hands and dappled grey. She is a fine beast, my favourite in fact. Her name is Belle."

"Really? You are so fortunate. I would love to own one like that," Miles said wistfully.

"And one day you shall," Patience said, handing her grandson a slice of delicious looking pie. "Now, eat, or you won't be big enough to climb on a large horse. You will only need a small donkey if you don't grow big and strong."

"Oh, Grandmama, you are silly sometimes," Miles said with a laugh, but tucked into the pie, nonetheless.

Julia had lowered her head slightly, completely embarrassed, but Gabriel, when seeing Anthony wasn't going to continue in the role of distracting Miles, decided to intervene himself. He had noticed his grandson responding to Julia's distress, and it gave him the smallest nugget of hope that Anthony wasn't completely void of feeling, which he so often seemed to be.

"Are you both going to the ball and the upper rooms tonight?" Gabriel asked.

"No," Julia responded.

"We are," Patience said quickly.

"But — " Julia started.

"I have changed my mind. We're going," Patience interrupted.

"In that case, may I have the first two dances, Patience, and the next two with you, Mrs Price?"

"That is too much dancing," Anthony interjected.

"Fustian! I've only not danced much because there has been no motivation to do so," Gabriel responded. "There are more ape-leaders in Bath than I have seen anywhere else!"

Anthony raised an eyebrow. "And yet you seem determined to find me a wife in this particular place?"

"Ape-leaders are more grateful than the diamonds one finds in London," Gabriel clarified.

Julia coughed to cover a laugh, but couldn't stop her eyes from dancing as Anthony shot Gabriel and herself a look that spoke volumes about his feelings at the comments.

Anthony didn't know quite how to retort. He was used to his grandfather's teasing, but to know he was being laughed at by Julia didn't rest easy with him. Normally he couldn't care less what people thought of him; it was something he never considered, but he'd experienced a revelation: He didn't want her to think poorly of him. He changed tack. "It is still too much dancing. You are here for your health."

"I'll dance once with you," Patience said. "And then no more. We are both beyond our prime."

"Nonsense! I am still as light on my feet as I was forty years ago," Gabriel insisted.

"Well I'm not," Patience responded tartly. "One dance from me is all you are getting."

"And if I could have the privilege of dancing the first two with you, I would be honoured," Anthony said to Julia.

Julia hesitated. She didn't want to spend an hour or more in the company of Anthony with no one else to provide relief, but she couldn't fault his reasoning behind asking her. He was trying to protect his relation, and that was admirable. Unless Gabriel approached someone else, he would have a rest between dancing with Patience and then herself. It was admirable to be protecting his grandfather. "Of course. And, like my Grandmother, I shall dance one dance with you at some point during the night, after you've rested from the effects of your other dance," she said firmly to Gabriel.

"Don't try to bamboozle me," Gabriel said, turning to Anthony. "You are engaging Mrs Price to dance because of your own motivation. It has nothing to do with protecting me."

Anthony looked decidedly discomfited, but Julia took pity on him. "Whichever reason it is, I'm glad of a dance partner, and that is the end of it, Mr Bannerman," she scolded gently. She didn't relish the time with Anthony, but wasn't going to stand by whilst Gabriel tried to make them both uncomfortable.

Gabriel chuckled. "Fine. I'll withdraw gracefully, but it is for your sake, Mrs Price."

"Good! To do otherwise wouldn't reflect well on you, and I would be disappointed to find out you were not the lovely character I had first thought," Julia said firmly.

"I apologise for my brutish behaviour," Gabriel said, chastised.

Anthony had the distinct impression that Miles would struggle to win any argument with his mother as he grew. She seemed perfectly able to put Gabriel in his place,

38

something Anthony had never quite succeeded at. He felt a modicum of empathy with the boy.

Chapter 4

Gabriel was thankful he was at the bottom of the set at last. It gave him time to catch his breath. Patience looked as flushed as he felt; she breathed heavily as she stood facing him.

"This wasn't one of your finest schemes, Gabriel," she said, using her fan, which had dangled from her arm during the dance.

"No. I admit to having forgotten how strenuous skipping is. I will have to think up less taxing ways of pushing those two together."

"I could see this afternoon that was your plan," Patience acknowledged. "Your actions were very transparent."

"Are you surprised? Beauty clearly runs through your family, and she seems as feisty as you are, my dear," Gabriel said with a smile.

"I am not convinced they will suit. Julia needs a man who loves her dearly to try to repair some of the damage Bruce did. Added to that, his Lordship doesn't seem the type of person who would take on another man's child. He was clearly at pains to distance himself from my grandson. Miles needs love just as much as Julia does," Patience cautioned.

"Anthony probably needs it more. I think they will make a splendid family. They just haven't realised it yet. It is up to us to show them what's best for them all," Gabriel said confidently.

"I hope you know what you are doing. If I have the slightest inkling that Julia will be hurt by any foolish matchmaking, I will not hesitate to remove us from your company and Bath if I must," Patience cautioned. She wasn't so convinced that Julia would be attracted to Anthony on any level, if any of the conversation they'd shared after the balloon outing was anything to go by. "I think you are hoping for something that won't happen, which at the moment is not likely to harm either of them, but I will not stand by and let Julia be hurt again, whether you are an old friend or not."

"I understand completely," Gabriel soothed. "I wouldn't want your granddaughter hurt at the expense of Anthony."

"Then we are of one mind."

"But if they should fall in love as a result of spending time together… "

"Gabriel, you're irrepressible!" Patience groaned, before taking his hands and re-joining the set.

*

It would have perhaps reassured Gabriel to know that Julia in fact *did* find Anthony attractive, but it didn't follow that she *liked* him. He was the quintessential meaning of tall, dark, and handsome, but his eyes were cold and his manner mostly offensive. Being in a long-ways set of over an hour with him proved that, on closer acquaintance, he didn't improve. He might be dressed in the finest clothes to have been made at Weston's, but his manner didn't encourage warmth in those around him. Julia wasn't dressed as finely as Anthony. In fact her dress was a number of years old, but with some fresh embroidery brightening the pale blue material, she thought it not too shabby. She had worked on updating her wardrobe from the moment her grandmother had suggested they remove to Bath. She had neither the funds nor the beauty to cause much of a stir wherever she went. She would be described as handsome, rather than pretty, but her personality was easy-going and welcoming, traits that masked her wounds as well as hiding the fear, uncertainty, and worry that haunted her quiet moments.

41

The two unlikely partners had spent a lot of their time in silence as they danced. Julia tried to school her features into an expression of mild amusement, but she wasn't convinced she'd achieved it when passing some of the other dancers and noticing their curious glances in her and Anthony's direction.

She sighed. "My Lord, we'll have to at least pretend we are enjoying our time on the dance floor, or neither of us will be requested to dance further dances. We are giving the wrong impression of ourselves, and it is doing neither of us any good."

"Not having to dance for the rest of the evening would be a welcome outcome for me," Anthony admitted.

Julia rolled her eyes in exasperation. "I would have understood if you'd just explained that your grandfather should not dance rather than sacrificing yourself by asking me to stand up with you. I am sorry that having me as a partner is such a trial."

"Dancing with you is pleasant," Anthony admitted honestly. Julia was light on her feet and was a confident, able dancer.

"My goodness! Is that a compliment, my Lord?" Julia asked, shocked.

"It is the truth. Whether it is flattery or not, I'm uncertain. Most ladies strive to dance well. I am just telling you that you have achieved your aim," Anthony explained.

"Goodness me, you smooth talking devil," Julia said wryly.

"I am presuming you're mocking me?"

"You presume correctly, my Lord."

"I don't find giving insipid comments or compliments comes easy to me," Anthony replied.

"Conversation in any form is slightly uncomfortable for you, isn't it?" Julia asked, her tone gentler than it had been. She was coming to suspect that he was socially awkward rather than arrogant and aloof as she had first thought.

"Yes."

"And I am not helping with my teasing?"

"No."

"I'm sorry."

"My grandfather would say it would do me good to be tortured somewhat," Anthony responded.

"I hope I am teasing, not torturing," Julia couldn't help smiling at the words.

Anthony smiled a little, once more unusually responding to his new acquaintance. "Is there any real difference between the two?"

"I hope so, but possibly not for whoever is receiving it."

"Quite so," Anthony said grimly, but for the first time since meeting him, Julia detected a hint of amusement. She felt surprisingly pleased to have broken through the stiff exterior, however slightly.

When they re-joined Patience and Gabriel, it was time to seek refreshments. Gabriel didn't mention his dance with Julia, and as she'd noticed his flushed cheeks, she didn't push the point. They found a table in one of the ante-rooms, and Anthony obtained tea and small cakes for the four of them.

They seated themselves comfortably, and Gabriel launched an attack on Anthony. "So, my boy, when are you going to take young Miles out on Belle?"

Anthony glared at Gabriel before replying. He had no idea how to respond to such a request, but the thought of taking Miles out horrified him. The delayed reaction gave Julia the opportunity to intervene.

"My son will not be riding his Lordship's horse, nor any other horse," she said primly. "We cannot afford to stable an animal. There is no point in raising his expectations. He has to learn to live within his means, as we all do."

Gabriel was immediately repentant. "I am sorry, my dear. My words were not said to cause you distress. I was merely trying to bring my grandson out of that toughened shell he wears."

"I would imagine his Lordship is quite capable of doing whatever he wishes whenever he wishes," Julia continued. She was mortified that once again her lack of funds was out in the open; it was embarrassing and demeaning, and she didn't react well to such feelings. "He, nor I, like being told what to do."

"I am able to speak for myself," Anthony interjected.

"I was defending you!" Julia exclaimed, turning incredulously towards Anthony.

"I realise what you were doing, but I am able to guard against any foolish comments aimed in my direction," Anthony responded.

"You are insufferable. Do you know that?" Julia snapped. The fact that her poverty had yet again been brought into the open and added to Anthony's ill-natured ways had finally tipped her over into responding angrily when she would normally have held her tongue. She could no longer keep her emotional balance and keep smiling and pretending that all was well.

"Yes. I've been told that many times," Anthony admitted.

"I have always thought honesty to be a commendable trait. I am rapidly reassessing my opinion on the matter. Please excuse me," Julia said, standing and walking out of the room.

Anthony's eyes followed her, a frown marring his puzzled expression.

"Have I taught you nothing these last years?" Gabriel groaned.

"If one speaks the truth, surely that is better than deceit? Yet I am being condemned for my honesty," Anthony said, genuinely confused.

"There's a time and a place for restraint dear boy. A pity it seems beyond you to realise when that time is," Gabriel said with a shake of his head.

"Julia is normally far more placid. It isn't usual for her to lose her temper so," Patience defended her granddaughter, slightly stunned that Julia would have spoken out so vehemently in front of their new acquaintances.

"I clearly irritate her," Anthony said.

"I hope not. Your grandfather has invited us all out to Wells tomorrow," Patience responded.

Anthony thought it was best not to comment on that piece of information, having been lectured once already about airing his honest opinions.

*

The party of three entered once more into the main room of the Assembly Rooms. The chandeliers were aflame with light, and the musicians on the balcony were in full swing, playing to an appreciative crowd. Patience and Gabriel managed to find two seats facing the dancers and were happy to watch the progression of the dance, neither mentioning again wishing to dance. Gabriel was content to introduce Patience to those he knew in Bath, and they soon had a gathering around them. Patience was as gregarious as Gabriel, and there were soon many guffaws of mirth and merriment coming from their seats and those around them.

45

Anthony was restless. He didn't wish to speak to anyone, much less dance, but he skirted the dance floor until he saw Julia dancing with an older gentleman. He had thought she hadn't any other friends in Bath and wondered about the man. Anthony moved to the side a little, so Julia wouldn't catch sight of him watching her, but he followed her movements with fascination and something else. He wasn't sure what the feeling was, but it felt like regret. Julia was laughing and being teased. Her heightened colour made her look younger than her six and twenty years. Anthony might not be able to commune with others as he would wish, but he could tell when someone was being flirted with and enjoying themselves. To observe it was to increase his feelings of remoteness.

He wondered what it would be like to be so easy with someone. He'd never been able to master social interaction to the satisfaction of the person to whom he was talking. Many times he'd caused offence without having any intention of doing so. It added to his sense of being isolated in the world, and the result was that he would withdraw further and further. Oh, he had seen his peers act with arrogance and derision to those they deemed unworthy, but they could as easily be charming and engaging. His actions were as a result of not feeling a part of the society he'd been born to, or any society for that matter.

Only the conditions of his father's will had forced him to leave the security of his country estate to take this trip, although one could hardly call being in Bath throwing oneself into the throng that was the London season.

He pondered if it was worth letting Giles have the extra inheritance. Anthony was no expensive man with a list of creditors as some in society were. He could quite easily live off the money he would have if he didn't marry.

46

The thought disturbed him. It didn't rest easy somehow to have the estate split in such a way. Anthony had a strong sense of what was right and wrong. No. The estate should remain intact. It should remain as it had been for the generations previously. He would not be the cause of its decline. The marriage stipulation would have to be adhered to. How hard could it be to gain a wife when one had title and fortune?

Anthony set his shoulders. It was time to marry.

Chapter 5

Julia was relieved that Anthony had decided to ride down to Wells, rather than join them in the carriage. They hadn't conversed much after she'd stormed away from their tea table. She wasn't proud of her immature actions. She should have apologised for her behaviour; it had been rude, even though Anthony's comments had been offensive to her. She'd been brought up to know that two wrongs didn't make a right, and she was ashamed of her conduct. It had done her no credit.

She'd known the moment he'd returned to the large assembly room and had wondered if, after her dance with a Mr Prescott, he would approach her, but he hadn't. In fact, he'd had the master of ceremonies introduce him to two young ladies and their families and danced with both. It had surprised Julia and annoyed her at the same time. So, he could be charming when he wished to be. It was clearly she who brought out the worst in him.

Now, he was riding alongside his carriage, much to Miles' delight.

"That is as fine a horse as Papa had, isn't it, Mama?" Miles asked excitedly, watching Anthony from the window.

"It is," Julia responded, barely looking at the horse and rider.

"When I grow, I am going to have a stable full of horses! The best high steppers for me!"

"Of course you are," Julia responded dully. She wished she could give him everything he wanted, but he would have to learn that to be able to spend money, he would have to earn it first. She didn't repine the choices her son would have to make. An intelligent young man had options. For her it was slightly different. She was mainly living off her grandmother, and although Patience was comfortably off, Julia feared that supporting the three of them would eventually be a strain on her relative's finances.

"Today is not for worry, my child," Gabriel said gently to Julia. "A frown shouldn't be marring those pretty features."

Julia flushed a little at openly betraying her inner turmoil. She knew her grandmother worried about her, and she worked hard to hide her concerns, but she smiled at Gabriel's words. "I am unaccustomed to being called pretty."

"You were considered very handsome when you had your season," Patience reminded her granddaughter.

Julia laughed. "The best I have ever been referred to is handsome. I always thought it was a little insulting. If one is not good enough to be referred to as beautiful, a diamond, or pretty, I think one should resort to singing the praises of a personality or musical ability rather than resorting to being called handsome. It is such a masculine term, don't you think?"

"You are as spirited and pretty as your grandmother. Don't let the ninnyhammers tell you any different," Gabriel responded.

"I can see why she likes you so much," Julia responded.

"He has always been full of fudge," Patience admitted. "But he has some charm."

"I'm almost overcome with emotion at such praise," Gabriel said, feigning being wounded.

"Get away with you. I don't believe you have turned into a shallow rascal!" Patience responded. "Now, are you going to be honest as to what has brought you to Bath? What ails you my old friend?"

"Less of the old!" Gabriel spluttered.

49

"The aging process is happening to us all," Patience pointed out.

"I find avoiding gazing into looking glasses relieves the pain of seeing the passage of time."

"Well, that young man does not strike me as one who'd be worried over nothing, and he was concerned about you exerting yourself last night, so I want to know what is going on," Patience persisted.

"Does she ever get side-tracked?" Gabriel asked Julia.

"No."

"I suspected as much. You have turned into a termagant, my dear Patience."

"Answer my questions, and I will shut-up."

"No you won't. You will start harping on as Anthony does." Gabriel held up his hands in defeat when it appeared Patience was going to speak. "Fine! The doctor says I have been doing too much and need to reduce the port and rich food I eat. A plain diet he has instructed and taking the waters. Do you know how unappealing that is? I'll have a plain enough diet when I am dead."

"Which could be soon if you don't do as you are told," Patience pointed out.

"Have you been talking to Anthony? Those are the exact words he said."

"He's clearly a sensible boy," Patience said with approval.

"He is. Too sensible sometimes. I wish he would just let go occasionally, if that makes sense? Just act the young man before a lifetime of responsibility weighs him down even further than it has already," Gabriel admitted.

"The head of the family always has the most responsibility," Julia said quietly. The words Gabriel were saying were revealing an insight into the new acquaintance that couldn't help but intrigue her.

50

"Yes. And to know your stepmother wishes you an early demise so her own son can inherit does not add to one's sense of being part of a family," Gabriel said grimly.

"Surely not?" Patience asked.

"She was desperate for him to join the military in some form, and I am convinced it was her hope, when Napoleon was rampaging across Europe, that he would buy a commission and wouldn't return. I sincerely believe she was saddened when the tyrant was defeated, for it took away the urgent need for men to join the military. She is barely civil to him, although I know his manner does not necessarily attract warmth," Gabriel said, seeing Julia's wry look.

Julia smiled. "He clearly cares about you, so he cannot be all bad."

Gabriel harrumphed. "He needs something to focus his attention on other than me."

"I can help ease his burden whilst we are in Bath," Patience said. "I don't mind assisting him in making sure you are doing what you are supposed to be doing."

"Good God! I'm doomed!" Gabriel moaned as the carriage continued.

*

The party walked around the cathedral in Wells, Gabriel once more encouraging Miles to join himself and Patience as they explored. Julia and Anthony followed behind, one of them wishing she was part of the threesome, the other wishing he was somewhere else entirely.

"I think you have an ally with my grandmother. She was quizzing Mr Bannerman about what ails him whilst we travelled here," Julia said, purely for something to say.

"My grandfather can be as stubborn as a mule, even when faced with sound medical advice," Anthony responded.

51

"Not many people take advice as kindly as it is meant. It is sometimes easier to ignore it than to face up to the reality of a situation," Julia defended Gabriel.

"Most advice is given with some sort of motive behind the words," Anthony admitted. "In my grandfather's case it wasn't."

"True to some extent," Julia acceded. "Although, I suppose keeping someone alive longer is still a motivation, albeit, a good one," she said quickly, seeing Anthony's frown increase. "My grandmama will certainly be encouraging a plain fayre from now on."

"I hope he listens to her more than he has listened to me so far."

"He must be very precious to you." Julia probed a little.

Anthony paused before speaking. "He is my grandfather."

Julia laughed. "Yes. Any family is bound to us, but it does not follow that we have to like them."

"No," Anthony admitted. "I find it very hard to feel much affection for my stepmother." He blinked after uttering the words, as if surprised he'd voiced them.

"We all have at least one of those relatives, I feel," Julia said quietly.

"You seem to adore your grandmother," Anthony was stirred into asking for clarification.

"I do," Julia said quickly. She flushed and then looked away in mortification.

"I've made you feel uncomfortable again. I apologise," Anthony said stiffly.

Julia smiled slightly. "For once it is not you who has said the wrong thing. I should not have mentioned anything, but when I mentioned relatives I wasn't fond of I was referring to my husband, if I am being honest. Which makes me the

52

worst wife in history — to demean a spouse who cannot defend himself."

"If your words are true, you cannot be pilloried for that," Anthony said.

"Be careful; your words could be classed as reassurance, my Lord. Is this a crack in your aloof demeanour?" Julia teased.

Anthony shook his head in disbelief at Julia's familiar way of talking to him, but for once a slight smile played around his lips. "I find my aloofness an excellent guard against impertinence."

Julia laughed, pleased she'd caused a smile, even a small one. "I would distance yourself from me then. I've been accused of far worse."

Anthony thought he could detect a seriousness behind the words, but for once he didn't utter exactly what he was thinking. Swallowing his words and suspicion, he smiled at Julia. "I am forewarned. Thank you for the advice."

It was now Julia's turn to pause. She'd never seen Anthony smile fully before. He was prone to be grave and frown, but the effect of his smile was disarming and surprising. His whole face lit up, and his eyes lightened from the dark tumultuous grey they usually were. There wasn't exactly a sparkle there, but there was a definite shimmer of amusement, and it was extremely appealing.

"Smile like that near the young ladies in Bath, and you will soon be fighting off potential wives," Julia acknowledged before realising she'd been as blunt as he could be. She laughed self-consciously at her own forwardness.

"Now you are sounding more like my grandfather," Anthony admitted, the smile disappearing as quickly as it had appeared.

"He wants you to marry?" Julia asked.

Anthony faltered. He'd never confided in anyone other than Gabriel, and even then it was on a basic level. Somehow, he didn't feel as if he would be judged by Julia and confessed some of his private affairs to her. "My father's will has a stipulation in it that, if I am not wed by the time I reach thirty years old, I lose a portion of my inheritance."

"What happens if you spend it in the meantime?" Julia asked, not unreasonably.

Anthony let out a crack of laughter for the first time in a long time. The sound surprised him as much as it seemed to do Julia. "Unfortunately, the money is inaccessible until I marry. My father knew me well enough to ensure there was no getting out of it." His words, although blunt, hid the brutality of the terminology that had been used in the will.

Julia smiled before becoming serious. "That's an unfortunate turn of events. Do you wish to marry?"

"My stepmother is hoping I don't, so my brother, Giles, receives a bigger portion," Anthony admitted.

"It is unfair that your father should potentially cause a rift in your family," Julia said. "Oh! I do beg pardon. I should not criticise your father, especially as he's a person I have never met."

Anthony waved his hand in a small, dismissive gesture. "Don't worry. You have said nothing my grandfather hasn't already cursed, and with far more colourful language, I assure you. There was not really a family unit to destroy before the terms of the will were known," Anthony admitted, once again surprised he was confessing so much.

"That is a shame. I am an only child, as is Miles, and I feel it would've been nice to have had a sibling—for both of us," Julia admitted.

"You are young enough to have more children," Anthony pointed out.

"I suppose I am," Julia admitted, but her tone wasn't enthusiastic.

"You don't intend to marry again?" Anthony asked. "I presumed you'd be looking to marry now as it is some time since your husband passed."

"Is that a proposal, my Lord?" Julia teased.

"Good God! No!" Anthony said emphatically.

Julia's eyes widened in shock at the forcefulness of his words. She felt anger bubbling up, but managed to suppress it. After all, she'd been the one to utter the comment that had caused his panicked response.

"I was attempting a joke, my Lord," she eventually replied, speaking through gritted teeth. "Don't worry that there is any danger from my setting my cap at you; the thought repulses me as much as it does yourself."

Anthony seemed momentarily confused, before sighing. "I have upset you again, haven't I?"

"Yes, but as I know to expect only brutal honesty from you, even on such a short acquaintance, it is my own fault for trying to fun with you. I shan't be foolish enough to do it again," Julia responded.

"I am sorry," Anthony said.

"What for? Your honesty, or that I shall endeavour to be nothing more than distantly polite in the future?" Julia asked.

"Both," Anthony answered.

"My damaged ego cannot take constant rebuttal, my Lord," Julia admitted. "I think it would be safest for us both if we merely nod to acknowledge the other on meeting. Anything else is likely to cause problems for at least one of us. And I think it would more than likely be myself," Julia admitted.

"I cannot explain why, but that depresses me a little," Anthony admitted.

"Not as much our continuing the way we have begun would downcast me," Julia admitted. "Call me foolish in not wishing to be the one who is constantly put-down or dismissed, but I am not that self-sacrificing. Not anymore."

"I am sorry my presence causes you so much pain. It is not my intention to distress you," Anthony admitted, giving a rare, sincere apology.

"I was hopeful it was not intentional. I presumed you were not such a cad as to be purposely cruel."

"Not at all. I beg your pardon for giving such a poor impression. I find I am usually at somewhat of a loss in social situations."

"Let us just leave it at that," Julia said. "I don't wish this to become an attack on your personality. You have apologised. I have accepted it. We can now part amiably."

"If only we could be friends," Anthony said, realising with shock that he wanted her friendship.

"I don't think that would work."

"That is a great pity."

"But it will protect me," Julia said, not realising the compliment she was being given.

Chapter 6

I feel things I've never felt before. Admittedly, most of it is confusion, but there is something else. It scares me, and yet I feel a curiousness I've never felt previously. What is it that makes one want to share inner thoughts with another? Is it recognising another lonely person? I think it might be. She laughs and smiles, but there is a sadness about her, and something else — a vulnerability that I have never detected in anyone else. A widow, especially a poor one, does have limited options open to her, so that could be causing her uncertainty, but I don't think it is. This vulnerability goes deeper.

Perhaps one damaged soul can detect another.

Pah! I am becoming as ridiculous as those who go around spouting sonnets. If this is what happens when one starts to look for a wife, I am destined to become a besotted fool, and I refuse to let that happen. The dances I've shared with perfectly suitable young ladies made me want to leave this society and head off towards my hunting lodge and remain there for years, let alone days. The conversation was insipid and tedious for the whole of the two dances I spent with each young woman.

At least there is intelligent conversation from her. I just wish it did not upset my equilibrium quite so much. I have always thought it important to be honest, but it sometimes upsets her, and I dislike how that makes me feel, especially when her expression betrays the hurt I have caused. That she tries to hide it when she's hurting seems worse somehow. Why has she had to hide her feelings?

She promises to be aloof in future, but I long to see her eyes warm with laughter. I want to see them warm when they look at me. This must be some sort of madness; she annoys me to the devil, yet I am drawn to her. I am glad she will not seek me out anymore.

I think.

*

Anthony had remained lagging behind the rest of the group after Julia separated herself from him. He watched the easy interaction between the four people, and not for the first time, wondered how people could be so comfortable with each other. It baffled him; yet if he dwelt on it too much, it would increase the emptiness he felt so often.

At one point Gabriel had joined his grandson. "What happened between the delightful Mrs Price and yourself? She seems determined to remain attached to her grandmother and son."

"I don't understand why people are repulsed so much when I speak," Anthony confessed.

Gabriel sighed. "Perhaps if you did not utter *everything* that you think?"

"I try, but it seems wrong to be deceitful."

"Not causing offence is hardly being deceitful, my boy." Sometimes Gabriel thought Anthony's inner maturity was far less than his years, and yet at other times he seemed older. He was a confused, mixed-up man. "Please try to be friendly. These are decent people, and they would offer you friendship and expect little in return."

"Except non-insulting conversation?"

Gabriel smiled. "It is such a little thing to ask."

"From your perspective maybe."

58

Once more Anthony felt adrift from those around him. Why did the world seem full of people who were so different from himself?

On leaving the cathedral, they explored Wells with Miles running ahead constantly. He chattered and was full of excitement for the whole day. After they'd eaten at one of the inns in the town, Miles seemed to sag.

"Mama, I am very tired," he complained, cuddling up to Julia and laying his head on her lap.

"You've had a busy day," Julia said, looking fondly at her son and stroking his head of constantly tousled hair.

"Can I go to sleep now, Mama?"

"Not quite yet. When we return to the carriage," Julia said.

"But it is such a long way away," Miles moaned.

"I will race you," Gabriel said, trying to instil some energy into the boy.

"I cannot," Miles said quietly. "My legs are trembling."

"I could send for the carriage," Anthony offered.

"Thank you, but there's no need," Julia said coolly. "He will be fine once we start to walk."

The party soon moved out of the inn and trudged slowly towards the cathedral area where they had alighted from the carriage.

Miles started to complain bitterly about needing to rest. Julia shushed him, but it was apparent the boy had spent his energy and was close to tears because of feeling exhausted.

Julia stopped. "Very well. I can see you are truly tired. I will carry you the rest of the way."

Anthony stepped forward from his usual place at the rear of the group. "Miles, come here. I will carry you," he said stiffly.

Miles looked hopefully between the pair. Having two offers of assistance was a relief to the bone-weary seven-year-old.

"There's no need, my Lord. I am quite capable of carrying my son," Julia responded to Anthony's words.

"I am sure you are, but I am even more able to do so. There's no advantage to tiring you both." The words were said without any emotion, something Julia was becoming used too. She wasn't sure whether there was any warmth behind the words, but it was a considerate gesture. She would struggle to carry Miles for any distance; he was a growing boy, and she was of slight build.

"Thank you. That is very kind of you," she responded, indicating to Miles that he should approach Anthony.

"It is the practical solution," Anthony responded, bending and lifting the boy into his arms.

"Take the praise, boy," Gabriel scolded. "He will never learn," he said in a stage whisper to Patience.

Anthony glowered at Gabriel before turning to Julia. "It is my pleasure."

Julia's eyes sparkled with merriment but she refrained from commenting. It wasn't fair for them all to single him out, and she was fully aware of how his words could just as easily sting.

"Mama! I am so tall!" Miles said with glee at being the same height as Anthony.

"Yes, you are," Julia said. "Now stay still. His lordship does not want a wriggling eel in his arms."

Miles giggled but, thankfully, was so daunted by Anthony's impassiveness that he was a little more restrained than normal. Julia walked close to the pair, worried that her son might upset Anthony in some way. It was clear the man had little experience of children. There was no conversation between the threesome as they walked.

Anthony faltered a little when Miles placed his head on his shoulder. Julia had looked in alarm at her son's action but had said quietly, "He must be truly worn-out. I can take him from you. He will be a dead weight if he sleeps," she said.

"There is no point disturbing him," Anthony responded. "We aren't far from the inn."

"Thank you," Julia replied quietly. "I should have let you send for the carriage. It's not fair to inconvenience you so."

"It is no hardship," Anthony responded.

"I don't think your cravat would agree," Julia said unable to stop herself teasing, even though she'd promised she wouldn't interact with him further. It seemed there was something about him that tugged at her in such a way that she couldn't ignore it.

Surprising himself, Anthony smiled in return. "I shall have to pacify my valet's lamentations. I will probably regret my offer of assistance when I'm subjected to his ministrations later."

Julia laughed. "Tell him you cannot be perfect all the time. It is your duty to keep him on his toes, or he'll likely become lax in his role."

"I shall repeat those words exactly," Anthony said with a raise of an eyebrow.

"As I will never meet your valet, my Lord, you cannot frighten me with such threats!" Julia teased.

"Hmm, why am I not surprised that you can't be easily browbeaten?"

"Because you consider me a lost cause? No! Don't answer that! I don't think I want to know," Julia said quickly.

61

"You make me sound positively brutal," Anthony admitted.

"I think it best to say there are one or two areas for improvement," Julia responded.

"One or two?" Anthony knew he was being teased, and for the first time in his life, he was trying to respond appropriately to it.

"Your words and the tone of voice you use," Julia answered.

"Is that all? A trip to my hunting lodge is becoming more appealing by the moment."

Julia smiled. "If you went, just think how dull our lives would be."

"And how less insulted?"

"Well, now you come to mention it..."

"No more!" Anthony groaned.

Julia's laugh was interrupted by their arrival at the coaching inn. Anthony strode ahead, still carrying the sleeping Miles, to give instructions to his coachman. If his long-time member of staff suffered astonishment at his master holding a sleeping child as if it was the most natural thing to do, he showed not a flicker. Gabriel and Patience entered the carriage first, before Anthony held out his spare arm to guide Julia into the vehicle before he climbed the carriage steps.

Julia seated herself nearest the door and indicated that Anthony should pass Miles to her. She was surprised when Anthony shook his head in the negative. He placed his free hand on Miles' back to hold him in place as he climbed into the carriage. It was a little more difficult being encumbered with the child, but he managed not to disturb the sleeping boy. Sitting opposite Julia, he nodded to the footman, who lifted the steps and closed the door. There was a slight delay whilst Belle was secured to the rear of the carriage for transporting home now she'd lost her rider.

"I can take him now. You have been very obliging," Julia said.

"He seems content," Anthony responded.

"Yes, and you should always let sleeping children lie," Patience interjected.

"I thought that was dogs?" Anthony asked.

"It is as relevant to both," Gabriel said. "A sleeping child is far preferable to a crying one."

Julia smiled in defeat. "You've convinced me. I shall enjoy my freedom."

"Talking of which, what are we all planning to do tomorrow?" Gabriel asked, keen to maintain contact with the people who were bringing Anthony out of his shell.

"Nothing," Anthony responded quickly. "You will not bully me into any foolish scheme. You will rest for a day."

"I feel fine," Gabriel insisted.

"In that case, we shall remove ourselves from Bath," Anthony said, his face impassive.

"I don't feel that fine," Gabriel said mulishly.

Anthony acknowledged the twitch of Julia's lips with a slight raise of his eyebrows. He was sure she was amused, but also approved of his words. "I prescribe a quiet day at home with nothing more strenuous than a trip to the Pump Room."

"He'll be telling me he is a qualified quack next," Gabriel said to the group as a whole.

"If I lose my inheritance, it is a profession I am sure I can enter into. I seem to be a natural at pandering to foolish old men when they should know better."

Patience laughed. "He knows you well, Gabriel."

63

"He thinks he's a court jester now," Gabriel muttered, knowing there was no point in arguing.

"I was being serious," Anthony said, but the twinkle in his eye made Julia's smile widen.

Chapter 7

Anthony flung the letter on the dining table in front of him and leaned forward, rubbing his hands over his face.

"What is it, boy?" Gabriel asked as they both sat at the breakfast table. Until Anthony had started to go through his correspondence, they'd been enjoying a quiet morning, filling their stomachs with the finest breakfast fayre Bath had to offer.

"She is coming to stay with us and is bringing Giles with her," Anthony said through gritted teeth.

Gabriel did not need to ask to whom Anthony was referring. The older man pushed his plate away and nodded to the footman to leave them alone. Only when the door had been closed did he speak.

"What is her excuse for visiting?"

"To see how I do," Anthony said.

"She has never cared about you for the years she has been your stepmother," Gabriel said with derision.

"You will have to hold your tongue when she is visiting," Anthony cautioned.

"Tell me she's not staying here," Gabriel pleaded.

Anthony smiled slightly despite being unhappy at the situation he was facing. "I can no more turn my stepmother away from the house I have leased than I could you."

"I suddenly feel an improvement in my health."

"I thought you wanted to find me a wife in Bath?" Anthony asked.

"I did, but the company has just become less appealing. When does she arrive?"

"Tomorrow. She sends the letter whilst she is en route. I suppose she wanted to ensure that I could not have the time to think up an excuse that would delay or prevent her arrival. It will be good to see Giles. A pity he is inclined to bow to Fanny's every wish," Anthony said of his younger brother.

"Why is she not bringing the other brat? Might as well fill the whole house and live off you," Gabriel said sarcastically.

"Wilfred is still at school," Anthony said. "As they live in the ancestral home, you can't say removing themselves to Bath would be any different than remaining in Worcestershire," Anthony reasoned.

"She'll be up to no good, that one. She has one motivation: to get as much as she can out of your father and you respectively. Watch yourself boy," Gabriel cautioned.

"I have been aware of Fanny's feelings since I first met her when I was nine," Anthony admitted. The quiet boy had soon found out that the woman his father had introduced to him as his new mother would not look upon him with affection. From the first moment, she'd been open with her disdain and mockery at Anthony's awkwardness.

As he'd grown, their mutual dislike had continued, and with Anthony responding honestly whenever spoken to, things had come to a head when he was fifteen. That was the time Gabriel had been brought back into the family, and Anthony had spent most of his time with his newly discovered grandfather.

"Yes. Well, I intend to go about our business as if she were not here," Gabriel said.

"I will have to spend time with her. If you choose to abandon me, that is up to you, but I cannot walk away from my obligations," Anthony said.

"If you insist on being honourable, I'll only put up with her, so I cannot be accused of deserting you," Gabriel responded. "I don't trust her motivation. She would likely try to sabotage any wedding plans you might have."

"She has little to worry herself about. I am no closer to marrying than I ever was," Anthony said with a shrug.

"That is because you can't see what is under your nose," Gabriel muttered, but it was quiet enough that Anthony didn't hear or at least he pretended not to hear. As the young man could guess the sentiment behind the whispered words, he chose to refrain from commenting.

*

Two days later, Julia and Patience were standing at the edge of the Pump Room, watching the bustle of people, when they were approached by Gabriel and his entourage.

"Ah, Patience! It is *so* good to see you!" Gabriel said with heartfelt warmth, clasping the hands of his friend and squeezing them to convey a meaning he could not voice.

"Good morning, Gabriel, my Lord," she responded to the two gentlemen. "We have missed your company these last few days," Patience replied honestly.

"Mrs Hancock, Mrs Price, please allow me to introduce you to my stepmother, Lady Lever and my half-brother, The Honourable Mr Giles Russell," Anthony said.

Bows and curtseys were exchanged, giving Julia time to look at their new acquaintances. Fanny must have been a lot younger than her deceased husband. She was still a pretty woman, blonde haired and blue-eyed, with a slim build. The dress she wore was made of the finest silk, excessive for a day dress, but it matched perfectly the flamboyant hat she wore. She was clearly out to give the impression of a woman of importance and wealth.

67

Julia wasn't fooled by the angelic look of the woman. Lady Lever had assessed shrewdly and openly the new acquaintances at their introduction. Julia managed to contain the smile that threatened when it was clear that their new acquaintance didn't seem to approve of those to whom she was being introduced.

Giles appeared to be about twenty. In looks, he was like his mother, but he was instantly friendly and pleasant. Next to Anthony, they would never have been taken for brothers, if not being introduced as such. It seemed each brother had taken after his maternal side. He was dressed in the height of fashion, clearly aspiring to be, if not already a member, of the dandy set, if his cravat and high, stiffly starched collar was anything to go by.

"Have you recently arrived in Bath, Lady Lever?" Patience asked, when it seemed obvious Gabriel wasn't going to be his usual gregarious self.

"Yesterday. My son expressed the desire to visit his brother," Fanny responded coolly.

"You were keener than I was," Giles responded and received a glare from his parent at his words. "Well, you were!" he responded defensively. "I was happy enough to rattle around at home."

"Not intent on moving down to London, Giles?" Anthony asked.

"Well, no. Sometimes, it is best to rusticate for a little while," Giles said, with a rueful grin at his brother and a slight colouring of his cheeks.

"Pockets to let again?" Anthony asked dryly.

"You know how it is. I have expensive taste," Giles responded unrepentantly.

"Giles! Hush!" his mother demanded, mortified to have her son's habits aired most unfavourably.

"Ah, Anthony needs to know if he is to advance me some blunt," Giles said with a nonchalant shrug and a winning chuckle.

"You have been here since yesterday and have not mentioned anything. I'm surprised you delayed," Anthony pointed out.

"I didn't want to announce it as soon as I walked through the door," Giles responded with a good-natured smile.

"Giles! Hush!" Fanny urged.

"You should check with your tailor; your pockets must have holes in them," Anthony said, ignoring his stepmother as much as Giles had.

"A week or two in Bath will help matters," Fanny said, finally giving up on the notion that their business shouldn't be discussed in front of strangers.

"I had rather return home sooner," Giles responded.

"My grandfather tells me the ladies outnumber the men. Vastly," Anthony informed his brother.

"Really? So that is your aim, is it? Good for you," Giles laughed at his brother, failing to notice his mother's eyes narrowing at the exchange.

"I came here with no aim, other than to stay with grandfather until he is fit to leave," Anthony answered honestly. Only after they arrived did Gabriel admit his motivation in choosing to recuperate in Bath.

"We shall be here a while. My condition is not so easily overcome," Gabriel interjected mischievously. "Are you going to the assembly tomorrow night, Patience?"

"Yes, but I shan't be dancing, so you can save your breath to cool your porridge," Patience responded before Gabriel could utter any foolishness.

"I will not make that mistake again," Gabriel confirmed.

69

"Could I have the first dance with you, Mrs Price?" Giles asked gallantly.

"Of course, it would be my pleasure," Julia responded.

"Fanny, if you would do me the honour of standing up with me for the first?" Anthony asked. He was not going to tie himself to his stepmother for two dances, although etiquette was that he should stand up with her for the first.

"I should have liked to see if it was the type of assembly I should stand up in before committing myself, but in principle, yes," Fanny responded. "I am not sure Bath has the calibre of society we should be seeking out. I saw no one of note on our journey here, and I don't recognise any names in the visitor's book."

"If you would dance the second with me, please, Mrs Price?" Anthony asked Julia, once more completely ignoring what his stepmother had uttered.

"That would be lovely, thank you, my Lord," Julia responded. She was watching the scene with interest. The family dynamics were fascinating.

"We should go," Anthony said to Gabriel.

"Yes, I suppose we should before we insult the whole of Bath," Gabriel responded grimly.

"Be thankful it isn't my words causing offence, for once," Anthony responded, his face showing no emotion as he bowed his goodbye to Julia and Patience. Fanny looked ready to burst at her stepson's words, but followed the three men out of the room.

"Well! I can see why Gabriel has a low opinion of those two," Patience said once the party were out of earshot.

"Mr Russell seemed pleasant enough," Julia admitted.

"With a mother like that, he cannot be untainted," Patience said.

"Don't say that," Julia interjected. "Comments like that reflect badly on the person who had no say in who they are born to. Think how you would feel if someone said something similar about Miles."

Patience touched her granddaughter's arm. "I am sorry, child. I should mind my tongue."

"I prefer to treat people how they treat me. Looking into any of our backgrounds is a sure way to find some badly behaved relative or another."

They were interrupted by the gentleman with whom Julia had made an acquaintance at the last assembly she'd attended. The master of ceremonies had introduced them at the request of the said gentleman.

"Mrs Price, how lovely to see you again. Is this your grandmother you were speaking of so fondly the other night?"

Julia smiled in welcome. "Good morning, Mr Prescott. This is indeed my grandmother, Mrs Hancock. Grandmama, please allow me to introduce Mr Prescott to you. I danced with him at the last ball we attended."

"It is a pleasure to make your acquaintance," Mr Prescott said with a flourish. He was an older gentleman, probably slightly younger than Gabriel, but looked more aged with his pure grey hair and eyebrows. "You see me alone in Bath and newly arrived. I was so happy to make the acquaintance of your granddaughter at the assembly. I thought I was to spend the whole night without speaking to a single soul."

"No one would be left so alone if the master of ceremonies had anything to do with it," Patience said. "Are you here for a long visit?"

"A few weeks," Mr Prescott said. "Do you intend to attend the next assembly?"

"We do," Julia replied.

71

"Could I accompany you ladies in to supper? It would be a pleasure to enter the room with two pretty fillies on my arm."

"That would be lovely," Patience responded. "We look forward to seeing you then. Good morning to you, Mr Prescott."

The two women moved away from their new acquaintance to leave the pump room. As they walked past the Abbey, Julia took hold of her grandmother's arm. "It seems you have another admirer in Bath. Although his turn of phrase isn't as flattering as Mr Bannerman's. I have never been compared to a horse before!" Julia laughed.

"At my age, flattery is flattery. One must take it where one can," Patience said with an answering smile. "If that means being compared to a fine four-legged beast, so be it."

Chapter 8

Anthony had never looked forward to an assembly as much as he was looking forward to the one to be held in the Lower Assembly Rooms that evening. He'd locked himself away with his valet earlier than he normally would just to escape his stepmother. She drained him.

Gabriel was inclined to be more antagonistic and argumentative towards her, not having the same familial constraints that Anthony had. It didn't lead to a comfortable atmosphere, especially as Giles looked torn in two. Anthony was not close to his brother, but he didn't like it when his stepmother was constantly trying to set them against each other. Anthony would always be honest, however brutal his comments were. It didn't make sense to him not to be, but he could see Giles was of a nature to please, and the situation they were in upset the younger man.

Walking down the stairs of the large townhouse, which had suddenly seemed to shrink since his relations had arrived, he fixed his cuffs to his satisfaction. At least after the first dance, he had no need of spending time with his stepmother. He would be seeking out Julia; she would be a welcome relief after the last day.

Fanny insisted on employing a Sedan Chair and men to convey her to the Assembly Rooms, but the brothers and Gabriel chose to walk. All three were glad of the slight respite, although none voiced their relief. As they reached the end of Henrietta Street, Gabriel suggested they should call in at number ten.

"Mother will be waiting for us," Giles pointed out.

"Feel free to go on ahead," Gabriel suggested. "I'm going to offer to escort my friends."

"Ah, no. I will join you. I have the first dance with Mrs Price after all," Giles said, knowing his reasoning was laughable, but neither Anthony nor Gabriel ridiculed him for it. For the first time, Gabriel was actually developing some sympathy for the young boy. It was clear Fanny wasn't an easy person to please, even though Giles tried his best.

Patience and Julia were surprised but delighted to be escorted into the assembly. The group filled the wide pavement as they walked. Once they'd crossed the narrow street that made up Pulteney Bridge, Giles soon offered his arm to Patience and became engrossed in the conversation between Gabriel and the older woman.

Julia and Anthony followed on behind. "Your brother seems a nice boy," Julia opened.

"He is, in the main," Anthony admitted. "A pity Fanny does not share some of his characteristics. I don't recall my mother, but from what grandfather says, I don't think she was anything like Fanny. I wonder at my father marrying two women so different in character and looks."

Julia realised how confiding Anthony was being, and it surprised and pleased her. "Oh, I think I can see what attracted him; a pretty young face framed by blonde curls is a strong inducement to forming an attachment for a lot of men," she said with a smile.

"It shows a want of character on my father's part," Anthony said with derision.

"Perhaps he was motivated in wanting a mother for you?"

Anthony snorted. "I doubt that. He barely saw me from week to week. I think most of the time he forgot I existed."

74

"That is a shame," Julia said gently. "It can't have been easy for you."

Anthony paused as if considering the notion for the first time. "I suppose one should not miss something if it has never been there, but I did feel there was something lacking. But I didn't know what. The feeling of being separate increased when Fanny had Giles and then Wilfred. I saw their lives were different than mine had been."

"You shouldn't have had to suffer alone," Julia said, her maternal instincts surging to the fore.

"I had nannies to take care of me. I was not neglected."

"There is more than one form of neglect," Julia responded.

"My grandfather said something similar recently. I never considered it as such, but it appears it is seen differently when other people view my upbringing," Anthony acknowledged before their conversation was stopped because of their arrival at the Assembly Rooms.

The group separated once they were through the large welcoming doorway. Julia and Patience disposed of their shawls and pattens and moved through the throng into the main room. Gabriel had remained with them, reluctant to rejoin Fanny, who'd glared at them all when they'd entered as she'd been waiting some moments without company.

"Is there a spare chamber at your address?" Gabriel asked Patience through gritted teeth. "I might need to move if that woman remains in Bath."

"Tsk. You are there to protect your grandson. I'm sure a silly young woman cannot put you off," Patience scolded.

"She is constantly criticising him and everything around her. Goodness knows how Anthony has not exploded before now."

"Perhaps he has more restraint than you give him credit for," Patience suggested.

"I couldn't honestly answer whether he has or not. I wish I understood him more," Gabriel admitted.

"He is a complex boy. Just like his grandfather was. Come, let's find a seat where we can watch all the high jinks of the evening."

Julia was approached by Giles as the musicians indicated the dance was to start. They took their places in a different long-ways set to Anthony and Fanny.

As Julia curtseyed and was honoured by Giles in return she smiled. "I don't think your mother is too fond of Bath and its people."

Giles grimaced. "Mama is not fond of anything these days."

"Perhaps she will be happy when you and your brothers have found wives? She must be a little outnumbered at home, having all boys," Julia was curious about the family, but it wouldn't be *de rigueur* to probe too deeply.

"I pity any chit Anthony brings home. She is doomed to be disliked from the get-go," Giles admitted.

"That is a shame. I have a boy of my own, and although he's only seven, I hope to like the wife he eventually chooses."

"Your boy is lucky. Fortunately, I don't intend to marry for at least the next ten years, so I have no need to fret yet. I would much rather flirt before becoming leg-shackled. It's just that young ladies seem to want serious flirtations that lead to marriage. It is daunting being young in society, I can tell you."

"You are very young to marry quite yet," Julia admitted, with a smile. She might be only six years older than Giles, but it was clear he thought her an elderly matron in comparison to himself. It amused her rather than insulted her.

They danced, both enjoying the other's company. Giles was an entertaining partner, even though he was a little innocent. Julia felt a lot older as the dance progressed. It felt a lifetime ago since she'd been that unworldly.

Giles led her back to their party at the end of the dance, and Anthony grabbed hold of her hand and almost dragged her back to the dance floor. Julia laughed at the action despite being manhandled, for she guessed his motivation and couldn't berate him for trying to escape.

They started the dance in silence, but soon Julia was forced to speak. "My Lord, this is our second time of dancing, and you are frowning once more. I beg you consider my reputation before you condemn me in society's eyes for being the worst dance partner in the whole of Bath."

"For once it is not you making me frown," Anthony admitted.

Julia smiled. "You old flatterer, you!"

"I'm being teased again."

"Yes, you are."

"I am happy to be dancing with you," Anthony admitted.

"I would hate to see your expression if you were not," Julia responded.

Anthony grimaced, for once understanding the comment. "Yet again, I am not being very gentlemanly. I apologise. After half an hour confined with my stepmother in a dance, I don't think I will ever smile again."

"As I have observed that you are one who smiles rarely, I have to point out that you are being a tad overly-dramatic, my Lord," Julia said.

Anthony smiled in genuine amusement. "I can't argue against you."

"Good. There is progress in our friendship."

"Is that what we are? Friends? You seemed so against me at the start," Anthony said, seeming to be genuinely curious and a little confused.

"I never thought that I would consider us as such," Julia admitted. "But I suppose we are. You helped me with Miles in Wells. I have helped to lift your mood a little tonight. That is the type of services friends give to each other. They help when either one needs it," Julia said gently.

Anthony paused, seeming to ponder. "I do believe you are right. I don't think I have ever considered anyone a friend before now." He didn't add that he hadn't wanted a friend until he had met her.

"You can be quite difficult to get to know."

"Yes. I am not very approachable, and my words cause upset. I just don't understand the nuances of people, I suppose. I have no idea why not," Anthony admitted. "Perhaps there should have been more people in my life on a day-to-day basis. Nanny and myself were kept apart, in the main, from Giles and Wilfred and their nanny."

Julia's heart ached the more she came to know Anthony and his background. "Not wishing to sound patronising, or condescending, I feel the need to say that I'm honoured to know you, and the others don't know what they are missing." He was far from perfect, but Julia was beginning to realise that underneath the brusque exterior there lay a decent man. Despite his wealth and consequence, he'd had the type of background she wouldn't wish on any child.

Again, the smile appeared that lit his eyes. "You can't fool me into thinking I would be anything other than a difficult companion."

"I have always liked a challenge," Julia said with an answering smile. His previous misdemeanours excused, if not forgotten.

"As my ally, I need to ask your advice. How do I deal with my stepmother? I can feel her glaring at me even as we dance."

Julia laughed. She'd also seen the looks aimed in their direction, but they amused her rather than troubled her. "Confuse her. Dance every dance, speak to people. Don't make yourself an easy target for her glowers; don't keep still."

"But that would mean exerting myself and trying to be polite," Anthony responded.

"Trying is a start. Who knows were it might lead? You could discover a whole new world of excitement and new friendships."

"I doubt that very much," Anthony responded with a wry expression. "But I suppose talking to others prevents me from being cornered by Fanny for the evening."

"See, you are already realising the advantage of the scheme. You will soon be a veritable social butterfly," Julia smiled.

Anthony shuddered dramatically but smiled at Julia. He was coming to understand some of the enjoyment that could be gained by being teased and teasing in return. There was a serious vein underneath the funning, but to one who could probably never be completely carefree, it didn't seem to matter. In some respects the feeling of Julia having hidden depths made it easier to relate to her.

After their dances, Anthony returned Julia to Patience before leaving the group and seeking out the young ladies he'd danced with previously. Any of them were preferable to spending time with Fanny. Julia was pleased her advice had been listened to, even if she suffered a pang when it was obvious Anthony was being flirted with by his dancing partners, who were younger, prettier, and dressed in finer clothes than she. Julia ran her hands down her dress self-consciously; there was no point in wishing for the impossible. She couldn't afford fine clothes. She was the age she was, and even in her younger days, hadn't been as pretty as those young women who were keen to dance with Anthony. Julia straightened her shoulders; wishing for the impossible made no one happy. She turned back to her companions with a smile on her face; she was determined to enjoy her evening.

Julia wasn't the only one to notice Anthony's popularity with the young ladies. At the edge of the ballroom, Fanny was silently fuming. She indicated to Giles to step to the side, away from their new acquaintances.

"It seems your brother is a hit with the desperate souls of Bath," Fanny hissed at Giles.

"I am hoping he'll introduce me to the beauty he is dancing with at the moment. It seems Bath has more to offer than I thought when we first arrived," Giles responded, cheerfully watching his brother's partner closely.

"Anyone of true breeding will not be visiting this outdated place, but it is up to you to get to know anyone whom Anthony is spending time with," Fanny instructed.

"I don't mind dancing and a little dalliance or two, but why does it have to be with whomever Anthony is spending time?" Giles asked in genuine puzzlement.

"Time is running out for him to find a wife. If we can help things along a little, you will become the rightful heir," Fanny whispered angrily, annoyed at her son for being slow on the uptake.

"Mother, that isn't good *ton*. Anthony is the first born and a generous brother at that. Some of my school friends are taken to task when they find themselves without a feather to fly with, whereas when I am cleaned out, Anthony always provides a few extra guineas. He doesn't even advance it from my allowance. That is top of the tree in my book!" Giles defended his half-brother.

"You'll be — how would you phrase it? — swimming in lard if you inherit," Fanny responded.

Giles laughed. "I never thought I would see the day when my own mother was speaking cant! This is famous! I shall have to write to Wilfred. It will send him into raptures," Giles said with glee.

"Be serious," Fanny scolded. "I want you to stick by your brother and be charming and flattering to the chits Anthony is friendly with, whether they are the daughters of 'cits' or whoever they are."

"So, I have your permission to have a good time?" Giles asked, his eyes twinkling at realising his mother had given him carte blanche.

"Just stop your brother making an offer to anyone," Fanny instructed.

"Anything for you Mother," Giles responded, giving his mother a kiss on the cheek, before leaving her to move further into the ballroom. His visit had just become more interesting. He didn't take his mother's motivation seriously. Since he'd been a boy, she'd bemoaned the fact that it would be Anthony who inherited, whereas he'd just accepted it. Not seriously considering that the money would pass to himself, he relished the opportunity to enjoy himself with his mother's blessing and Anthony's financial support.

Julia was approached by Mr Prescott, who with a flourishing bow, came to claim his companions for supper.

81

Julia and Patience took an arm each and were escorted into the room that was laid out with tables for those who wished to enjoy some of the sustaining fayre on offer.

Mr Prescott ordered tea for himself and the ladies. "My, this is a fine evening," he said, settling himself between the two women. "I am not one for dancing every dance, but I enjoy watching the young ones having a good time. You dance very well, my dear, and I hope you have space for another dance with me," he said addressing himself to Julia.

"I have. It would be lovely to dance with you again," Julia responded.

"Have you settled on how long you are to remain in Bath, Mr Prescott?" Patience asked.

"A few more weeks. I am here to sort out a little business, but then I hope to return to my home over the border in South Wales," Mr Prescott explained. "I don't like being away from home for too long."

"We've never travelled to Wales," Patience responded.

"It is a beautiful country and not too distant to travel to Cheltenham, Bristol, and Bath. I would recommend a visit; the countryside is very picturesque."

They were interrupted by the arrival of Gabriel and Anthony. "Is there room for two little ones?" Gabriel asked, sitting down before being invited to do so.

Julia wondered at the flicker of annoyance that flashed across Mr Prescott's face before he welcomed the two gentlemen. She didn't think it would be too long before the two older men were seriously vying for her grandmother's attention, which pleased her. More drinks were ordered and a silence descended on the group.

"Mr Prescott was just telling us how beautiful Wales is," Julia started. "I haven't travelled much so every new place is of interest to me," she finished.

"I would be willing to act as host if yourself and your grandmother would like to visit there," Mr Prescott quickly offered.

"Thank you, but at the moment we have no firm plans because of my son," Julia said quickly. She didn't want to make any commitment to such a new acquaintance, nor did she want to commit to spending money on another trip.

"I shall leave the offer open, if the young chap should require country air," Mr Prescott said easily. "Where are your family from, my Lord?" he asked Anthony.

"Worcestershire," Anthony responded.

"A fine county," Mr Prescott acceded.

"It is very similar to those around it, although Birmingham is expanding rapidly. I travelled quite a bit over the border when I was younger. The river Wye provides a good fishing ground for an eager angler," Anthony said almost eloquently, astounding those in his party who understood his usual reticence.

"It does indeed! I've spent far too many hours there myself over the years," Mr Prescott responded. "My fishing lies in another direction these days, but I have happy memories of spending fine days there."

"I would prefer to be in a warm ballroom," Patience said. "I have never understood the fascination with outside sports when it always seems to take vast amounts of brandy to warm up afterwards."

"One look at you Mrs Hancock, and brandy would no longer be needed," Mr Prescott said.

Julia saw Gabriel and Anthony exchange a look, but smiled to herself. It was good for her grandmother to be flirted with.

Giles approached their table and smiled at the group. "I hope everyone is having as good a time as I am. The ladies here are delightful! I am hoping you will be staying for a while, brother. Mother is determined to stay as long as you do."

Giles had inadvertently spoiled Anthony's evening with his innocent words, but for once, Anthony didn't respond as he would have done normally. "Who has captured your interest?" he asked, genuinely puzzled as to how his brother could be so enthusiastic about the ladies he'd been introduced to.

"Why Miss Stock in particular and Miss Carruthers, of course!" Giles responded. "I think we should suggest a trip out with them soon, brother. I'm sure the surrounding areas will offer some entertainment for a day's excursion."

"Don't get carried away with your plans. If they don't come up to snuff, mother will have something to say," Anthony cautioned.

"She's turned over a new leaf," Giles said. "She is speaking to Miss Stock's mother now."

Anthony rose from his seat. "Let us go to mother, Giles. It is not fair to leave Mrs Stock alone to her fate."

The two gentlemen left, and Mr Prescott broke the silence once more. "These young cubs do run around so; they both seem intent on many flirtations whilst they are here."

"As we all did in our younger days," Gabriel defended his grandson.

"I have found that the older I have got, the more I've appreciated our fairer sex and learned how to treat them with care and affection," Mr Prescott continued.

"I am sure the ladies of your acquaintance appreciate your consideration," Patience responded.

"I hope so. It is my aim to provide only the best for those I care for," Mr Prescott said.

"Flummery and fudge," Gabriel muttered under his breath.

Chapter 9

Spending time with Giles as an adult was certainly interesting and challenging for Anthony. His half-brother bordered on being a dandy but had enough charm to not repulse those prone to dismiss the more flamboyant dressing that Giles favoured. If his collars were a little too high, his smile and sincere address enabled his excessively starched collars to be ignored. If he spent more time over the fall of his cravat than most people took to dress, he was indulged as a young man not yet learned about the important aspects of life. Even Gabriel took to the boy despite his initial protestations when hearing of his arrival.

Miss Stock, Miss Carruthers, and their mothers were to join the now large group of friends. Giles had insisted they would have a 'swell time of it' if they all planned their days to coincide with activities. As a result, Anthony found himself completely discomfited by being surrounded by people he barely knew.

As the brothers rode on horseback along with Miss Stock and Miss Carruthers to Wells, whilst their mothers, Fanny, Gabriel, Patience, Julia, and Miles travelled in Anthony's carriage, Giles congratulated himself on pleasing his mother for once. She had actually smiled at him that morning and told him he was a good son.

Giles rode between the two ladies; Anthony was left to follow behind a little way. Giles felt no compunction about excluding his brother; it was not through malice but the eagerness of a young man to be in the company of two pretty ladies.

Eventually, Miss Stock separated herself from the leading grouping and joined Anthony.

"Forgive us, my Lord, for neglecting you," the engaging young woman said. She was blonde haired and blue eyed and quite fetching in her blue riding habit.

"I was quite happy alone," Anthony admitted.

"Oh — That is good. Hah. Well. Your brother is very entertaining," Miss Stock continued.

"Is he?"

"Why, yes! Are you funning with me, my Lord? Trying to make out you don't find him amusing?"

"No. I'm being perfectly serious. I spend little time with him; therefore, I don't know if he is of an amusing character or not. To be fair, he has always been pleasant around me, but that might have something to do with him usually requiring funds, which I hold," Anthony admitted.

"Goodness me!" Miss Stock responded in surprise. "I suppose not all families are in each other's pockets as mine usually is."

"Indeed."

"Are you not missing the joys of the London season?" Miss Stock asked, keen to learn more about a handsome, unattached member of the aristocracy.

"Not at all. I would rather spend my time in my hunting lodge."

"Are you more of a country lover than town?"

"I prefer places that are not filled with people, who insist on being shallow and duplicitous in many cases. I don't understand the games they play, nor do I wish to."

"Ah. My father said he isn't inclined for me to have a season in London. He said although we have enough money to buy half of— ah, I shouldn't be so crass in talking about money. Forgive me, but what I mean is, our situation in life would be looked down on by London society. And now because of my uncouth utterings, you will be assured of the fact that 'cits' and the aristocracy should never mix," Miss Stock admitted.

"Not at all. You have money. There is no point in lying about the fact. I don't lie about my circumstances, so why should you?" Anthony said.

"Thank you." Miss Stock shot him a grateful smile. She decided it was time to move the conversation onto safer grounds, where she wouldn't show her ill-breeding in quite the same way. "It must be nice to be able to spend time with your brother whilst you are all in Bath. I miss the rest of my family, but it was only right to support mother whilst she takes the waters."

"I am supporting my grandfather in the same way," Anthony admitted.

"It was a pleasure to make your acquaintance so early in our stay, my Lord. At least now we can look forward to the entertainments. My mother's cousin, Mrs Carruthers, decided she would join us with my cousin, Lucy, but we were afraid we wouldn't make many new acquaintances. Even in a place like Bath, there would be some people who would not like the fact we are of trade," Miss Stock explained honestly.

"My stepmother might have some prejudice in that regard, but the rest of our party is more accepting," Anthony admitted.

"Oh, but Lady Lever has been nothing but welcoming! She spoke to my mother for a full half-hour last night and was all politeness."

"Then I stand corrected," Anthony said. "She isn't usually so keen to please."

Miss Stock smiled, a little unsure as to how to respond to such direct comments. She rode on for a little while without speaking.

Julia had been unable to prevent herself from watching the exchange, partly out of curiosity and partly out of slight jealousy. She cursed herself, but although Anthony annoyed her most of the time, she was attracted to him, and it wasn't purely physical. He seemed as damaged as she sometimes felt, and she was self-aware enough to know she was undoubtably drawn to him.

She pondered on the fact that it might not be an attraction to Anthony that was causing her present feelings of jealously but envious feelings towards his two female companions. She couldn't actually remember a time when she'd been as carefree as the two young women who were accompanying them. Bruce's impact on her life had been so brutal that thinking back to a time when she could remember being light-hearted and innocent meant looking back over too many other memories. It was hard enough being herself at the moment, or the person she was projecting as herself. Looking to her past was for another time. She held Miles a little closer as he sat, not very still, on her knee. He was all that mattered now.

Anthony looked relieved once the conversation ceased, and just once, Julia's eyes met his. Was it a long-suffering glance he'd given her, or was it her imagination? He waved to Miles, who eagerly returned the salute, babbling excitedly about Lord Lever's horsemanship. Smiling slightly, she agreed with her son before turning away from the window.

The arrival of the party into Wells, saw them splitting into different groups. Giles headed towards the cathedral with the Misses Stock and Carruthers, their mothers, and his own.

Anthony helped Gabriel, Julia, and Patience out of the carriage before their usual group of the eldest and the youngest of the party joined ranks, leaving Anthony and Julia to their own devices. The pair followed behind with Julia trying to smooth down the front of her pelisse.

"The problem with having a seven-year-old on your knee is that they just cannot keep still. I look a mess," Julia groaned. Her clothes weren't as fine as the others in the group, and now that she was creased, she felt even more the outsider.

"You look like a mother who does not try to rid herself of her child. It's a commendable trait. You should not worry about a slight crumpling of your attire," Anthony replied, once more surprisingly quick to reassure her.

"Oh well, I suppose there always has to be a poor relative in a group. I shall have to content myself with my role," Julia sighed dramatically.

Anthony chuckled quietly. "Don't let your grandmother hear you, or you shall be taken shopping. I am sure of it."

"You are right. She is always trying to spend her money on me, but I am enough of a drain on her resources. I won't let her spend more than she has to," Julia admitted.

Anthony looked sideways at Julia. She wasn't saying the words to stir sympathy; he knew that without a doubt. She, like him, very often stated the truth even if it was uncomfortable to say or hear. "Was no provision left for you and your son?"

Julia sighed. "No. I didn't know how bad things were until Bruce died. I don't know what would have happened if he had lived. I suppose we'd have ended in the debtor's prison." It was the first time she'd voiced the words to anyone.

90

"Your grandmother would not have helped if your husband had lived?" Anthony was driven to know more about Julia's background. He hoped it would help him understand why he was drawn to her.

"No. She could not have given as much as we needed. It sounds terrible to say that Bruce's death meant we could sell everything and reduce our outgoings to a minimum. My grandfather had left me a small legacy, which I had no idea about, but it was only to be paid out on my husband's demise," Julia said.

"That is an unusual specification. I'm presuming your family did not approve of your choice of life-partner?" Anthony asked.

Julia let out a sigh. "They did at the beginning. There was no one so charming."

"But when they got to know him… " Anthony's words were left hanging.

"The little that he showed them of his true character was enough to create a deep dislike," Julia admitted, her words only hinting at what her homelife had been like.

Anthony remained quiet. He was angry that someone could misuse the person they were supposed to love. It convinced him further that marriage was a flawed state into which to enter.

"It seems our favourite place to visit is Wells," Julia said, changing the subject onto safer topics. "I have warned Miles about saving his energy for the walk back."

"I have instructed the carriage to meet us at the inn where we will be partaking of refreshments, although he was no weight to carry," Anthony admitted.

"You are very kind to consider him," Julia responded. When it appeared that Anthony was going to speak, she jumped in quickly before he had a chance to. "I realise it is the sensible option."

Anthony smiled. "Am I that predictable?"

"A little, although hearing logic and truth whenever you speak can still be surprising. Most people say what is expected of them, rather than be honest," Julia admitted, once more appreciating the change on a person's features that a smile could bring.

"I am trying to consider what I say before I say it, but I'm afraid it is harder than it would appear."

"I'm sure it is. And I will try not to torment you about it, although I cannot promise completely!"

"I would not expect you to."

"Your stepmother seems more pleased with Bath than when we first made her acquaintance," Julia probed a little.

"I cannot fathom the change; then again, I don't understand why she came to visit in the first instance," Anthony admitted.

"Perhaps she wanted to see you?"

"In the hope that it was I who was ailing," Anthony said grimly.

"Surely not?" Julia asked. "Are you making a joke?"

"I wish I was, but I would not know how to. By my father putting the clause in the will, it was inevitable that it would drive a further wedge between myself and my relatives. I don't blame her for her desire to see her son inherit a large portion; most people would react in exactly the same way. I sometimes just wish she was not quite so open about it," Anthony said quietly.

Julia remained silent, but in a forward action, she slipped her arm through Anthony's. He looked in astonishment at her, but didn't pull away from the touch.

Julia smiled. "As a mother, if I see a child who is upset I have to respond to that hurt," she explained.

"I can hardly be considered a child."

"If your mother had lived, you would have been her child even if you reached the ripe old age of sixty!" Julia smiled.

"I do sometimes wonder if life would have been different if she had survived," Anthony admitted in a rare moment of candour.

"Without doubt it would have been, but there is no use languishing over maybes and perhaps," Julia said gently. "We have to spend our time dealing with what life throws at us, not waste energy on what could have happened."

"Why do I tell you these things?" Anthony asked, genuinely puzzled.

"Because I'm no threat to you. I am not a young flighty thing who will break your heart and reveal your secrets," Julia teased.

"No. You would not," Anthony responded seriously.

"I don't know whether you are referring to my breaking your heart or divulging your secrets, but I think it prudent not to ask for clarification. We have been getting along relatively well, so there is no point in spoiling it," Julia said.

Anthony chuckled, but put his hand over Julia's and squeezed it gently. It was the tenderest touch he'd ever given to anyone.

Chapter 10

Giles was very pleased with himself. Miss Stock was a wealthy heiress, and although at first he'd thought she was determined to set her cap for Anthony, over the last few days, she'd seemed to show a decided preference for himself. As a younger son, he was well used to being overlooked for the richer, titled, elder brother, so he was enjoying this new state of popularity.

Miss Carruthers didn't seem too smitten with Anthony either, which suited Giles just fine. He could report to his mother that neither young lady was in danger of receiving or accepting a proposal from Anthony.

Unfortunately for Giles, his news wasn't as well-received as he'd hoped. "Of course they aren't going to declare their feelings to you!" Fanny snapped at her eldest child. "You could run straight to your brother and tell him they were trying to ensnare him. No one would be fool enough to do that. Just think of the extra advantage Anthony would have if he married either of those wealthy chits. It grieves me to think what combined fortune they would have. No. You have to make sure they are under no doubt that Anthony is not a suitable match."

"How the devil am I supposed to do that?" Giles retaliated, one of the rare times he had spoken back to his mother.

"Whilst I would never agree to your marrying someone so base born, you need to get them both to fall in love with you. Do whatever it takes," Fanny responded, leaving the astounded Giles alone.

94

The young boy fulminated for an hour, becoming angrier with his mother as he thought over her words. Eventually, he took himself off to Sydney Gardens to try to cheer his mood.

Walking down the pathways of the well laid out gardens, he absentmindedly pondered on the problem of his mother and Anthony. He liked Anthony. Oh, he was an odd fish, but he'd never been a cruel older brother as some of his friends had experienced with their siblings. Whenever Giles had sought Anthony's help, it had been given, sometimes with a few stern words, but never with derision and ridicule. For one who had been indulged by his mother and nanny, Giles was a gentle soul. Now, as a young man, who had tastes that exceeded his income, he was even more inclined to look favourably on a brother who allowed the excesses to go without much comment. This havey-cavey business his mother was encouraging didn't sit well with him. Although, flirting with two pretty ladies wasn't much of a hardship, it was the deceit that surrounded it that was causing him discomfort.

As he walked, an exclamation of surprise brought him to his senses.

"Miss Carruthers! I did not see you there! I do beg your pardon," Giles said, with a welcome smile at the young woman who'd spoken his name as he almost walked past her.

"You appeared deep in thought. I was not sure if I should leave you be," Miss Carruthers admitted. She was two years older than her cousin, taller, darker, and surer of herself, but Miss Stock had the advantage of being the prettiest of the two, which Lucy was not jealous of in the slightest.

"I'm glad you did. I dislike melancholy, especially when it is I who is in the doldrums," Giles admitted. "What brings you here?"

"I am an earlier riser than my cousin," Lucy explained. "I like walking through the gardens and taking a stroll down Great Pulteney Street; it is my favourite area of the city as it leads out towards the countryside around."

"Are you lodging close by?"

"In Laura Place," Lucy admitted, expressing how wealthy her group was by staying in one of the most sought-after addresses in the city.

"Just down the way from where we are staying. My brother's house is on Great Pulteney Street," Giles said with pleasure. "Would you like to join me for a walk? I can return you home after we have explored these pathways."

"That would be delightful, thank you," Lucy responded, indicating that her maid should fall a little way back, to allow for some privacy with her companion.

Giles gallantly offered his arm, and Lucy placed her hand on it as they started to walk.

"Are you enjoying Bath?" Lucy asked.

"I am now that I've made yours and Miss Stock's acquaintance," Giles answered honestly.

Lucy laughed. "That is very sweet of you to say so. I am sure you are very sought after."

"That is where you are wrong," Giles admitted. "The younger son is never as sought after as his older brother."

"Surely that depends on the merits of the brothers?" Lucy asked.

Giles smiled. "You really have not spent much time with the *ton*, have you, Miss Carruthers? It is a veritable shark-infested sea in Society. The richest rise to the top while the

96

rest of us have to scrabble about on the sea bed for the left-overs."

"A man with charm and family connections cannot achieve greatness?" Lucy asked incredulously. "Now, I'm convinced you are bamming me with a Banbury tale!"

"Maybe a little," Giles said with a smile. "Are you not to have a season as Miss Stock is not?"

"No, but it has nothing to do with my father's wishes," Lucy admitted.

"Oh?"

"If I tell you a secret, would you keep it?" Lucy asked, a twinkle in her eye.

"Of course, as a gentleman, I would never divulge a lady's confidences," Giles said, his curiosity well and truly piqued.

"I don't want a season because I don't intend to marry," Lucy admitted in a mock-whisper.

"No!" Giles was genuinely shocked. "I thought every young lady wanted to wed."

"I have the advantage of being independently wealthy. I have no need of a husband," Lucy explained.

"But a family," Giles protested. "Surely you would want that?"

"I see I have shocked you, Mr Russell; I suspected I would," Lucy laughed. "I am quite happy at the moment, planning my life out as I would wish it to be without needing to bend to anyone else's wishes or will. That would change if I were to marry. I find my present situation suits me perfectly."

"When you say it like that, it does sound appealing. My mother was convinced you were hankering after my brother," Giles admitted perhaps a little too truthfully.

"Lord Lever? No! We would never suit even if I were to join the marriage mart. He needs someone meek and mild, I feel," Lucy said with authority. "My cousin would be far better suited to someone so strident in his opinions."

Giles's face fell. "Do you think so?"

"I do," Lucy responded, but she'd noticed Giles's reaction with interest. "But my cousin doesn't have to marry someone with a fortune, as her own portion is large. If she were to find a person she preferred *more* than Lord Lever, I am sure, as long as she were to be happy, my aunt and uncle would be content. They are not longing for her to have a grand title."

"Oh, that's good. Nice to know when one's parents want only the best for you," Giles said, his mood a little lighter. It was good that Miss Stock had the potential to be persuadable from her focus on Anthony. It would console his mother and make his job easier. Failing to realise he was inordinately pleased on his own behalf, he continued to chatter with Miss Carruthers.

*

When Lucy returned home, she sought out her cousin. "Nancy, I have just spent the most enjoyable half-hour with Mr Russell in Sydney Gardens. He really is a delightful companion."

Nancy stretched languidly on her bed, not yet quite ready to get up. "You have the best luck, Lucy. He is very handsome and charming."

"Yes, he is," Lucy continued, her tone teasing. "And if you continue in the way you are at the moment, I think you will have both of the Russell brothers in love with you!"

Nancy laughed. "I doubt that. Lord Lever is very grand, but he's very aloof and top-lofty. Mama would love for me to marry a man who is a full member of the aristocracy, but I am not sure I would ever be suited to Lord Lever or he be interested in me. Mr Russell is very agreeable though and has his own title. One would hardly believe they were brothers."

"Yes. They are very different. Just think, if you marry Lord Lever, you will have a title and a fine estate in Worchester, and if you marry Mr Russell, you will produce the most angelic looking children who ever lived! Two sets of blue eyes and blonde hair combining can do nothing other than produce celestial offspring," Lucy pointed out.

Nancy giggled. "Oh, stop! We have known them only a few days."

"But how long does it take for two souls to collide and realise their destiny is to be together?" Lucy asked dramatically, with her hand on her heart.

"For someone who is so pragmatic about love and marriage, you read too many romance novels," Nancy said, tugging Lucy's hand away from the mock-dramatic pose.

"I have to know what's happening, even if it does not appeal to me. You never know. When you have decided which husband to choose, I might decide that I will console the brother you disappoint and marry him out of pity," Lucy said.

"Do you like either of them?" Nancy asked seriously. "For I would never seek favour with someone you could lose your heart to, Lucy. I truly could not."

"And that is why you are the best cousin in the world. Fear not my dear; neither of your gentlemen has made an imprint on my heart, I can assure you," Lucy said seriously. "Feel free to ponder over both of their attributes before you decide which one to have, for either would be very lucky to have you."

"Thank you, Lucy. You are very kind," Nancy replied. She twisted her hair between her fingers, a sure sign she was troubled.

99

"What is it, poppet?" Lucy asked gently.

"We have money to recommend us, but do you think I aim too high?" Nancy asked, her expression full of doubt. She was no longer the teasing, laughing twenty-year old, entertaining her dance partner or riding companion, but an unmarried young woman in a world, where she was just one of many equally pretty and rich debutantes, all with much to offer potential beaux.

"Oh, Nancy, my dear, no!" Lucy said immediately. "You have every right to aim for whomever you wish. They would be fortunate in having you as a wife — and I am saying that as an impartial observer. Obviously."

Nancy laughed. "Of course you are. Very unbiased! But seriously... "

"No. There's no seriously about it," Lucy said firmly. "Our money is just as good as theirs; in fact it is better. We've earned it; it has not been handed down through generations or obtained from their tenants who live in poverty whilst paying high rents in many cases."

"Our papas have a workforce as well. It is only the same as having tenants," Nancy pointed out.

"Who earn a good living for what they do," Lucy responded. "I'm not saying our trade is perfect, but it is not for anyone else to shun us when they don't actually know us."

"You have always been braver than I at not caring what others think."

"It is not that I don't care about other opinions; it's just that I think respect has to be earned," Lucy explained. "I am always going to give the rank the deference it deserves, but for me to admire an individual, they have to earn my good opinion. One thing that does concern me a little is your attitude."

"Why is that?"

"It is clear you like at least one of our new gentlemen friends aside from my teasing," Lucy said gently.

"Y-yes," Nancy admitted.

"Are you going to admit which one? Is it Mr Russell or are you considering both of them? I wouldn't condemn you if you were. You have pointed out they offer different attributes, and I admit, Lord Lever could be more appealing on closer acquaintance."

Nancy smiled. "They are both fine gentlemen, but only one has caught my attention, and before you ask which one, I'm not going to say who it is because it will only make me even more self-conscious in his company. It is hard enough to remain coherent and try to be charming as it is."

"Then I will not press you — for now — although I know you'll chose the one who suits you best rather than the one your mother would prefer," Lucy said with a smile. "My concern is that if you don't feel worthy enough about the society to which Lord Lever and Mr Russell belong: is it wise to develop a tendrè for either of them? If anything came of an attachment, you would be thrust into their world whether you liked it or not," Lucy cautioned.

"I know. It is too early to say, but his position in life has put doubts in my mind. I don't feel that I can just let my feelings grow naturally. I have to think through the consequences of an attachment before anything has actually happened," Nancy admitted. "All this worry, and he might not even like me!"

"He would not like you? How on earth would you think that? If that were to be the case, you could not possibly marry him because he would be a clod!" Lucy responded firmly.

101

Chapter 11

Giles was keen to be in the company of the two pretty young women with whom he was now acquainted, and he enjoyed the company of Patience and Julia, so he encouraged his brother and Gabriel to plan further outings as a group.

They watched a concert in the Assembly Rooms and a fireworks display in Sydney Gardens. On the second time they all joined in a public breakfast there, Julia smiled at Lucy and Nancy. "We are becoming one of the regular faces at these events," she said as she helped herself to a bath bun from a pile on a groaning table of food.

"We are going out on a ride with Mr Russell and Lord Lever, so it's a perfect way to start the day," Lucy said, helping herself to a large portion of ham and bread. "You don't join us, Mrs Price?"

"No. I am not what could be considered a fine horsewoman and so would hold everyone else back. I know how much you more experienced riders like to burn off energy, whereas I'm more content on an old mule," Julia responded good-naturedly.

"My brother has bought a few of those over the years," Anthony said, joining the threesome.

"Of which you have informed him," Julia responded.

Anthony smiled slightly. "On many occasions."

"With great delight," Giles said, never too far away from the younger women of the group.

"An elder brother would always seek for supremacy," Lucy acknowledged. "I have seen it with my father and his brothers many times."

"Yes, but do they do it with such glee?" Giles asked with a mocking glare at Anthony.

"Glee? Are you sure you are referring to me?" Anthony asked in genuine surprise. "I'm not sure I would even know how to describe that emotion, let alone, feel it."

Julia couldn't help her laugh escaping even though Nancy and Lucy looked a little perplexed. "An appearance of glee then?" she asked Giles.

"And smugness," the long-suffering brother responded.

"If you will not take the advice of a brother nearly ten years older… " Anthony shrugged.

"But does older mean wiser?" Julia asked archly.

Giles sighed. "With regards to horseflesh, yes," he admitted.

"Mr Russell! I thought we had his Lordship on the ropes then, but you have let me down," Julia teased.

"You are more than capable of tormenting me single-handedly," Anthony said without malice.

Julia smiled at the slight twinkle in Anthony's eyes. "I'm glad you see it, my Lord. I would hate all my hard work to go to waste."

Anthony shook his head in defeat. Although becoming used to being teased by Julia, he couldn't always parry with her. He was still very much learning in that respect.

Julie didn't carry on the conversation; she was happy to have had her banter with the complicated Anthony but knew things could quickly become misunderstood. For some reason, she didn't want him to be at a disadvantage in front of their young friends. She continued to tuck into her food and lapsed into a comfortable silence whilst she and Anthony watched Giles entertain Lucy and Nancy.

"Your brother seems to be a hit," she said quietly, as once more the three started to laugh at something Giles had uttered.

"He is fortunate in that he has an easy nature and is well liked wherever he goes," Anthony admitted.

"I think that is often the case between the eldest and the other siblings," Julia continued.

"In what way?"

"A man with a title is sure to receive a warm welcome, but a younger son, who cannot rely on a grand title or stately home and inheritance has to rely more on his own charms to recommend himself to strangers," Julia explained, her serious countenance not quite hiding the flicker of amusement in her eyes.

"Thank God I was not the younger son. I would have been ostracised even more than I have been," Anthony said.

"Really? If that is the case of your experience in society, I can't tease you about it," Julia said becoming serious.

"It is a fact of life; there is nothing to languish over. Brooding on past happenings will not change anything; it didn't change me. I am not sure I could have changed if I'd wanted to," Anthony admitted.

Julia had stepped a little further away from their group, not wishing for the others to overhear the conversation. She knew Anthony enough to have the suspicion that he was not used to speaking openly. "Why do you feel so excluded?" she asked quietly. "From an outsiders' perspective, you have everything."

"I have much," Anthony admitted. "But you know me well enough that you know I cannot communicate as smoothly as perhaps I should be able to."

Julia's lips twitched. "Yes. Direct, is a word that immediately springs to mind when thinking of you."

"Yet my brother would attract flowery words, such as appealing, charming, personable," Anthony countered.

"I suppose so. Even though you are different, it must be advantageous to have brothers," Julia said. "There were times when I would have liked to have someone close to talk over my concerns."

"You didn't seek out your grandmother?"

"No. There are some things, a parent, or grandparent should not know," Julia admitted. "At those times I would have welcomed a brother or sister from whom to seek advice and support."

"I feel it would depend on the brother," Anthony said. "I can't say I really know Giles or Wilfred. They seek me out when they want something — and I say that with no bitterness — but in the main we rarely meet or commune."

"Do you at least write when you are separated?"

"No. We have nothing to say to each other," Anthony admitted.

"That is a shame," Julia responded. Everything she learned about Anthony made her heart ache for him. He seemed so set apart from everything around him, and yet, the more she had contact with him, the more she suspected there was a heart and feelings under his stiff exterior. "Were you close to your father?" She probed further.

Anthony laughed bitterly. "Not at all. He thought me the oddity I was, expressed eloquently through the final terms in his will."

"You explained the terms previously, which to an outsider are quite shocking," Julia admitted.

"He expressed them in a way I was hardly likely to forget — or forgive — in a hurry," Anthony said.

Julia remained silent but watched Anthony. There was a flicker of hurt, which was quickly hidden behind a derisive

105

expression. It didn't seem as if he were going to say anything further, and then he put down his plate and offered her his arm.

Giles noticed they were moving away from the table and delayed their departure. "Brother! Where are you going? We are promised on a ride!"

"I shall return shortly. I'm walking Mrs Price to the entrance, and then we can depart," Anthony answered.

"I am leaving then?" Julia whispered.

Anthony faltered. "Am I being too presumptuous? I am, aren't I?" he asked, his tone for once full of doubt.

Julia squeezed his arm under her hand. "You want to tell me something, and I want to listen. I tease too much. I am sorry."

"I should be used to your teasing by now."

"As I suspect you haven't been teased much over the years, it must take some getting used to," Julia said gently.

"It does. But it is not always unwelcome," Anthony admitted.

"That gives me hope that I am not causing too much consternation. Now what do you want to tell me out of earshot of our friends?" Julia asked.

"I don't honestly know why I want to tell you this. My grandfather knows about it, as does my stepmother. It is of no one else's concern really," Anthony started.

"But… "

"But I feel compelled to tell you. I think I must be going soft in the head, wanting your sympathy or compassion," Anthony confessed, as confused at his feelings as he'd ever been.

"We are friends, remember? After our disastrous start, it is what we decided to be, and friends share their thoughts, whether good or bad."

Anthony sighed. "I have always been the outsider. Even my father couldn't cope with what he considered my insubordination, but to me, it was just pointing out the obvious," Anthony started. "It resulted in me spending a lot of time alone. Even at school I did not make friends easily and eventually requested I be home tutored instead of being subjected to the trials of life with others," he finished.

"It must have been a very lonely upbringing," Julia said.

Anthony looked at her, for the first time looking vulnerable and not trying to mask his expression. He looked younger and unsure. "I've always been alone. At least by now I am used to the sensation."

Julia fought the tears of pity springing to her eyes. He would not respond well to such a reaction, so although she blinked slightly more than she would normally, there was no overtly outward reaction from her. "Your grandfather adores you. That must be of some comfort."

"He is a blood relative. I am the only connection to his daughter; he feels the familial obligation of that. I can and do understand his motivation in being with me," Anthony said in explanation of his grandfather's presence in his life.

"No!" Julia said forcefully. "I cannot let a statement that is so wrong pass unchallenged. I see how he feels about you and can only be sorry that you don't view his affection for what it really is. He might not gush and be overt with his fondness, but believe me, there is adoration in all his looks and in his actions towards you. I doubt he could feel more," Julia defended her new acquaintance.

Anthony stopped walking, a deep frown marring his features. "Do you think so?" he finally asked.

"I know so," Julia confirmed. "You say you are not aware of people's feelings and how to read a situation, and that must have much to do with your upbringing. But believe me when I say I have learned to read people very well. I see clearly how much he cares for you."

Anthony glanced at Julia, once more being reminded that her history was not a happy one, but now was not appropriate to probe further. He mulled over her words.

"Thank you," he eventually said. "I will consider what you have said, but I trust you enough to know you wouldn't have uttered the sentiments without being convinced of their certainty."

"I would not. Give yourself time to look back over everything he's said and done. I think you will come to realise you haven't been quite so alone after all."

"Maybe not," Anthony admitted. "It is a novel thought. I have never considered an alternative state. You have certainly given me lots to mull over, Mrs Price."

"Good. But you were going to tell me about your father's will," Julia continued. "I hope I can convince you that you might have misinterpreted that as well."

"I doubt that," Anthony said with derision. "My father was as clear with his thoughts as I can be with my words. I hate to say it, but perhaps I was not so different from my parent as I would like to think I am, after all."

They walked around the side of the hotel, passing many people but not acknowledging any. As they strolled slowly down one of the side paths, leading away from the hotel and towards the road surrounding Sydney Gardens, Anthony continued. "My father was clear in his opinion of me. Oh, I know you will try to persuade me I'm wrong, but believe me, in this instance, I am not. When the will was read, I was stunned. 'As the only way to see the family line continue from my firstborn, I am forced to offer an incentive to the unfortunate soul forced to marry him. Three quarters of the inheritance will be held back until my eldest marries, prior to his thirtieth birthday. That should give him enough time to persuade someone to shackle themselves to him. If not, although he will keep the title, as I cannot change that, the unentailed inheritance will go to my second born to make use of it. A pity I can't leave the home and lands to him as well if my eldest fails to marry. Prove to us all, Anthony, that you are not the oddity we know you to be. Some women will be tempted by your money if nothing else.' There, I think his words make his feelings extremely clear. I feel even your good-nature cannot find a way of softening those words," Anthony said with a grimace.

Julia remained quiet.

"I have shocked you," Anthony probed her silence.

"No. You have not. And it isn't shock that is keeping me silent; it is the absolute disgrace of putting such hurtful words into a legal document! How could someone do that to their own child?" Julia fumed.

"I was not a child when my father died."

"I've said before that we are our parent's children until the day we die! You are right. I cannot find a way to excuse his words, and it grieves me that he hurt you so deeply."

"He didn't," Anthony said, but for the first time he was beginning to realise that the words had hurt him. It was as if they'd been seared into his mind and haunted many of his thoughts — too many to ignore that he was not unscathed by them.

"Of course he did," Julia responded. "You would have to be completely inhuman not to be affected. I could damn him to the devil for being so cruel!"

Anthony chuckled. "I like having you as my defender, Mrs Price," he said, genuinely amused.

"With experiences like that, you are guaranteed of my being so," Julia said, but she smiled in return. "It was a

109

horrible thing to do, and you are far more magnanimous than I would be in the same situation."

"It has put all my family in a difficult situation," Anthony admitted.

"Pfftt!" Julia snorted. "Not in my opinion. They should all be supporting you."

"That is certainly not going to happen," Anthony said drily. "Not with regards to Fanny anyway. My brothers follow her instructions. They wouldn't dare challenge her, so it is a lost cause to try to find me a family who cares, Mrs Price."

"Brother! Come! It's time to go," Giles said, approaching the pair with Lucy and Nancy on his arms.

Anthony sighed and pressed his lips together in annoyance at being disturbed. "Forgive me. I must go."

"Of course, you must," Julia said, but she was sorry that their conversation was coming to an abrupt end. She wanted to convince him that his family's treatment of him said more about the individuals' selfishness than it did about him when he was struggling with the fall-out from his father's will.

"Thank you for your understanding and support. I did not know how much it would mean to have someone who appreciates some of my difficulties," Anthony admitted quietly.

"You are very welcome," Julia responded as Anthony bowed over her hand, and taking it in his, he kissed it quickly before smiling into Julia's eyes.

"Miles has a lioness for a mother. He will never feel a lack of protection, and I envy him that and am glad of it at the same time," Anthony said before joining the others and leaving Julia alone.

110

As Julia walked down Great Pulteney Street to return to her lodgings, she mulled over the new revelations. Anthony was complicated to be sure, but he was also something else. Something more worrying. He was becoming more and more important to her, and she was afraid to acknowledge those deep feelings. Blowing her cheeks out to try to relax herself, she picked up the pace of her steps.

"Come, Julia," she muttered. "He likes you for a friend, nothing more. You have nothing to offer a man of his rank, even one who is a little out of the ordinary. You are even more damaged than he."

She was disturbed from her musings by a movement from across the street. Mr Prescott was waving his cane to attract her attention. Julia smiled in answer and waited until the gentleman had crossed between the carriages that were using the busy thoroughfare.

"Mrs Price! You are wandering around Bath alone!" Mr Prescott said with surprise.

Julia smiled at his words. "I am hardly a debutante who needs a constant chaperone, Mr Prescott," she said. "My grandmother insists on my taking a maid when we are in London, but in Bath, I can walk around unaccompanied without shocking the Bath gossips."

"I commend you for your independence, and if you don't mind my saying, I do like a spirited filly," Mr Prescott said.

Julia raised her eyebrows at the reference, but didn't respond.

"I was going to call into your house after visiting a friend in Sydney Place," Mr Prescott started to explain. "I have a box at the theatre tonight, and I would be honoured if Mrs Hancock and yourself would accompany me."

"That is very kind of you," Julia said.

"Not at all. I get to spend the evening with the two most attractive women in Bath. The benefit is all mine, although I will ensure there are refreshments enough to make-up for your being with me for the evening," Mr Prescott responded with a self-deprecating laugh.

"I'm not sure your description of us is accurate, but I thank you for the compliment," Julia said. "My grandmother loves the theatre."

"That is something we have in common then," Mr Prescott said. "Shall I arrange transport for you?"

"No. That won't be necessary. We can walk."

"But if it rains, as it so often does in Bath, you would catch cold," Mr Prescott fussed.

"If the weather turns inclement, we shall employ sedan chairs to convey us, but there will be no need; it has been so fine lately, I doubt if it will change by this evening. Your invitation is kind enough in itself. Don't concern yourself about our travelling there. Thank you."

"I realised early in our acquaintance that you are a very capable woman. It's sometimes easy to forget how young you are," Mr Prescott said.

"When I am near Miss Stock and Miss Carruthers, I feel almost maternal, our differences are so marked," Julia admitted. She came to a stop in front of her lodgings on Henrietta Street. "Would you like to come in, Mr Prescott? My grandmother would be pleased to see you."

"You are very kind, but I shall forgo the pleasure of Mrs Hancock's company until later. I am promised at my friend's home," Mr Prescott said, taking hold of Julia's hand and bowing over it. "I shall look forward to this evening with a great deal of pleasure."

"As will we," Julia said.

Chapter 12

Why do I feel more at peace when I've spent time with her? She is not as pretty as some of the others; she is not as charming — more tormenting in many ways — but when we speak... It is as if she speaks directly to my soul, soothing my inner self. It feels as if nothing is impossible when I have spent time with her, and yet I feel calmer — less detached from the world and other people.

She must think me an idiot. Unable to stand up for myself. To be at the mercy of a twisted, bitter man who only wanted to ensure that our family was permanently fragmented. He must have known with the personality of my stepmother that she would never support me in her hope that Giles was the beneficiary. I see that now. Julia has shown me that.

My grandfather. She says he adores me. How would I recognise that to be true? I don't know if I could, but the thought comforts me, nonetheless. Someone alive in the world who actually cares about me. What do I feel about him? Can I care about someone? Is it possible?

I think perhaps I could if I let go of the tight hold I have on my inner turmoil. If I try just a little to allow myself to feel, I wonder what it would be like? Terrifying perhaps, but worth the risk? Possibly. Maybe.

And what of her? Does she feel pity for me, or is there something else? Could there be something else? That thought alone is enough to scare me witless at the moment.

*

"What are you staring at?" Gabriel asked his grandson later that day.

113

"Nothing."

"Don't try to bamboozle me. Something is going on," Gabriel said.

"I am observing you," Anthony responded with a sigh.

"I know that! You have been watching my every move since you entered the room," Gabriel pointed out. "It is beginning to worry me. Do you know something I don't, boy? Am I not long for this world?"

Anthony smiled slightly. "That's more in your control than mine. I am trying to work out if something Mrs Price said is true."

"And what was that?" Gabriel asked, suddenly very curious.

"That you care deeply about me. It was something I had never considered until she mentioned the fact. I was trying to work out if she was correct and I had misunderstood your looks, expressions, and actions," Anthony admitted.

Gabriel paused. He didn't wish to frighten his grandson with his words, but he felt his next utterances were vital for their future relationship and understanding. "I see," he said, delaying for time.

"Is she wrong?" Anthony asked, suddenly feeling the fool.

"No. She is not at all wrong; in fact she's perfectly accurate," Gabriel admitted quickly. "I do care very much."

"But as I pointed out, you have familial obligations towards me."

"Fustian!" Gabriel scoffed. "If you think that has kept me by your side for these last fourteen years, you are as much a nodcock as your father was."

"You really didn't like him, did you?" It was a rhetorical question.

"No. He kept me from you and Eliza, for which I hope he is facing retribution," Gabriel admitted. "But I am grateful he sought me out when you were proving to be particularly difficult."

"I can understand you wanted to be in touch. I know when you look at me, you see your daughter in my features. That must give you some comfort or connection to her in some respects." Anthony wanted to give his grandfather the easy way out. He was voicing the reasons he'd convinced himself over the years that they were in touch.

"At first I was thinking more of Eliza than I was of you, because we were strangers after all," Gabriel admitted. Anthony would know immediately if he started to lie to him. "But very soon, my affection for you as my grandson was as deep, as any love I had for your mother."

"Oh."

"Eloquent as always," Gabriel responded, trying to maintain his usual banter with Anthony.

"So you like me? Despite my lack of finesse?" Anthony asked, needing the further clarification.

"You buffoon, of course, I do. You put up with my foibles, with only very little complaint. I would not be without you boy. You mean everything to me. And I would not change you," Gabriel said gently.

"I'd change myself," Anthony admitted.

"That is something for you to do if you wish, but know this: My affection is consistent and irremovable. Always. Whether you change or don't."

"Thank you," Anthony said. "It is surprising to realise this, but it actually means a lot to hear that."

"I know you will ponder over our conversation, but don't let doubts start to creep in when you are staring at the canopy of your bed tonight. Remember there are people who care for you in this world for being just as you are now," Gabriel said.

"Don't get carried away," Anthony said with derision. "I will not be convinced that there are a mob of people who adore me!"

"No. Perhaps not. But your brother looks up to you, when he is not being browbeaten by Fanny, so I am presuming Wilfred does as well. Then there are Mrs Hancock and Mrs Price. They both think highly of you. See? We aren't far off a mob already," Gabriel said, trying to maintain a lightness.

Anthony smiled. "You are a deluded old man."

"I am happy in my world, and one day I hope you will be able to feel real happiness too," Gabriel admitted.

"Let's not run ahead of ourselves. I doubt I would recognise joy if it were to hit me around the face. In the meantime, I have heard that the Mrs Price and Mrs Hancock are going to the theatre tonight with your friend, Mr Prescott," Anthony said, more than ready to change the subject.

"That blockhead!" Gabriel said. "If he thinks Patience will fall for his flowery words, he does not know what that woman likes."

"She likes him enough to let him accompany them on an evening out. Luckily, I have also secured a box and, although it will contain Fanny as one of the party, it is directly opposite that of Mr Prescott. Try not to glower at him for the whole evening," Anthony advised with a grin.

*

If Anthony had not been longing to be in the same seating area as Julia, he would have found the evening extremely amusing. Gabriel spent the first act glaring at the threesome in the box that Mr Price had secured. Fanny was ensconced with the mothers of the Misses Carruthers and Stock who had been invited at Giles' request. Anthony had no objections to his brother sitting at the front of the seating area between the Misses Stock and Carruthers, whilst himself and his grandfather watched the ladies they would rather have been with.

The other group consisted of just Julia, Patience, and Mr Prescott. He was making sure to be equally charming to both ladies. With not being a large group, it was easier to notice what else was going on in the rest of the theatre. All of them could see clearly into the box occupied by Anthony's family.

"I've kept you from your friends," Mr Prescott said, placing his ungloved hand gently on Julia's.

Julia moved her hand from underneath the rough, sweaty limb, feigning the need to use her fan. She didn't like the familiarity of the touch, or the contact itself, even through the material of her own evening gloves. "Not at all. Our connection is through my grandmother and Mr Bannerman. I would not expect for us to be in each other's company constantly."

"Ah, forgive me. I thought you were a favourite of his Lordship," Mr Prescott probed.

"We have become friends of sorts," Julia admitted. Anthony and herself did gravitate to each other; there was no point in denying that. "Although, I could not consider myself a favourite by any means."

"So, there is still chance for the beaux of Bath to try to conquer your heart?" Mr Prescott asked.

Julia laughed, a slight note of derision in the sound. "As I bring little other than myself to recommend me, I doubt I shall have the few men in Bath beating a path to my door."

"Mrs Hancock, you really need to speak sternly to your granddaughter. She is too quick to disregard what she can offer a suitable man," Mr Prescott said, turning to Patience.

"A modest girl will always be dismissive of her own qualities, I'm afraid," Patience responded. "She does not see what the rest of us do."

"You are slightly biased," Julia pointed out to her grandmother.

"Not at all. I would be as eager to highlight your faults if you had any," Patience retorted.

"I think that is reassuring," Julia said dryly.

"And you, Mrs Hancock? Are there competitors for your affections?" Mr Prescott continued.

"At my age, I'm happy with good company and intelligent conversation," Patience responded. "My days of swooning over some besotted man are well and truly behind me."

"What? Not even the charming Mr Bannerman can sweep you off your feet? I get the distinct impression that he would like too. I have been getting daggers ever since he entered the theatre."

Patience laughed. "Gabriel is a ninnyhammer sometimes. There is no harm in him, but we are very old friends, nothing more."

"Well, his loss is my gain," Mr Prescott said, before lapsing into silence as the second act started.

During the third interval, the Prescott box was filled with most of the group from opposite them. For once, Anthony had encouraged his brother to seek out their acquaintances. He had experienced the longing of wishing to be somewhere else, not unusual for him, but uniquely, he wanted to be with another person. He had watched Julia more than he'd watched the play.

After hellos were exchanged, Mr Prescott had been surrounded by Giles, Nancy, and Lucy, who were chattering ten to the dozen. Patience had been joined by Gabriel.

Anthony had nodded to the others, but immediately sought out Julia.

"Are you having a good evening?" Julia asked.

"Not really," Anthony admitted. "Although Giles is doing most of the entertaining, I still find it a tedious use of time."

Julia smiled. "Don't let your companions hear you."

"No. I am learning a little about restraining myself, rather than uttering everything that I feel."

"There is hope for you yet!"

"Mr Prescott seems an attentive host," Anthony said, unable to stop himself from letting the jealously he'd been struggling with rise to the surface.

"I think he is interested in Grandmama. He is very attentive towards her," Julia said quietly.

"I know one person who won't be happy about that," Anthony said, feeling a sense of relief at Julia's words.

"I am not sure what she feels about him in return. Mr Bannerman could be jealous unnecessarily," Julia admitted.

"You look troubled. More so than I would expect at the news your grandmother has two beaux. Are you envious?"

"Are you teasing me, my Lord?" Julia asked, a laugh in her voice.

"Quite possibly," Anthony responded.

Julia smiled up at him. "Good. Although, I'm not begrudging of her being sought after. Of course not! But I had hoped Miles could stay with her when he is at home from school during the holidays. I never presumed she would marry again, yet it seems she has a choice of gentlemen vying for her attention."

"Why would your son need to stay with Mrs Hancock?"

"I need to find suitable employment. A companion, or governess, but whichever I choose, they will not allow me to have my son stay with me," Julia admitted.

119

"And what does Mrs Hancock say of the scheme?" Anthony asked, with a distinctly uncomfortable feeling in his stomach at Julia's words.

"She doesn't know," Julia admitted. "But it is something I have been considering for a while. I am worried about being a drain on her resources. I need to provide Miles with the best I can."

"Yet you would desert him."

Julia looked sharply at Anthony, but she knew immediately his words were not a criticism about her, or her parenting skills. They were to do with Anthony's upbringing and his inner turmoil. "I would make sure he was with someone who loved him unconditionally and was open in showing him that affection. His situation would be completely different from yours," she finished quietly.

"I know," Anthony admitted. "But the thought of him not being able to see you… "

"He would manage," Julia responded. "He is old enough to understand."

"Of course. Forgive my impertinence," Anthony apologised. "I'm fully aware you have your son's best interests at heart."

"I understand why the thought disturbs you, and it does you credit, but really there is no need for you to be troubled. Miles will always be my first priority," Julia responded.

"I know. It was uncivil of me to utter anything that appeared censorious."

"You are forgiven. I know your words were not said with malice, but out of concern. Oh look, it seems your party is returning to your own box."

Anthony reluctantly left with the others. Julia's revelation had made him panic slightly. He wondered why. Miles meant nothing to him, as such, but to think he would be forced to spend most of the year away from the mother he adored saddened Anthony — yet another emotion he was unused to experiencing. He completely understood why Julia was thinking of securing employment. She was ultimately a woman alone, and there was only one sensible option for her if she were not to marry.

Marry.

He could offer for her.

Anthony separated himself further in the box on his return. He didn't watch another moment of the play or take part in any of the conversations going on around him. He was aware that Gabriel thought Julia was the perfect wife for him. Was she? Could they marry?

It would solve her problems, and it would certainly solve his.

He thought a lot about her. More than he did anyone else, apart from Gabriel, possibly. He shook his head – he thought about her far more than he did his grandfather. But marriage. Being with someone forever. Having to consider that person as well as himself. And what about Miles? Could he be any sort of father to the child?

Anthony took a long steadying breath. Attracted to Julia he certainly was, but to be married to her terrified him more than marriage to anyone else had. Perhaps it was that until now, those women had been faceless individuals, and she was very real. Or, maybe it was that he thought he was flawed enough that he would eventually hurt and be rejected by whomever agreed to marry him. With a stranger that didn't matter so much, but with Julia — that would hurt them both, and he wasn't sure he could ever countenance being the one to cause her such pain.

Chapter 13

Giles was to find an ally on his next excursion with the young ladies with whom he was spending more and more time during his stay. Lucy had feigned a need to sit down with the maid who was chaperoning herself and Nancy whilst Giles took Nancy through the labyrinth in Sydney Gardens the afternoon after the theatre trip. The maid had muttered darkly to Lucy for a full five minutes as they'd sat on the bench, and Lucy had patiently listened before going on to convince the worried servant that Mr Russell was a fine member of the aristocracy and was hardly likely to do anything untoward in the busy attraction.

When Nancy came out of the exit, laughing with flushed cheeks and sparkling eyes, Lucy was glad she'd let her cousin have the time with Giles. There was no suggestion that Nancy's feelings lay in any other direction, no hints now that she had affection towards Anthony. It was clear she was smitten with the young man she was presently with, and if his expression was anything to go by, he was half-way to being in love with Nancy.

The couple walked along, smiling at each other. "That was good fun," Giles said.

"Oh yes. I know Bath isn't fashionable any more, but I am enjoying myself. You must think me a rustic to think so," Nancy responded, a blush tinging her cheeks.

"What? No! Not at all!" Giles responded quickly. "I am finding Bath, well the company, to be honest, to be of the highest calibre. I am so glad my pockets were to let and Mama persuaded me to visit Anthony."

"But you must like London of all places?" Nancy probed.

Giles was under the distinct impression there was meaning behind her question, and he refrained from uttering his initial reaction. "I like most places I stay," he said cautiously. "My brother says it's because I am too easily pleased, but that is because he is rarely happy with his lot."

"I think an easy-going nature is to be commended," Nancy said.

"It can be a dashed incumbrance sometimes," Giles admitted. "Mother isn't the easiest person to please, and I can feel pulled between pillar and post with her constant demands. I try to agree with everything she says, but it is not always possible, and she tears a strip off me if I dare to go against her, I can tell you!"

"I am sorry to hear that. I'm lucky that mother and father want the best for me, but they do worry about our reception into higher society," Nancy said.

"Someone who is as pretty as you will have no trouble at all," Giles said gallantly. "I just hope you remember me when you don't have a dance to spare and are surrounded by the fops who frequent the balls in town."

Nancy blushed. "I doubt that would ever happen. I am sure there are far prettier ladies than I in London."

"I have yet to meet any," Giles said.

Their conversation was interrupted by Lucy, who had deemed they had spent enough time in their private tête-à-tête.

"I think it is time we were returning home," she said. "Mary is getting a little agitated."

"Oh, perhaps if I treat her to a nice pastry from the hotel, she will be more at ease," Nancy said quickly, not wishing the maid to be uttering anything of her excursion when they returned home. Nancy's parents were indulgent with their daughter, but they would not stand for inappropriate behaviour.

"It can't hurt," Lucy admitted.

"If you wait here, I will take her to choose one," Nancy said, before quickly approaching the maid and walking with her towards one of the hotel entrances.

Lucy was left alone with Giles, a situation for which she was grateful. "Mr Russell, might I speak to you in confidence?" she asked. There was no point in skirting around what she wished to say.

"Of course," Giles answered, intrigued.

"My cousin is a lovely, gentle creature, but my aunt and uncle are reluctant to take her into London society. They are aware, more than Nancy or I, about the prejudices against those who might not be seen to fit in quite as much as others do. If you understand my meaning?"

Giles frowned. "Miss Stock mentioned that only a few moments ago. I am sure they are worrying over nothing."

"It is to your credit that you are accepting of others from a different class than yours, but I would give credence to my aunt and uncle. They have stayed in London quite a bit over the years but are reluctant to return. I feel that hesitation will influence when they are accepting of offers from potential husbands for my cousin. I don't think I am mistaking their wish that, although a title sounds fine in principle, a husband who would be willing to remain in their social sphere rather than the other way around would be preferable," Lucy said, flushing at the forthrightness of her words. It had seemed an easy thing to say when she'd thought of them; not so when the words were actually uttered.

"Ah. I see," Giles said, looking crestfallen.

Lucy was worried that she'd said too much and put him off any tendrè he had been developing. "I don't wish my cousin to be hurt. If yours is a playful flirtation, I think you should let her know, so she can consider the spark you share in the same vein."

"I see. Yes. I would hate to give off the wrong impression," Giles said, his frown still in place.

Lucy's heart sank. "I had hoped my words would stir you into proving to my cousin that she was worth the sacrificing of the excesses of London Society."

Giles flushed and looked panicked. "I-I did not mean to raise any expectations… " he started to stutter.

"Of course not," Lucy responded coolly before turning away from Giles. She was aware that everyone in her circle was hopeful that Nancy and Giles would make a match of it; they seemed so well suited, but it appeared it had been nothing but a diversion for Giles. She was devastated for her cousin.

Giles remained quiet until Nancy and Mary, the maid, rejoined them. He offered his arm to Lucy and Nancy, and they walked in a threesome along Great Pulteney Street until they entered Laura Place. Bowing to them, Giles smiled, but his whole demeanour was strained, which was unusual for him.

"Miss Carruthers, Miss Stock, thank you for your company this afternoon. It has been a pleasure as always. I hope to see you both very soon," he said smoothly.

"Would you like to come in for refreshments?" Nancy asked.

"I'm afraid I cannot," Giles said apologetically, already moving to the iron gate that separated the front door from the street.

Both ladies wished him goodbye and dropped a curtsey before entering the house. When they'd been relieved of their bonnets and spencer jackets, Nancy put her hand on Lucy's arm. "What happened?" she whispered.

"I don't know what you mean," came the evasive reply.

"Don't fib, Lucy. We came out of the labyrinth as if we were the best of friends, and when I returned with Mary, he could not wait to escape from us. We have never walked as quickly down Great Pulteney Street. I almost felt like I was being dragged along," Nancy responded.

Lucy sighed. "I tried to find out a little more about Mr Russell, and I don't think he took kindly to my probing." It was a variation on the truth, but Lucy consoled herself with the thought that she had found out something about Giles — he wasn't holding any serious affection for Nancy. There was no possibility Lucy was going to admit that though; it would destroy her cousin's self-esteem. Better for them to leave Bath and let the flirtation fade with separation.

"Why did you do that? Do we not know enough about him? He is everything that is gentlemanly and all politeness. Mother is happy with him as a close acquaintance. Why are you not?" Nancy asked.

"I don't know. I just wanted to know a little more, I suppose. I am sorry for meddling and spoiling your time with him," Lucy said truthfully.

"Oh, I am sure it will not matter," Nancy said, quick to forgive her cousin. "He will have probably forgotten about it the next time we meet."

Lucy wasn't sure that would be the case, but for Nancy's sake she hoped Giles would find an excuse to return to London soon; it was clearly his favourite place. If he weren't going to come up to snuff for Nancy, Lucy didn't want her cousin to suffer any disappointment over unrequited feelings. For the first time since being in Bath, she wished they'd never met their new acquaintances.

*

Giles didn't immediately return to his brother's house upon leaving Lucy and Nancy. He walked down Henrietta Street and turned right at the top. He would eventually return to Sydney Place and then back into Great Pulteney Street, but for now he needed the extra time his longer route would give him.

As he walked, he pondered over Lucy's words. He was astute enough to realise he was being probed and tested by Lucy. It was an impertinence of the young lady, but he wasn't one who would object strongly to her interference. He had been going along with the situation; he acknowledged he was guilty of seeking them out at every opportunity. He supposed that it wasn't surprising there was some curiosity about his intentions. Whether Lucy had the support of Nancy's parents in her probing he didn't know. The whole situation made him feel a little unsettled.

Marriage.

It was such a daunting prospect. Terrifying in fact.

On the other hand, Nancy was by far the prettiest girl he'd ever wanted to spend time with. And she was rich, which helped. No. He shook his head as he walked. Her riches didn't matter to his feelings, he liked *her*.

He started to smile. Marriage to Nancy wouldn't be that bad, and he'd please his mother, for she wouldn't be able to marry Anthony if she was married to him.

As Giles entered Great Pulteney Street, there was a definite spring to his step. What would his friends say when they heard that he'd proposed to someone? It would cause a stir that he'd settled down so early, but perhaps when one met the right person, it wasn't so daunting after all.

127

In fact, it was quite exciting.

*

Fanny remained above stairs until well after the breakfast hour. She delayed getting dressed until it was time to leave the house or to endure morning calls from the few residents of Bath with whom she was now acquainted. When in London there was a steady stream of visitors, all of similar breeding, rank, and outlook as Fanny. She even enjoyed morning calls when on the estate in Worchester. There she was very much the lady of the manor and given due reverence by the local families. Bath had proved sadly lacking in suitable society for a woman who was fully aware of her standing in the community.

She refused to spend time in either Anthony's or Gabriel's company if she could help it. Anthony was still as much the oddity he'd been when she'd first met him. She'd never felt a modicum of affection for him, even when he was a boy. He had been constantly serious, and with his outspoken words, it had been a relief to realise her husband liked him as little as she did. A woman of limited intelligence was never going to feel an affinity with a person who found entertainment in learning and books. That the child might have spent less time at such noble pursuits if given more attention was never considered. There had been no effort on her part to be a surrogate mother.

She could understand the family connection when she'd met Gabriel even though in looks they were dissimilar. Gabriel was as obnoxious and rude as his grandson. It was only for her own son's benefit that she had moved into the enemy's stronghold.

Sitting back after sealing her daily letter to her youngest son, Wilfred — she felt compelled to write to each of her boys every day, giving them instructions and advice, whether they wanted it or not — she stretched. Although she longed for Anthony's thirtieth birthday to arrive with him still unwed it seemed to be taking twice as long as the normal passage of time. She was living on her nerves, and not one to appreciate struggle of any kind, she felt even more aggrieved towards her stepson.

She looked up when Giles entered the room. "Are you going to escort me to the Royal Crescent?" she asked, reclining on the chaise lounge that was positioned to get the full effect of the large fire. "I need to get out of this house."

"If you'd like," Giles said amenably.

"Even the society in Bath is preferable to spending time with Anthony," Fanny said.

"Oh, I thought you were enjoying yourself," Giles responded innocently. "You seem to be enjoying the company of Mrs Carruthers and Mrs Stock."

"A necessary evil," Fanny admitted. "The more time I spend with them, the more I am convinced any connection to my family with people of their ilk would be a mistake. Their company is unrefined and tiresome. Thankfully, I am not normally obliged to associate with their like. I cannot wait until Anthony reaches his birthday, and then I can retire once more to spending time with the more deserving members of society."

"Oh." Giles was crushed at her words.

Fanny failed to notice the effect her prejudice had on her son. "I think you should split your time more evenly between the younger chits and Mrs Price. There seems to be an increasing understanding between the widow and Anthony."

"I doubt it. She is a lot older than Miss Stock and Miss Carruthers and not as pretty. Why would Anthony choose her as a wife?" Giles asked innocently.

129

"Anthony is a desperate man. Any calculating doxy will do. We don't want him getting a special licence and marrying any of one them. Thankfully, there seems to be only those three in the frame. His usual propensity to upset people has worked to our advantage in this instance."

"They are all quite nice. Would it be so bad to see him marry?" Giles asked, never being comfortable with his mother's scheme, and although he didn't want to see Anthony chasing Nancy, his mother's actions seemed especially harsh now that he was considering marriage himself.

"Would you see yourself always at his command?" Fanny screeched. "The likes of him inheriting what is rightfully yours."

"Mother, he is the first born. He was always going to inherit; I accept that. I always have," Giles said placatingly. "Would it really matter if Anthony married someone he met here?"

"What? Marry the daughter of a 'cit'?" Fanny hissed. "If it was not bad enough him inheriting what should belong to you, he'd then besmirch the name and blood of the family! How can you possibly suggest such a thing?"

Giles had flushed a deep red at Fanny's words. "Don't dismiss our friends so harshly! They are just as good as you or I, Mother," he said through gritted teeth.

"Poppycock! They have made their money through *trade*. How on earth can you compare their likes to us? I think it is a good thing you'll be spending more time with Mrs Price. It will refocus your attention about socialising with people of our own kind at least. She is a gentleman's daughter, although that is her only recommendation."

"Is she more acceptable to you than our other friends?" Giles asked.

"Don't be foolish! She is a penniless widow trying to ensnare Anthony. You need to distract her for long enough that they don't come to some sort of arrangement that would be to our disadvantage. The sooner Anthony's birthday is reached, the better. My nerves are stretched to the limit. The sooner we can return home to how life should be, the better," Fanny responded.

"I shall go and change," Giles said, defeated and unable to carry on the conversation, using the change of clothes as an excuse to escape his mother's room.

*

Anthony looked up from the task of pulling on his gloves. He was dressed in a grey many-caped greatcoat in readiness for taking Belle for a ride over the hills surrounding Bath.

He paused. Giles was stomping down the stairs looking agitated.

"What's wrong?" Anthony asked.

Giles was startled, not having even noticed that his brother and the butler were in the marble hallway. He flushed a little at being caught acting childishly. "Mother."

Anthony gave a nod of understanding and quickly took off his gloves. "Tell Jackman to return Belle to the stables. I shall not need her for the moment." He addressed the butler before being helped out of his greatcoat. "Come. Let us retire to the study. We will not be disturbed there," he instructed Giles.

They both walked to the small room at the rear of the house. It was darker than the other rooms, and until Fanny's arrival, Anthony had hardly used it. Over the last few weeks though, he had used it more and more to escape his stepmother.

"Sit," Anthony commanded. Walking over to a side table, he poured two measures of brandy into crystal glasses. "You

131

look as if you need this," he said, handing Giles a glass before taking his own to the seat opposite his brother.

"Thank you."

"What has she done now?"

Giles took a swallow of his drink. He couldn't admit to the scheme his mother had, no matter how she'd upset his own plans. He wasn't a person who relished conflict and revealing the real reason behind their visit would risk causing a huge row. "She was lecturing me on who I should and shouldn't be socialising with," he admitted.

"I did not think our acquaintances came up to snuff for her," Anthony said unperturbed.

"No," Giles acknowledged.

"Which one does she think I will marry?" Anthony asked.

Giles's eyes flew to Anthony's in a silent admission of guilt.

"It was the only explanation for the real motive for you travelling all the way here," Anthony explained, unaffected by his brother's expression. "We are all aware my birthday is looming and of the feelings of Fanny on whom she thinks the wealth of the family should be bestowed. She has never hidden the fact that she wishes me to the devil because I receive the inheritance and not you."

Giles sighed in defeat. "I don't want your money."

"That is good to know," Anthony acknowledged. "But if it is any consolation, I did not seriously think you did."

Giles looked grateful. "I know we are not close, but — well, you are the first born, and I have told mother this. I have always objected to her views. They aren't mine at all."

"She is to be disappointed if she is still hoping you will inherit. I'd already decided to marry even before you arrived," Anthony admitted.

132

"Who?" Giles was all curiosity, along with feeling a nugget of panic on his own behalf.

"That is my business until I propose," Anthony said. He wasn't sure if or when he was going to propose, but he certainly wasn't going to open himself or Julia to speculation or pressure.

"But your birthday... " Giles murmured.

"Is not here quite yet," Anthony answered.

"Mother is convinced you are going to marry under special licence," Giles admitted, his tongue free now that it seemed Anthony had guessed correctly Fanny's motives.

"She knows more than I, then," Anthony responded drily.

"You are running out of time for a traditional wedding though," Giles pointed out.

"Maybe. But that's another consideration that has nothing to do with anyone other than myself and my bride, should she agree to marry me."

"I envy you. Being able to plan your future without the encumbrance of a forceful character like Mother in the way. It is so difficult having to consider how she will react to anything I wish to do. It can take the joy out of a situation," Giles said, thinking of his own plight.

"She tries to interfere. I just don't let her. You are a man, almost of age now. It's time to stand up for yourself and act on your feelings if you are truly fond of Miss Stock," Anthony advised.

Giles flushed once more. "I — How did you know?" he spluttered.

"Give me some credit for interpretation," Anthony scoffed. "Even a brute as unfeeling as I can see when someone is mooning over another."

"You make me sound a buffoon," Giles muttered, his colour deepening in mortification.

"I would only consider you that if you let your mother talk you out of attaching yourself to a perfectly decent young lady from a good family," Anthony said, trying to soften his tone a little.

"She is delightful, and the more I think of being with her for the rest of my life, the less scary it feels," Giles admitted.

"And does she feel the same way?"

"I think so. Although it did not end too well the last time we spoke. I'm afraid I was a bit of a cad," Giles said, remembering his cool tone.

"That sounds like a comment I would make, rather than you."

Giles smiled, once more relaxing at his brother's admissions. "Yes, you do tend to upset people without trying."

Anthony shook his head before taking a drink, unable to argue against his brother's observation. "What are you going to do to make amends?"

"I don't know. Speak to her I suppose."

"Should you not be speaking to her father first?" Anthony suggested.

"Probably. But I want to smooth out any misunderstanding between us before I do that. We are all meeting at the ball tomorrow. I shall speak to her then," Giles said cheerfully.

"I suppose you know her best. If it's of any value, I, as the head of the family approve of the match. If you need my support, you have it," Anthony said.

"That means a lot. Thank you," Giles said with a smile. He stood. "I think I need to spend some time alone. Mother wanted to walk to the Royal Crescent, but I am going to send my apologies. I don't want her to muddy my thoughts again."

"Good idea."

"And Anthony… " Giles turned back as he reached the door.

"Yes?"

"Why did you bring me in here instead of going for your ride?"

"You looked as if you were a little lost. I know how that feels, so I wanted to help. I have been overcome recently by the need to smooth things over when it is needed for those few people I hold in any regard," Anthony admitted.

"Oh. You haven't had a very good time of it, have you?" Giles looked uncomfortable, knowing it was his blood relations, including himself, who had treated his half-brother poorly.

Anthony paused before he spoke. He knew this was one of the times Julia would urge him to hold back before he uttered his immediate thoughts, and he modified what he was going to say. "My lifestyle was set before father met Fanny. You and Wilfred were too young to rail against your parents. I don't condemn you for enjoying your childhood, whether I enjoyed mine or not."

"That is decent of you to say, but I don't believe any of us is blame free. Thank you for today. You have really helped. It is yet another instance when I know I am lucky to have you as an older brother."

Anthony frowned. "There are other times when you've felt fortunate of the fact?" he asked, unable to keep the disbelief from his voice.

Giles smiled. "Oh, yes. My friends are green with envy that I don't get a roasting if I overspend and don't have a feather to fly with. You always pay my creditors or give me a little extra blunt if I need it. Most of the others have to beg on bended knee and go through the longest lectures and cursing. Their ears are still ringing when they return to town. They are definitely jealous of me."

"You are lucky because I spoil you?"

"Yes and no, but there are other reasons too," Giles admitted. "You always speak out if you see an injustice, even to mother or father. I was never that brave. I am lucky you were the firstborn. I would not be a good master of the estate or a good keeper of our heritage. You are far better at the job than I ever would be. I am more than happy being the second son."

"I never thought you were. I had always presumed you wanted what your mother did, although since your arrival in Bath, I had started to suspect that you had different opinions than Fanny," Anthony admitted.

"By Gad, I don't agree with mother! You can have the inheritance with my blessing! So for both our sakes and the sakes of all the tenant's we have, please marry soon," Giles said with a last smile before walking out of the doorway.

Anthony sat back in the leather chair he occupied, blowing out his cheeks as he rested his head on the high chair back. The conversation with Giles had revealed more than he'd expected. His brother thought highly of him and wished him to be the heir without any form of recrimination on Giles' part. It touched him. Pausing in his thoughts, Anthony rubbed a hand through his hair.

I'm touched? Yes. I am. It is a feeling I am not used to experiencing, and it's a little overwhelming to realise, that although I have battled to maintain a remote demeanour, since my arrival in Bath, it feels as if I am being hit by wave after wave of differing emotions. I did not know I was able to feel. It's not only confusing but to some extent terrifying. But there is a tiny part of me that feels freer. It is such a small part that I sometimes doubt its existence, but Giles's unexpected revelations have made the feeling grow a little.

Anthony smiled. His brother didn't resent him. He'd thought it didn't matter; it turns out it did. Suddenly the feeling of reluctance to get married didn't seem so strong. Giles had given his blessing, and it meant more to Anthony than he had supposed. What was even better was that he felt even more sure that marriage was the right course for him, especially if Julia would be his bride.

Chapter 14

Nancy and Lucy prepared for the ball. Lucy smiled at her cousin, who looked beautiful in a white silk gown edged in the finest Maltese lace that had been brought back by Lucy's father when he was on one of his many business trips. Her hair was a blonde bundle of curls, tumbling around her face, making her look even more angelic than she did normally.

"You are stunningly beautiful," Lucy said, knowing that, although she was considered pretty, she could never compete with her cousin.

"Thank you. I don't know whether or not it is too much," Nancy said, gently sliding her hands down the silky material of her dress.

"There is no such thing as overdressed," Lucy assured her. "Not when you look like you do. I think every gentleman in Bath will be fighting for a dance tonight."

"I haven't any taken at the moment."

"Don't worry. Within five minutes of our arrival, you will not have a dance to spare."

"I hope Mr Russell secures the first two," Nancy said longingly.

"Perhaps we should try to widen our acquaintance whilst we are here?" Lucy asked innocently. "We have kept ourselves to quite a tight-knit few."

"Oh. Are you tiring of our new friends?" Nancy asked.

"No! Of course not, but we should try to extend just a little the number of those we spend time with. We shall be sadly lacking if Lord Lever and his family leave Bath," Lucy said gently, knowing full well why her cousin was looking crestfallen. Nancy wanted nothing more than to spend time with Giles.

"With Papa sending word that he is to come and visit, it is more likely we will leave before they do," Nancy pointed out.

"I still think we should open ourselves up to making new acquaintances."

"I shall be guided by you if you think we should," Nancy acknowledged, always ready to trust her cousin on matters of society.

They took their carriage to the Upper Assembly Rooms along with their mothers. The walk up the hill to the ballroom was too great for the older ladies. Eventually reaching the rooms, there was a little delay while the coachman fought with the other carriages to deposit his cargo. Most people didn't opt for carriages when staying in Bath, but the journey from Laura Place to the Upper Assembly Rooms was of a distance enough to justify the usage in Mrs Stock's view.

Eventually entering into the large ballroom, they were immediately accosted by Giles who had been waiting near the doorway that led into the main room, determined his chosen one wasn't going to be snaffled by anyone else.

If he had any last minute doubts about seeking out Nancy, they flew out of his head the moment he laid eyes on her. She looked exquisite and smiled at him in such a warm way that he almost declared himself there and then.

Recollecting himself, Giles approached the party and made his bows. "Good evening. Miss Stock, I hope you aren't engaged for the first two? I would be honoured if you would join me in the dances."

"I would be happy to dance, thank you," Nancy responded.

"Excellent! And Miss Carruthers, could I have the honour of the third and fourth with you?" Giles asked.

"Of course, Mr Russell, I would be delighted," Lucy said, but her tone was cooler. She wasn't as convinced of Giles since their last conversation.

Giles led Nancy onto the dancefloor when the first quadrille was announced. He was barely aware of the other dancers in the many sets of squares that filled the floor space. All he was concerned with was the beauty whom he was partnering, although he did glare at anyone he saw giving Nancy appreciative looks. He wasn't secure enough in her affections yet to be amused and smug by the admiring looks. That would occur only if he could secure his chosen one.

As they danced, Giles became less afraid of the married state and more convinced of his choice. Now that he had Anthony's blessing, he felt supported and able to face the wrath of his mother.

"My father comes to Bath this weekend," Nancy said as they danced. "He is keen to see the sights we have been writing about."

"I'm keen to meet him, if you would be so kind as to introduce us," Giles said eagerly. "I am sure my brother would also like to make his acquaintance."

"Of course," Nancy said with a blush. She was aware of the compliment Giles was giving her family.

"We should plan some excursions to show him some of what we have seen and visited," Giles said enthusiastically, warming to a scheme in which he would win over the approval of the man who would hopefully become his father-in-law.

"That would be a very good idea," Nancy said. "Mama thinks he is visiting to see how she does and plan for our return home."

"Oh, really?"

"Yes. They don't like to be apart, and Mama is now feeling more the thing. Taking the waters has had a beneficial effect on her," Nancy confessed.

"Ah. I thought you would be staying a while to come," Giles responded, suddenly feeling the stirrings of panic.

"It was always going to be a short visit."

"Oh."

They continued to gaze at each other longingly until the first dance had ended. Giles decided it was time to take control of his destiny as his brother had advised him.

"Miss Stock, would you allow me to escort you to the refreshment room? I would like to speak to you a little more privately," Giles said.

"Of course," Nancy responded, her colour heightening.

The pair left the dancefloor, and Giles noticed that his mother and Lucy hadn't observed his movement, which suited him just fine. Leading Nancy into the much quieter room, he gallantly obtained two cups of lemonade, before sitting next to Nancy. He didn't want his important words to be overheard.

"I hope you don't mind me speaking so openly, Miss Stock, but the thought of you leaving Bath leaves me desolate," he admitted.

"It's very kind of you to say so. I shall miss you too," Nancy responded, her hands in her lap to hide the nervousness she felt. She wanted to hear the words it seemed Giles was going to utter, but that didn't prevent her insides fluttering.

141

"I like you, Miss Stock. I like you very much," Giles admitted, his own colour rising.

"And I like you," Nancy said quietly, feeling very forward at her admission.

"Do you like me enough to give me permission to speak to your father when he arrives in Bath?" Giles asked, her gentle encouragement giving him courage.

"Y-yes," Nancy stuttered, hardly able to meet Giles' gaze and flushing a deep pink.

"Good. My brother advised that I should speak to your father first, but I would like to know your feelings before I do that. I adore you, Miss Stock. I cannot face the thought of your leaving without being betrothed to me. Do I make a fool of myself in declaring myself to you in such a befuddled way?" Giles babbled.

The smile that lit Nancy's face would have been enough to convince him of her wishes, but Nancy reached out her hand. "Oh no! I don't think you a fool at all!" she said quietly, but with so much emotion that her words were choked. "I like you very well indeed, and I'm happy to know you return my feelings. I could only dream you held any affection for me."

"You are the only person I have ever fallen in love with," Giles admitted guilelessly. "Took me by surprise and frightened me half to death at first," he admitted artlessly. "But I cannot be without you. I know that for certain."

"Good. Because the thought of returning home and not seeing you again had me crying all morning," Nancy said. "As much as I am looking forward to seeing Papa, I couldn't face leaving you behind."

Giles took hold of Nancy's hand and kissed it with passion. "Oh, my dear, Miss Stock, your words make me the happiest of men! We shall not be parted. I promise you!"

142

"What on earth is going on?" came the clear, angry voice of Lady Lever.

Giles almost knocked over his chair as he leapt to his feet in surprise at the voice behind him. He immediately looked guilty, but at the worried expression on Nancy's face, he puffed out his chest a little and turned to face his mother. "Mama, I have just come to an agreement with Miss Stock and shall be speaking to her father when he arrives in Bath in the next few days. Subject to his approval, you will be able to wish me happy."

"What?" Fanny spat at her son. "Is this some kind of joke?"

"No," Giles responded firmly. He had moved to the side of Nancy's chair in an act of protection. "Be careful, Mother. I won't stand by while you insult my bride-to-be's family."

"There will be no wedding. I forbid you to continue this nonsensical talk a moment longer," Fanny demanded. "You know my feelings about the people we have been forced to associate with. I will not tolerate any formal connection with them, especially with my own son. It was bad enough when I considered that Anthony might marry one of the chits, but you? Never!"

Nancy gasped at the insult, but Giles rested a hand on her shoulder in reassurance. "Then you will lose me as a son, for I am determined to marry Miss Stock, with or without your approval."

"Is there a problem?" Anthony asked as he entered the room and approached the table. Noticing when Giles and Nancy left the ballroom, he'd also seen his stepmother follow. Leaving the party behind, Anthony had reluctantly trailed after his stepmother to support Giles if things didn't go well. From the expressions on the faces of the three people gathered, it seemed a full-scale explosion was about to take place.

"Your brother has it in his head that he's going to throw himself away on some daughter of a 'cit'," Fanny responded, almost shaking with anger.

"Don't insult my future wife by using such a derogatory term," Giles threatened.

Anthony noticed that a few people were taking interest in the scene in which he was now involved. Not one to relish any sort of attention aimed in his direction, he decided it was time to intervene to bring the situation to a close.

"Miss Stock, I sincerely apologise for any upset you have suffered during these last few moments. I think it is time you returned to your mother," he said gently.

Nancy looked at Anthony, her colour draining, as she interpreted his words as a rejection against herself. "Of course." She stood, trying to maintain her dignity, but tears filled her eyes and would not remain contained, spilling onto her cheeks.

"Anthony," Giles said through gritted teeth.

"Not here," Anthony commanded. "I suggest you return home with us."

Nancy started to walk away, but Anthony moved his hand to rest it on her arm, temporarily staying her progress. "Miss Stock, I am only not letting my brother accompany you because I don't want to create more speculation than there will already be because of this gathering of my family and yourself," he explained. "My brother will speak to your father as he planned if it is still what you wish."

Nancy looked at Anthony, and although he could see she was deeply upset, she nodded her head almost regally. "I do," she said.

"Good. Then all has not been spoiled," Anthony said, allowing her to continue out of the room.

Fanny turned to her stepson. "If you think I'm going to stand by whilst that doxy — "

"I suggest you don't utter another word," Anthony said angrily. "I will not allow you to offer insult to a defenceless young girl or her family."

"But I — "

"There is nothing more to say. Especially here," Anthony snapped. "You might be willing to make a show of yourself, but you shan't do it in my company. Giles, arrange for the carriage to be brought round. We are going home."

"I— " Fanny persisted.

"Enough!" Anthony bellowed.

Used to blunt comments from her stepson, but never anger, Fanny was finally stunned into silence. Although she wasn't meek, and in fact was silently fuming, she followed her relations into the entrance hallway of the Assembly Rooms and waited until the carriage was brought to the pavement, and the three entered into the equipage in silence.

When they moved away from the Assembly Rooms, Giles turned on his mother. "You can say nothing to dissuade me from marrying Miss Stock! I have made my decision, and she is happy to accept my proposal."

"I will do everything in my power to prevent the marriage," Fanny hissed back at her son.

"Then we shall never be in company together again, for I shall not give her up," Giles snapped.

"I wouldn't want you anywhere near me if you were connected to the family of a 'cit'," Fanny retorted.

"Then you will end a lonely woman because I am going to marry her. I only need the permission of Mr Stock. You hold no power over me," Giles said, no longer the meek and mild son he had been until his future happiness was threatened.

"You don't presume you would be the only one to speak to him, do you?" Fanny mocked. "I'm sure he would be interested to know of your wastrel ways and the lightskirts you have had. There are probably half a dozen by-blows with your looks strewn across London by now."

Giles flushed a deep red. "There are nothing of the sort! I have never done anything other than the usual larks anyone my age has become involved with. I have certainly not been rampaging all over town."

"He will not know that though, will he?" Fanny retorted, pleased that her dig had hit the mark.

"You would lie to someone about my character?" Giles asked, shocked beyond belief at his mother's words.

"If it will prevent you making a fool of yourself and bringing a slur onto the family name, of course, I would," Fanny said smugly.

"Then you've lost me as a son, anyway," Giles said, but the fight had been knocked out of him.

Anthony decided that to intervene would only add fuel to Fanny's fire. The more he looked to be supporting Giles, the more she would rail against them. He offered a small smile to Giles as a method to try to reassure his younger brother. He had been pleased that Giles was finally standing up to Fanny, who usually ran roughshod over both of her children. It seemed Giles was emboldened by his affection and that, for the first time in his life, he was prepared to fight for what he wanted.

Chapter 15

Julia entered the drawing room to find Patience hard at work on her embroidery. It touched her that her grandmother would spend hours updating her gowns while she spent time with Miles. They had argued about it good-naturedly, but Patience had insisted she would much rather sew, than try to wear out an active young boy.

"I am going to take Miles to Sydney Gardens. Would you like to join us?"

"I think I will remain indoors. It has been a hectic few days. I'd like to conserve my energy," Patience responded, looking up only briefly.

"Preparing yourself for when your beaux continue to fight over you? Mr Prescott has had no competition this last day or two," Julia teased. The gossip had reached her grandmother about what had happened during the ball. Miss Stock's group had been missing since the evening, as had the Russell's. It had been a very quiet few days for the pair. Julia, in particular, had missed the company of Anthony. She was worried about how he was dealing with a family crisis, wanting to be the one to support him, but knowing she didn't have the right.

"Ha! Gabriel is only toying with Mr Prescott; only our new friend cannot see it. Gabriel is feigning being smitten with me to antagonise Mr Prescott. He has never changed in all the years I've known him, causing mischief whenever he can," Patience responded without censure.

Julia took the opportunity of voicing some of the questions that had been bubbling inside her almost since Mr Prescott had started to dance attendance on Patience.

147

"Have either of them touched your heart?" she asked, sitting near her grandmother.

Patience looked up in surprise. "I have always loved Gabriel, and the decades of absence have not changed that," she said. "But as for what you are really asking, no, I shan't be marrying either of them."

"It would be company for you, more than a devoted granddaughter and great-grandson can give," Julia said cautiously.

Putting down her embroidery, Patience turned to her granddaughter and took hold of her hands. "What is bothering you, child?" she asked gently.

Julia flushed. "I am ashamed of my thoughts. They are so selfish," she confessed.

"Let me be the decider of that," Patience responded. "Come. Out with it. There's clearly something amiss."

"I was worried that, if you married again, there would be no place for Miles in your home," Julia said, not relishing what direction the conversation was going in, but knowing it had to be said before she could seek employment.

"He will always be welcome in any home I have, but why mention him and not yourself?"

Julia sighed. "I need to find some sort of position. I hate being a drain on your resources and even with grandfather's three hundred a year, when Miles goes to school, there will be little, if any, left after our day-to-day expenses. I know there will be many more bills than we have now once he starts his formal education. I want what is best for him, and if that means working for a living, I am prepared to do it. Don't think I repine over my need to find employment, for I don't."

Patience flung up her hands in horror. "Over my dead body!" she said. "No! No! No! Julia, I'm not so poor that I

148

cannot support you and add to Miles' upbringing. He shall go to the best schools without any need of you sacrificing yourself to a life of drudgery. Why ever would you consider such nonsense?"

"I hate being such a drain on your funds when you should be enjoying them. It is not fair," Julia admitted.

"If they are making the two most important people in my life more comfortable, then I shall be enjoying my money in the best way possible. I don't want to hear any more of this idiocy, do you hear me? Not another word about your searching for employment when there is no need whatsoever. Your place is with me unless you remarry. Only then will I happily let you leave me," Patience said firmly.

"I shan't ever remarry," Julia said.

"Then we are destined to be together until I turn up my toes and that is final," Patience said firmly. "Am I being clear enough, you foolish girl?"

Julia nodded, but she still wasn't happy. Bruce had told her time and again how much of a leech she was, what a drain on their resources, and her situation at the moment seemed to confirm his accusations, albeit with regards to her grandmother's money and not her husband's.

Thinking of Bruce always made her want to escape, and she soon excused herself and collected Miles. He was the perfect antidote to brighten her mood once more. Walking down the street, Miles trotted at her side, babbling about this and that. Once they reached the gardens, Miles spent his time running ahead of Julia and then returning to her, telling her of what was to be seen around the next corner.

It wasn't very long before Julia was smiling along with her son. His innocence and wonderment always brought her out of the doldrums. She thought again how, although she'd hated almost every moment of her marriage to Bruce, she

149

could never wholly regret the match because of the joy Miles brought her.

As they made their way towards the hotel, Julia saw that Anthony and Gabriel were walking along a path that would intersect with the one they were on. They were both striking in their own way. Although Gabriel was an old man, he was dressed in the height of fashion, not favouring the clothing of yesteryear as some of his peers did. Anthony drew the eye though. He was tall, handsome, and although his expression couldn't be considered as welcoming normally, when he set eyes on Julia, he smiled with pleasure, which she couldn't help but return, for it was very good to see him.

"Good morning, Mr Bannerman, my Lord," Miles said before Julia reached the pair. "We have been exploring the pathways."

"Have you indeed," Gabriel said pleasantly. "And have you any energy left to join me in the labyrinth?"

"Oh, yes!" Miles said, eagerly. "Mama, may I go with Mr Bannerman?"

"Of course," Julia smiled at Gabriel. "As long as you are sure?"

"He will provide me with the sanest conversation I have heard these past two days," Gabriel said. "Present company excluded of course," he grinned at his grandson.

"So aged, yet so impertinent," Anthony responded.

"I will clip you around the ear with comments like that," Gabriel said before seeing the alarmed expression on Miles' face. "Don't worry my boy. I am only funning. Anthony knows I tease him. Come, I have yet to go in the labyrinth. Lead on young Miles!"

Anthony offered his arm to Julia, which she took willingly. They walked in companionable silence for the first few moments before Julia broke the quiet.

150

"Has it been very bad?" she asked. There was no point trying to pretend she had not heard of what had happened at the assembly. She could only imagine what conversations had gone on once they'd returned home.

"Worse. I am glad that Giles is finally standing up to Fanny's unreasonableness, but she responds to his stubbornness and arguments with dramatics and hysterics," Anthony responded, barely able to repress a shudder at the memory of the last days.

"Oh dear. She's not come around to the idea of his marrying then?" Julia continued.

"No. She swears she will do everything in her power to prevent it happening. I have told Giles there is little she can do in reality, but he is used to her will being the law, so he's in fear of her visiting Mr Stock when he arrives at the weekend," Anthony explained.

"Surely she cannot influence a man who must be sensible. After all, he is extremely successful in business," Julia exclaimed.

"I would expect not, but from what Miss Stock has said, her father has a low opinion of the *ton*. Rightly so, now they have been subjected to my stepmother's prejudice. I don't think her father would look kindly on my family after he has heard what happened, especially in so public a place. It has been a poor show from the so-called 'betters' in society. I imagine it will fuel his preconceived ideas," Anthony said.

"She is such a lovely young lady. I think she would make your brother a perfect wife," Julia said.

"Yes. Even I can see they're well suited," Anthony acknowledged.

"It is a pity no one has been seen since the altercation," Julia continued. "Sometimes it is best to face the gossips.

That way they can perceive that there is nothing really amiss, and they can move onto their next victims."

"That sounds like the voice of experience," Anthony said, glancing at Julia. He was curious about her background now that he had concluded that only she could make him a suitable wife. He was still able to try to justify his decision in a cold way, pushing aside the effect she had on him or the depth of his feelings for her. His wish for them to marry made him even more curious to find out more about her.

"It is," Julia admitted. "Living with my husband was difficult on a number of levels, and for the first few months, I hid as you have all done. I soon came to realise that if I went about my business, it showed people what he was capable of more than words could." It was the first time she'd confessed anything of her previous life to anyone. Only Patience knew the true horror of what a marriage to Bruce entailed. Saying the words to Anthony suddenly didn't seem as frightening as uttering them had seemed previously.

Anthony frowned, not quite understanding Julia's meaning and mulling over her words before he responded. He knew without doubt he could not fail her in his usual way. Spotting Mr Prescott approaching them, clearly intent on interrupting them, he cursed under his breath.

Hearing the expletive, Julia almost choked in an attempt to stop the laugh bubbling to the surface. It would have appeared rude to have laughed at the approaching gentleman and too complicated to try to explain her mirth; she didn't wish to offend Mr Prescott as much as she was enjoying Anthony's company.

After greetings were exchanged, Mr Prescott turned to Julia. "And are you to attend the ball tonight, my dear?"

"Yes, I am."

"Ah, good — "

"But she's already taken for the first two," Anthony interrupted rudely.

Julia shot Anthony a look, but it was met with an innocent one of his own.

"That is a pity. Perhaps I could have the third and fourth?" Mr Prescott responded, covering his annoyance quickly.

"Of course. It would be my pleasure," Julia said. "I shall look forward to it."

"Ah, good. I must hurry," Mr Prescott said. "I'm to meet an old friend at the hotel, but I spotted you and wanted to secure our dances. It would not be the same if I did not stand up with you at each dance. You brighten the evenings, my dear."

Julia smiled and said her goodbye. She watched him as he hurried away, a slight frown marring her features.

"Does it trouble you, that if he were twenty years younger, he would have proposed to you by now?" Anthony asked, watching both Mr Prescott's retreating form and Julia's expression.

Julia blinked at his words. "Don't be silly! He's enamoured with my grandmother."

"I think you are wrong," Anthony argued gently.

"No! I am sure I am not. He is always so attentive to my grandmother, apart from his requests to dance with me at every event. But she does not dance since that first disastrous one with Mr Bannerman. He is being gentlemanly towards me because it brings him closer to my grandmother."

"And yet you don't like the attentive Mr Prescott," Anthony said.

153

"There is something — I'm just being silly… "

"I doubt that," Anthony defended her.

"It's just that sometimes I see barely suppressed anger, and it makes me feel uncomfortable," Julia admitted aloud for the first time. "I am probably overreacting, but I wish he would leave our circle. I don't trust someone who tries to hide so much of themselves. I think we never see the real man that I am sure lurks behind the polite exterior. I admit to being relieved that Grandmama doesn't seem to hold him any serious affection."

"I think while he's a resident in Bath, you will not be able to avoid him," Anthony pointed out.

"No. We don't spend too much time in his company, I suppose, so it is not too onerous. A couple of dances and the occasional conversation is not excessive in reality. He is not too bad. He just makes me feel wary, and I cannot wholly relax when he joins us," Julia explained.

Seeing Miles and Gabriel approach, they were prevented from continuing their conversation as the four of them walked together to Henrietta Street. Stepping into the house, they spent an enjoyable half hour until Julia forced her son to have a rest.

When Miles had left the room, Gabriel turned to Julia. "He is full of energy that boy. I can hardly believe that you came here because he was unwell."

"It was over-cautiousness on behalf of Grandmama," Julia responded, looking fondly at Patience. "I knew it would only take a few weeks, and he would be his old self once more. There really is no need for us to remain in Bath." There. She'd said the words that had been haunting her dreams. She would have to leave Bath sometime soon and in particular, Anthony.

"I'm enjoying myself," Patience intervened. "Is that not enough reason to stay?"

"If you leave, I shall follow," Gabriel said quickly to his old friend. "You are the only bright star on the horizon. Don't deprive me of your company, my dear delight."

Patience smiled at the words. "I shall not be deserting you in the foreseeable future, my friend."

"Good. These last few days have been hell," Gabriel admitted.

"You can join me with the chaperones tonight and tell us all about it," Patience said soothingly.

"I had rather he did not spread our family squabbles throughout the town," Anthony interjected.

"Better to tell his version than for people to make up their own," Patience cautioned.

Anthony groaned in defeat while Julia laughed at his reaction.

"Never mind. You can forget about gossip while we dance. I promise to be the most delightful of partners," Julia consoled.

"No teasing?" Anthony asked.

"None at all."

"I can hardly let myself believe that such a state of heaven exists," Anthony responded with a twitch of his lips.

Julia laughed. "That's outrageously bad form, my Lord! I am almost tempted to renege on my promise."

"I knew it was too good to last."

Gabriel chuckled. "I expect you to be equally as charming as Mrs Price, Anthony. Now come, we have stayed long beyond propriety. Even I don't wish those who tittle-tattle to have more fodder to chew on."

155

The pair left, and when they had turned the corner from Henrietta Street on their route home, Gabriel decided it was safe enough to speak.

"When are you going to offer for that girl?" he asked.

"Soon," Anthony replied. There was no point in trying to hide anything from Gabriel; he would only badger him until Anthony confessed all anyway.

"The sooner, the better. You are not getting any younger, you know," Gabriel pointed out.

"As you remind me daily how many days it is until my birthday, I am hardly likely to forget," Anthony said drily.

"Yes. Well. Some of us don't have the luxury of too much time. You especially. It is time you acted. There is no justifiable reason to dally."

"I suppose not."

"You suppose? Damnit boy, take hold of your destiny and act!" Gabriel said with despair.

"I will. It is a huge step to take though. It's a little daunting," Anthony admitted.

"But it is the right decision to make," Gabriel persisted.

"I know that, but leave me to choose the right moment. I refuse to go blundering in and mess up everything. You know how easily I could make a faux pas."

"For once I cannot argue against you. It is not often you make sense, but I acknowledge this is one of those occasions," Gabriel said.

"Damned by faint praise," Anthony responded.

Chapter 16

Julia wore a new peach dress. Patience had bought the material and presented the dress, already made, to her, poo-pooing her granddaughter's protestations at the expense. The skirt was decorated with scalloped edges with bunches of small white flowers at the gathers. It was stylishly elegant and the most expensive item of clothing Julia had worn in a long time. She ran her hands down the smooth material and cursed her materialistic tendencies as she sighed at the feel of the soft fabric under her fingers.

Patience entered the room and stopped when she saw Julia. "You look beautiful, my dear," she said.

Julia touched her curls; she'd had the maid spend more time on them than usual. "Do you think it's too much?" she asked, a note of uncertainty in her voice. "I should be beyond trying to act the debutante."

"Nonsense. It compliments what is already visible to those who value you," Patience said gently. "You shall be the most sought-after young woman in the assembly tonight."

Julia laughed in genuine amusement. "I do love your conviction, but I know my place even in Bath society."

A frown flitted across Patience's face but she suppressed the comment she wanted to make. She would not spoil Julia's evening by mentioning the past. Tonight was for enjoying. "You will look fine on Lord Lever's arm. He has become a very attentive young man," she probed gently.

"We are good friends, which is a surprise to us both after the shaky start we had," Julia said, ignoring the fizz in her insides when she imagined herself dancing with Anthony. He was becoming more important to her every day, and the feelings frightened and excited her in equal measure.

"He seems to be a decent young man, bearing in mind what he has faced. I am not sure I could stand to be in the company of Lady Lever for many hours if she was hoping for my death. He's had to live with that knowledge since his father's will was read," Patience said. "I hope he checks the stairs before he descends them. It wouldn't take much to attach something across the top one."

"You have definitely been reading too many gothic novels!" Julia laughed. "Lady Lever's behaviour is inexcusable, but I don't think even she would stoop to such low tricks as to try to kill her own stepson. There is a huge difference between wishing someone to perdition and actually taking measures to achieve that!"

"One never knows what a person would do when money is involved," Patience cautioned.

"Come. Let us go and enjoy ourselves," Julia said, linking her arm through her grandmother's. "I feel the urge to dance every dance."

"It's going to be a good night. With you looking so becoming, I am sure it can only be wonderful," Patience said as both walked through the doorway and down the stairs.

*

Anthony had arrived at the Assembly Room early. He couldn't remain at home. Tonight was important for him. He had never felt as nervous in his life, and it wasn't resting easy on a man used to feeling remote and in control.

He moved to intercept Julia and Patience as soon as they entered the ballroom. "Good evening, ladies," he said with a bow. "You are both looking very well indeed."

"Thank you," Patience responded. "Have you all ventured out this evening, my Lord?"

"My grandfather and brother have, but my stepmother has decided to remain at home. She no longer wishes to partake of Bath Society," Anthony responded, his words hiding the tantrums and hysterics Fanny had thrown when Giles had refused to leave Bath at her request.

"Oh dear. That is a shame," Julia responded.

"Not really. Giles is relieved to be away from her. He says he feels battered by her constant rantings. He has admitted he never considered her a termagant until all this happened," Anthony admitted.

Julia laughed at Anthony's openness.

"I should not confess to that, should I?" Anthony asked with a rueful twitch of his lips.

"No. But you are among close friends, so it does not really matter in mentioning it to us," Patience said. "Now, I shall leave you two to prepare for the first dance while I seek out Gabriel."

"Prepare yourself to hear lots about my stepmother. He is in a ranting mood," Anthony warned.

"I shall refuse to indulge him. It won't do his constitution any good to get so agitated. He can be so foolish sometimes," Patience tutted as she left Anthony and Julia.

Anthony watched the formidable woman's progress towards Gabriel with raised eyebrows. "I don't know whether to feel sorry for my grandfather or just wish your grandmother would put him out of his misery and marry him."

Julia smiled. "I know what you mean. She can be quite scary sometimes, but she insists she is happy with the way things are at the moment and has no intention to marry. They would make a redoubtable couple though, I grant you."

"On second thought, I am not sure the world is ready for that. Come. We have two dances to enjoy," Anthony said offering his arm and leading her into the set.

"Be careful, my Lord. You will be accused of gushing, hinting that you will actually enjoy our dances," Julia teased.

"With you looking so beautiful and your skill as a dancer, my enjoyment is guaranteed. I was not using flowery language, only speaking the truth," Anthony admitted.

Julia was silenced by the words, a blush tinging her cheeks, but smiled at Anthony's chuckle.

"The great Mrs Price lost for words?" Anthony asked.

"I do believe you're teasing me, my Lord."

"Not when I say you look beautiful. I have not the intention to be anything but honest in that regard."

Julia flushed deeply at the second sincere compliment he'd uttered and smiled at Anthony. "Thank you. I have to point out that you are in danger of being beguiled by my sinister plot to convince you that I am something I am not. I discovered many years ago that handsome was the best I could hope for in the levels of attractiveness," she admitted, but she was funning with him. Her heart was warmed by Anthony's words.

"Ah, a plot to entrance me. I see how it is," Anthony continued, enjoying the banter they were sharing. "In that case, would you care to join me on a carriage ride tomorrow? I would like to enjoy your company some more without the eyes of a ballroom watching us."

"We are not doing anything tomorrow. Grandmother likes to rest after a ball," Julia replied.

"As much as I like your family's company, I don't want them to accompany us on that particular trip," Anthony said, becoming serious.

"Oh."

160

"Do you object to my request?" Anthony asked, suddenly unsure of himself.

"No. I am just so used to us being in company," Julia admitted. She could have cursed as, at that moment, they were parted in the dance. Julia could see that she'd caused doubt within Anthony, and although her heart raced at the possibilities of him requesting to see her alone, her overriding instinct was to reassure him. It was a few moments before she could whisper to him. "I am really looking forward to our excursion."

"Are you sure? I don't wish to force you into a situation you would not enjoy," Anthony responded.

As their hands touched to enable them to make a full turn in the dance, Julia was emboldened into squeezing Anthony's hands. "I look forward to spending some time with you without interruptions and distractions," she said honestly.

"That is a relief. Thank you," Anthony said.

Julia laughed and spoke throughout the remainder of their dances, but inside, her mind was racing. What could he possibly want to say to her? Was he experiencing the same attraction she'd been feeling recently? She tried to convince herself that it would be something to do with his family, but there was enough warmth in his looks and his actions that she didn't think so.

When their two dances came to an end, Anthony escorted Julia to the side of the room. "I expect I won't see you for the rest of the evening. You are going to be a very desired partner."

"As I have two dances with Mr Prescott and then two with your brother, that does not leave much of the evening left for anyone else," Julia pointed out.

"Good. I don't want any strangers coming along and turning your head. Know that I will be enjoying watching you dance," Anthony said, a twinkle lighting his eyes.

Julia flushed, but smiled. "Watch yourself. You are becoming positively charming. Those hordes I spoke about when we first met will find out and bear down on you."

Anthony laughed, but didn't comment as Mr Prescott had approached them.

"I have come to claim my delightful partner," Mr Prescott said with a bow. "You are looking exquisite tonight, my dear."

"Thank you," Anthony responded. "I try my best."

Mr Prescott shot Anthony a look that spoke volumes that could not be uttered in a ballroom. Julia coughed slightly, desperate to let out a laugh but knowing it would be gauche to do so. She placed her hand on Mr Prescott's offered arm, and they left Anthony to stand alone.

Mr Prescott didn't speak much as they danced. He was more rotund than Gabriel, so the energetic activity made him slightly breathless. It wasn't until they stood out of the dance at the bottom of the set that he uttered more than the usual pleasantries.

"I am to leave Bath soon," he stated.

"Oh? We shall miss your company," Julia said politely.

"I was hoping you'd say something on those lines because I think there has always been an understanding between us," Mr Prescott said, his voice low.

"I have found your company pleasant," Julia said. "You have been very kind to my grandmother."

"I am willing to be fond of anyone who is connected to you, my dear," Mr Prescott continued. "I would like to speak to you alone, but your friends seem persistent in never leaving your side, especially Lord Lever."

"I've mentioned previously that our grandparents have known each other for a long time, therefore, there is a close family connection," Julia said, her tone a little abrupt. She was becoming wary of the direction of the conversation and felt trapped that it was occurring in a busy ballroom.

"Quite so. I am glad you don't seem to favour the young Lord, for I think he is destined for someone of a higher rank than you, my sweet," Mr Prescott said.

Julia felt herself stiffen with indignation, but tried to keep her expression bland. His words might be true, but it was impolite to point it out.

"I realise your position in life is not as you had hoped it would be, and I have a suggestion that I think would be appealing to you," Mr Prescott said.

"Mr Prescott, I — " Julia started, panic in her voice.

"Please, my dear, let me finish. We are about to rejoin the set," Mr Prescott persisted. "I would like to offer you my protection."

Julia paused. "I'm sorry. I don't understand your meaning." She had a horrible feeling that she did, but apart from the colour draining from her face, she showed no outward sign of apprehension.

"You are a widow without a decent living. I could offer a home for you and your boy and funds to live quite comfortably," Mr Prescott said, his words now urgent. "We could have the most convenient arrangement. I would even be agreeable to you being hostess at my home on some occasions, depending on the company, of course."

"You cannot be thinking straight, Mr Prescott. You cannot be offering what I think you are. Consider your words," Julia choked out. "Please."

163

"Don't be shocked, my dear. It is the perfect solution. I knew from almost the moment I saw you that you would be perfect for me," Mr Prescott said warmly.

"You had the master of ceremonies introduce us because you thought I would make a good *mistress?*" Julia gasped.

"Don't make it sound so sordid," Mr Prescott said, annoyance flitting across his face. "We would be the perfect companions, and I would care for any children we produced. They could not inherit of course, but I would provide for them." He held out his hand as they were to rejoin the dancers, but Julia stepped back.

"No. No. Never," Julia said, choked.

"Don't throw away the best offer you are likely to get," Mr Prescott hissed, but more loudly he said, "Come my dear, we have missed our cue."

"I feel ill. I must leave," Julia said, not looking at anyone, but turning on her heel and walking away from the dancers.

Anyone leaving mid-dance would cause curious glances to be cast in their direction, but the paleness of Julia's complexion and her expression of shock and anguish led them to suppose that she'd been taken suddenly ill. Mr Prescott made no attempt to follow her, but he looked furious with being left alone at the bottom of the set. The other dancers had soon altered their positions to compensate for the change in the number of dancers and continued without delay.

Julia blindly walked through the crowded room and into the ante-room that led to the outside. Her pace increased, as did her need for fresh air. She felt as though she would cast up her accounts, and she couldn't face the shame of that on top of everything else.

As she leaned on the outside wall of the Assembly Rooms, her shaking body welcomed the cold of the stone.

She closed her eyes and took great gulps of air to try to settle her insides.

"Mrs Price, what is it?" Anthony asked. He'd been watching her dance as he had said he would and had noticed her change in demeanour. It had taken all his willpower not to interrupt the dancers as soon as he'd realised she was uncomfortable. When she'd left the dance floor, he'd almost pushed his way through the crowds in an effort to reach her.

Julia didn't open her eyes. "I need to go home," she said quietly.

"I shall escort you," Anthony said immediately.

"No. I need my grandmother," Julia said quickly.

"Promise me you will stay here, and I will go and seek her out," Anthony said.

"I cannot move anywhere at the moment," Julia admitted.

"Can I get you a glass of wine first? You look very pale," Anthony asked.

"No. I don't need anything," Julia assured him, but her eyes remained closed.

Anthony was undecided for a moment, but after a short pause, he entered the doorway that led back into the Assembly Rooms. He soon found Gabriel and Patience, and after only a few words, they left the people they had been sitting with and followed him out of the building. It pained yet relieved him to see that Julia had not moved an inch since he'd left her.

"Julia! What is it? Are you ill?" Patience asked, immediately alarmed.

At the sound of her grandmother's voice, Julia opened her eyes. They were swimming in unshed tears, but none fell. "I have been a fool, Grandmama," she said quietly.

"I doubt that very much," Patience said with authority. "Let us get you home."

"I want to leave Bath. We should never have come," Julia said, anguished.

"We can leave whenever you wish, but you have been enjoying yourself. Whatever's happened tonight should not spoil the weeks of fun we have had," Patience soothed.

"It has all been based on lies," Julia said.

"What has?"

Anthony wanted to demand what had gone on, but he could see that Patience was getting to the cause of the upset. It was just in a more roundabout way than he would have preferred, so he had to grit his teeth and listen.

"It has all been a farce. No one is as they seem," Julia said, rubbing her hands over her face to try to drive away the expression on Mr Prescott's face as he'd made his lewd offer.

"Now, you know that not to be the case," Patience scolded gently.

Julia looked angry. She was more annoyed at herself for being a fool once more, but at the words Patience uttered, she turned the feelings onto her grandmother. "So, Mr Prescott has not just offered to provide a cosy little place for myself and Miles to live and to wait for him to visit? He's promised to provide for any children we should have, so at least he is not expecting me to have them adopted or offered up as foundlings. I suppose that is the indication that he is a decent man — I mean, he has been honest in saying they cannot inherit his wealth, but I suppose him not sending them away is a positive. He contrived an introduction to me because I gave him the impression I'd be perfect for his needs," Julia said bitterly.

166

The three standing around Julia went silent at Julia's words until Patience broke the stillness. "He has asked you to be his lightskirt?"

"Apparently it is the best offer I am going to get," Julia responded dully.

"I'm going to kill him!" Anthony almost shouted. "I'm going to separate his foul-spouting head from the rest of his body!"

Gabriel tried to grab Anthony's arm to prevent him re-entering the assembly to find Mr Prescott, but he was shaken off. "Oh, dear Lord!" Gabriel said, before following his grandson into the building.

*

Anthony strode across the ballroom. The dark colour of his frock coat was nothing to the blackness of his expression. Anger vibrated off him as he strode through the crowded space. For Anthony there was only one person in that room, and he was aiming straight for him. Dancers stepped out of Anthony's way, rather than having their satin slippers trampled on by a man immune to any distress or annoyance of those around him.

The dancing stopped, and the musicians came to a floundering halt when it was clear that there was something amiss. Anthony didn't pause until he stood in front of Mr Prescott. The older man looked wary but tried to maintain an air of slight amusement.

"My Lord?" he asked in question. "What is all this? You are disrupting the entertainments."

"How dare you insult her?" Anthony ground out, completely oblivious that he was putting on a show for the attendees of the evening. It wouldn't have stopped him even if he had noticed the large audience he had

167

accumulated. Nothing would have distracted him from his task of protecting Julia.

There was no gain in Mr Prescott pretending no knowledge as to what Anthony was referring. He shrugged. "It is a good offer for someone with no connections and little to recommend them other than a pleasing face and body. What's wrong? Did I beat you to it? If you wanted to try her delights yourself, you should have made your move earlier."

The punch made the onlookers gasp and exclaim in shock when it connected squarely to the older man's jaw. Mr Prescott was flung backwards, unavoidably colliding with some of the stunned crowd before he crumpled to the floor.

Anthony stood over him, his fist still clenched, daring the man to move. "It is a good thing you are an old man, or you would be receiving the pummelling of your life," he growled out.

Mr Prescott took a few moments to come to his senses. He remained on the wooden floor, but he glared up at his attacker. "I could call you out for that!"

"Go on! Let these people be witness to your death wish, by all means," Anthony mocked, but anger was still oozing from him.

"What's wrong with you? Defending a penniless widow. Is she worth fleeing the country if you were to kill me in a duel?" Mr Prescott sneered in return. Someone had handed him a handkerchief, and he was wiping at his bloodied lip, but he remained on the floor.

"There would be no 'if' about it," Anthony snarled. "My father was probably the worst parent in the world, but he certainly insisted on my knowing how to shoot a gun with deadly accuracy. There would be no deloping on my part; I promise you that."

"You are young. You don't realise that she is one of many you could have," Mr Prescott said, finally realising he perhaps was in more danger than he'd first thought. He was no sharpshooter and had used the threat of a duel to try to frighten the younger man. It seemed he had underestimated his opponent.

"She is the only one I am going to marry, and if I see you even looking in her direction in the future, you will have more than my fist to worry about. Do I make myself clear?" Anthony snapped.

"Perfectly. I apologise, my Lord. There is no need for us to fall out over this. It's a misunderstanding. If I had known you were betrothed, of course I would never have presumed to infringe on your property," Mr Prescott responded.

"You are a spineless fool who preys on the weak," Anthony said. He stood straight, and for the first time, looked at the hundreds of faces who were all watching the events with fascination. "If this is the type of person allowed within these walls, then this establishment is not the place any decent person should be frequenting." He turned back to Mr Prescott. "You are the worst kind of snake, and you'd best keep out of my sight. I have a good mind to give you a taste of what to expect if I see you near her ever again."

"Brother, no," Giles urged. He'd appeared at Anthony's left, the right being taken by Gabriel. "He is not worth it."

"He insulted her," Anthony ground out, glancing at his brother.

"And you have shown him what the consequences are for that. Come. She needs you." Giles had only the same information as everyone else, but he was astute enough to guess it involved Julia.

"He's right, my boy. Come," Gabriel encouraged. Both men took hold of Anthony's arms and gently led him away

169

from the fracas. People were openly watching what was going on, but the threesome ignored the looks and whisperings that followed them out of the room and through the corridor.

Returning to Julia, Anthony approached the women, who were now standing together, Patience having wrapped her arm around her granddaughter's shoulders. "He will not approach you again," he said gruffly.

"I just want to leave," Julia said, her haunted expression upsetting Anthony further.

"There is just one thing," he said.

"What is it?" Patience asked, eager to take Julia home.

"I announced to the room that we were to marry," Anthony admitted.

"What? No!" Julia exclaimed.

"No?" Anthony said in disbelief.

"No. I… " Julia started.

In frustration, Anthony raised his hand to run it through his hair, but he paused mid-action at Julia's reaction to his movement. She'd flinched and turned her head towards Patience in an attempt to shield her face.

There was a deadly silence from Anthony whilst he processed what Julia had done.

"You thought I was going to strike you," he eventually said, his voice devoid of emotion.

"My Lord, you don't understand… " Patience started.

Anthony never took his eyes off Julia, ignoring Patience's words. "After all that we've shared, you thought I could hit you?" He'd said the words, but he knew he wasn't going to get a response. Julia hadn't opened her eyes and was shaking like a leaf. He turned to Gabriel. "I have been a fool. I am going home."

Gabriel and Giles followed Anthony's almost marching steps as he returned to Great Pulteney Street. Neither said a word.

Chapter 17

Patience had tended to Julia herself when they returned home. She'd been worried about the way Julia didn't seem able to stop shaking, and Patience had eventually admitted she didn't know what to do for the best and sent for a doctor.

"She's had a severe shock," the doctor advised after examining a silent Julia. "I suggest a strong sedative for tonight, and we will see how she fares tomorrow. She is young and you say usually well. I expect her to rally after a night of rest."

"Thank you. I shall remain with her," Patience said.

"She will not waken after taking the draught," the doctor assured Patience.

"Even so, I would like to be here."

Patience settled Julia in her bed, and once the laudanum had taken effect, she was relieved to hear her granddaughter's deep, even breathing.

Taking up a book, Patience prepared herself for the long night ahead.

*

Julia awoke to the sounds of whispering. She felt groggy and as if she'd lain in bed for too long. Trying to concentrate on the voices, she forced herself into consciousness and smiled wanly when she saw Miles' worried expression when she opened her eyes.

"Mama! You're awake!" Miles said, with a lunge at Julia, wrapping his arms around her as best he could and squeezing his mother tightly.

"Miles! Come away!" Patience scolded. "Let your mother be!"

"It is fine. He does no harm," Julia croaked out.

"Mama, you sound funny," Miles said, looking in concern at his mother.

"I just need something to drink. Would you be a good boy and order me some tea please?"

"Yes, of course," Miles said, running out the door and down the stairs.

Julia grimaced at the noise level against her throbbing head. "What time is it?"

"Mid-afternoon. The doctor said you would sleep well, but I did not expect it to be quite this long," Patience smiled in an effort to stem the worry she'd felt at watching Julia's still body all through the night and into the morning.

"What a lazy-bones I am!" Julia said, trying to sit up even though her head still throbbed.

"I hope you feel better for it. You were very upset."

"Yes." Julia paused, the events of the previous evening flooding back. Her cheeks flamed, and eventually she turned wide eyes to meet Patience's worried ones. "I thought Mr Prescott was attracted to you," she said simply. "I didn't mean to give him a false impression of me."

"There is no need for recriminations on your part where that man is concerned!" Patience said briskly. "We were all taken in by his motives. I thought he was an honourable gentleman. What a fool I was to think that!"

"Did you regard him? I am sorry if his duplicity has hurt you," Julia said quickly.

"I liked him well enough as an acquaintance but nothing else. I have told you this already, my sweeting. I will not be marrying again. My Hancock cannot be replaced," Patience said gently. "My anger at that man's actions are on your behalf not mine. That anyone could offer you such an insult fair makes my blood boil."

"I suppose I'm not the first widow to receive such a proposition. It was just so shocking, and for him to make it in a ballroom! I could barely comprehend his meaning at first. Although I should not have reacted so badly. Leaving the dance mid-way through is a sure way of attracting unwanted gossip," Julia admitted.

"It certainly stirred Lord Lever into action," Patience said, watching her granddaughter closely for her reaction at mentioning Anthony.

Julia put her head in her hands and moaned. "I treated him so poorly," she admitted with shame.

"You realise now that he was not going to strike you?" Patience asked.

With an anguished look, Julia sank back onto her pillows. "How could I have reacted in such an hysterical way? I know he's so different from Bruce, but when it came to it, I gave him no credit for being such. I could not help it. I just panicked when I saw his hand rise and the expression on his face."

"It is a natural reaction after all you have been through," Patience reasoned.

"Two years ago maybe, but not now. Not with him," Julia responded dully.

"He'll understand, I am sure."

"No. He will not. He has been through so much himself, I would not expect him to be able to grasp the reasonings behind my reaction. It is too much to expect of him."

"What are you going to do?" Patience asked.

"I would like to leave Bath. I cannot face anyone. I just want to try to forget about everything that's happened and hope I can forget how much I must have hurt Lord Lever," Julia said.

"I will agree to leaving in a few days, once I am convinced the journey will not make you ill," Patience said firmly.

"It won't," Julia assured her.

"I will decide that," Patience said. "I saw how you were last night. I accept it would be best to leave but I am not departing immediately as if we have something to be ashamed of. Everything last night was as a result of Mr Prescott's actions. I refuse to react as if we have done something wrong."

"I cannot leave the house," Julia appealed. "I can't see anyone."

"That's perfectly acceptable," Patience soothed. "I will not allow any visitors, but I wish to say my own goodbyes."

"You will miss Mr Bannerman," Julia stated.

"Yes. But you are more important to me than he is. As long as I say my farewells, that is all I require," Patience assured her granddaughter.

"Who are you saying goodbye to, Grandmama?" Miles asked as he entered the room ahead of the maid who carried a tray of tea and scones.

"Mr Bannerman. We shall be leaving Bath in a few days," Patience informed her grandson.

"Aw, no! I like Mr Bannerman," Miles wailed. "He said we could visit the tea rooms at Sally Lunns."

"I'm sure I can fit in a visit with you before we return home," Patience said. "But your Mama is not well, and we need to leave soon."

"But I came to Bath to get well," Miles pointed out not unreasonably.

175

"Sometimes people need different things, other than taking the waters," Patience explained. "Now, come. Let us leave your Mama alone to rest."

The pair left Julia in peace. She drank the tea as if she'd not drunk for months, letting the warm liquid sooth her insides. Whilst enjoying the sweet beverage, she couldn't help but go over the events of the night before. Mr Prescott she could dismiss to some extent. He was obviously a scoundrel, but when she considered his actions, she could not exonerate herself completely.

He had made more of a fuss of her sometimes, but she'd not considered his motivations beyond that of being pleasing towards Patience's family in order to promote himself further. Upon reflection, Julia remembered some of the instances when Mr Prescott had seemed to avoid Patience in preference to herself.

Putting down the empty tea cup, Julia rubbed her hands over her face. She'd been a naïve fool and could curse herself. If she'd been less intent on worrying if her grandmother was going to marry, she might have actually noticed that Mr Prescott favoured herself. She felt no honour at being singled out; she'd never been so insulted.

She'd overreacted to the proposal. Everyone will have noticed her leaving the dance. It was behaviour that would draw the curiosity of the gossips and goodness knows what story would be racing through the people who were in attendance. They had seen Anthony return to the ballroom and the exchange between the pair. She could only imagine what had gone on, Patience not going into any details if she knew any. All they were sure about was that Anthony had announced he was to marry Julia. Her cheeks burned at the thought that one who was used to blending into the background would be the talk of the evening.

176

Forcing herself to face the memory of the worst part of the evening, she remembered the expression on Anthony's face when he'd realised why she'd flinched at his actions. He thought she'd kept her eyes closed, but she had seen his expression as she'd flinched and turned away. How could she have thought he would be of a similar tendency to Bruce? They were nothing alike. She felt sick to her stomach — she had done him wrong and could never excuse her behaviour. How could she ask for his forgiveness when she had treated him so poorly? She didn't deserve his understanding, and she certainly couldn't ask for it.

The sooner they left Bath, the better.

*

It was a full day after the events at the Assembly Rooms, and Miles was bored at being restricted to remain within doors. He moaned and was restless until, eventually, Patience secured Julia's agreement to take him for a walk to Sydney Gardens to burn off some energy.

Unbeknownst to Julia, Patience also intended calling at Great Pulteney Street to speak to Gabriel and see if the unexpected situation of estrangement between their grandchildren could be overcome.

After spending an hour in the Gardens with Miles acting as if he'd been constrained for months instead of a day, the pair started to walk down towards Anthony and Gabriel's abode.

Patience faltered when she saw Mr Prescott walking towards her. At first she was going to cross the road to avoid him, but then decided that she was not in the wrong, so she would not skulk away from the situation. Setting her shoulders, she held Miles' hand a little tighter and walked with her head held high down the busy street.

She thought they were going to pass without incident, but just when she thought she could relax, Mr Prescott stopped her progress by putting his hand on her arm.

"Get your hand off me!" Patience snapped quietly, not wishing to draw attention to the exchange.

"Mrs Hancock. Please. Let me explain," Mr Prescott said. He was all hesitant smiles and nervous movements. Patience took some pleasure in the large bruise that covered one side of his jaw. Anthony had clearly made his displeasure felt in the most effective way possible.

"There is nothing to explain," Patience said stiffly. "You are a rogue, sir, and we don't wish to have anything more to do with you."

"My aim was not to insult you or your family," Mr Prescott persisted. "In fact, in the cold light of day, I am surprised you cannot see the benefits of my offer."

"You proposed that Julia become your lightskirt," Patience hissed, trying to shield Miles from the words being said. "What possible way would we consider that as an advantageous proposal?"

"I would have looked after her and her son. I know how much Miles wants a stable of his own. Don't you, my child?" Mr Prescott asked, ignoring the glare he was receiving. "I am sure I would soon have you driving around in my curricle."

"Oh yes!" Miles said eagerly. "With the finest team."

"Of course. Nothing less than the best horseflesh for you," Mr Prescott said.

"Enough!" Patience said. "You are playing an underhand game that will get you nowhere. My granddaughter was clear in her message to you, and if not, I feel Lord Lever's actions drove the message home."

"Yes. I believe felicitations are in order. Little did I know that Mrs Price was intent on securing herself a title. I must congratulate her on her double-playing. She has turned out to be rather more scheming than I expected," Mr Prescott said.

"If we were not in a public place, I would slap your face for that comment," Patience responded. "Come, Miles. We are not going to speak to Mr Prescott ever again." She tugged on her great-grandson's hand, and they walked away. She was aware that Mr Prescott was watching her with amusement, which made her dislike of him increase, if that were possible.

"Why don't you like Mr Prescott, Grandmama?" Miles asked innocently.

"He was not very nice to your mama," Patience said, with possibly the vaguest response to a question, she'd ever given.

"I thought it was because he mentioned me having horses. I know Mama does not want me to have horses," Miles responded.

Patience sighed. "It is not that, my sweeting. She would love you to have a full stable, but unfortunately since your papa died, there aren't the funds to keep horses. They are very expensive."

Miles pondered her words before speaking. "Mama is sometimes worried about money."

"Yes, she is, but if I help with funds and you don't ask for horses, among the three of us, we should be able to manage just fine," Patience said, not wishing for Miles to start bombarding Julia with requests for horses once more.

"I will try," Miles said. "But I would like so much to have a horse of my own."

"I know, my love. I know."

Chapter 18

I am a fool. A buffoon of the highest order.

I have managed to make a complete idiot of myself by allowing someone to get under my skin, to start to affect me in ways that I would never have believed a few weeks ago. I was idiot enough to think there was an understanding between us. Yet she reacted towards me in the most repulsive way she could.

She recoiled from me.

Am I truly so bad? I never expected to have much to offer, but her reaction showed a repulsion even I did not suspect.

I don't understand what our time together has meant if that is how she felt about me. Why have the conversations we have shared, the time together, if I sickened her so much? It meant so much to me. I am ashamed at how easily I was taken in. As if I were some green horn.

It all adds up to one thing — I should have kept to my first intention: of keeping my feelings, for what they are, in check and marrying someone to whom I have no connection, for I will not let another's misleading behaviour cost me my heritage. After all, it is all that I have.

Today I shall ask Miss Carruthers to marry me.

I refuse to depend on feelings anymore. They can be false, misleading and misguided. I need certainties in my life.

*

Gabriel was concerned. Anthony had completely withdrawn into himself. Nothing the grandfather said or did drew Anthony out of his self-enforced removal from those around him.

After another unsuccessful attempt to bring his grandson out of his study, Gabriel entered the morning room, to find Giles standing in front of the fireplace. Dressed finely, he might have been, but the action of rolling on the balls of his feet was a clue that he was upset, even if the expression on his face had not betrayed him.

"What has you looking so blue-devilled?" Gabriel asked, making himself a large drink from the decanters on one of the side tables in the room. After his conversation with Anthony, he needed the fortification to face the rest of the day.

"Mother wishes for us to depart tomorrow," Giles explained.

"So, she believes he will not marry?" Gabriel asked.

"No. Yes. She believes he will not marry."

"I have some bad news for your mother. He has just announced he is going to offer for Miss Carruthers," Gabriel said.

"Really?" Giles asked, temporarily shocked out of his maudlin mood. "Well, I'll be — can he do that? He is technically betrothed to Mrs Price, is he not?"

"I tried using that argument," Gabriel admitted with a sigh as he sat on a sofa near to where Giles stood. "He laughed in my face at that. Mrs Price has hurt him deeply. A pity she's the first person to be able to get through that shield he wears. He is suffering badly because he is not used to the massive emotions being in love creates, but he can't see it and refuses to listen when I try to explain why he is in such turmoil."

"It was a strange way for her to react. We all know Anthony's a decent sort," Giles admitted.

181

"Yes, but we know nothing of her past except the little that has been hinted at. I believe it was not a happy one," Gabriel said.

"All the same, there was no need to fear Anthony!" Giles defended his brother.

Gabriel smiled, his initial dismissal of Giles as a weak, inconsequential fool completely forgotten since his arrival in Bath and their time together. "No. But she'd had a shock. I wish they could see each other to sort out this misunderstanding, but it is impossible."

"We are all doomed to be miserable," Giles said forlornly.

"What have you to be sad about?" Gabriel demanded.

"Mother insisting on leaving, which she will now she believes Anthony won't marry. Even if he manages to persuade Miss Carruthers, Mother's likely to still leave. I think she has reached the conclusion that events have not turned out quite in the way she had hoped. And if we leave, it means I don't get to convince Miss Stock's father that I am a worthy suitor," Giles bemoaned.

"You youngsters are enough to give me a chronic bilious temperament, never mind it being blamed on my eating rich food," Gabriel grumbled.

"What do you mean?" Giles asked in surprise. Gabriel was usually the one to keep the mood light, and yet here he was being as cantankerous as Fanny.

"Just because you have received one set-back, you are willing to give up. You can't think much of your young lady if you abandon her so easily. I would leave her be if that is the case; she deserves someone with more backbone," Gabriel mocked.

"I do think highly of her!" Giles protested hotly.

"It doesn't look like it to me," Gabriel continued.

182

"Mother said she is going to whisper poison in Mr Stock's ear if she has to. How can I convince him that I am worthy of his daughter if my own mother is spouting lies and tittle-tattle? What sort of a start would we have with our parents against the match? Even if I could persuade Miss Stock to marry me in those circumstances," Giles fretted.

"Do you think marriage is easy, you foolish whippersnapper? Let me tell you this: It is the hardest thing you'll ever embark upon, but it is also the best thing to happen to any of us," Gabriel said. "In most aspects to do with marriage, you have to fight for what you want, and to me, it does not look like you have an ounce of fight in you, you nodcock."

"It sounds like a lot of hard work," Giles said.

"It is and yet it is the best thing on this earth to share your life with the woman you truly love."

"I do love Miss Stock," Giles admitted, reddening.

"Well, get out there and fight for her!" Gabriel commanded. "Show her that you will do anything it takes to prove that you are worth her faith in you. And if all else fails — elope!"

Giles laughed. "That certainly would shock Mama! I have never gone against her wishes."

"Don't marry Miss Stock because you want to rail against your mother," Gabriel cautioned. "You are a young man. The rest of your life will hopefully consist of tens of years. It is a long time to be married to the wrong person and too short if she is the perfect one."

"I cannot imagine being married to anyone else," Giles said. "It's only since meeting her that I have even thought of becoming leg-shackled. I never believed I would seek out the state for years to come, if at all, but I can't do without her."

183

"Then I suggest you see her as soon as you possibly can and work out what's best between you," Gabriel said.

"Thank you," Giles said, as he walked to the door. "I really did not know what to do to resolve this conundrum, but in some respects you have made everything clearer."

"I'm glad to be of help. I only wish I could help Anthony in the same way. I am sure Mrs Price is the best person for him," Gabriel said, not quite as upbeat as he had been moments before.

"If that is the case, I will try to keep him away from Miss Carruthers. I know she has no intention of marrying, but we don't want to take the risk of her changing her mind," Giles offered.

"No, we don't. Good idea. Do what you can, and God speed with your own quest."

"Thank you," Giles said, leaving the room.

*

"A trip to Wells would do you good," Lucy said to her cousin as they gathered their outdoor wear from their bedchambers.

"All it would do would be to bring back memories of being there with Mr Russell," Nancy said pulling a face, as she tied her bonnet ribbon under her chin.

"It is understandable that they have not been seen for a few days. We also have not been socialising as we did," Lucy said gently.

"No," Nancy acknowledged. "Why couldn't this trip go smoothly? It all seemed to be going so well and then... "

"You will see him again."

"Papa wishes to leave as soon as possible," Nancy said. "And mother seems happy to return home. I knew Papa wanted to see how she fared, but I did not think he would want us to vacate our premises quite so soon."

184

"Should I feign a sudden bout of illness?" Lucy offered.

Nancy smiled. "You might have to."

"A day out will do you good," Lucy persisted.

"No it won't. I have no other option than to seek out Mr Russell myself, and being away from Bath for the day can only cause further delay."

"You are not going to his home are you? You could not be so brazen!" Lucy exclaimed.

"Not at all," Nancy laughed. "I might just have to walk the length and breadth of Great Pulteney Street until he notices me."

"How are you going to shake off Mary? You know she will report anything to Aunt Susan," Lucy cautioned.

"As far as Mary is concerned, I will be on my way to Wells with everyone else. As far as mother is concerned, I am going to pretend I need to abandon the trip to Wells due to a prior engagement," Nancy said.

"You'll never get away with it!"

"I have to. Too much relies on my seeing Mr Russell. I cannot leave without saying goodbye. Please support me in whatever nonsense I utter."

"I will try. I hope you know what you are doing," Lucy said with a shake of her head.

*

Giles turned the corner of Great Pulteney Street into Sydney Place and nearly collided with Nancy. "Miss Stock!" he exclaimed.

"Mr Russell. What a surprise to see you out and about," Nancy lied. She was beginning to think herself of criminal bent with the amount of deception she'd undertaken since confessing her plan to her cousin.

She'd entered into the carriage and travelled with the group along Henrietta Street as they'd set out for a final day

185

in Wells before leaving Bath once and for all. Falsely remembering an arrangement with Julia, she'd persuaded her father to stop the carriage and let her out. Waving to her family as the carriage moved away, she'd pretended to enter the wrought iron gate of number ten before watching as the carriage turned the corner at the end of the street. Retracing her steps, she'd skirted the buildings and cut through to the rear of Henrietta Street. She didn't want to be in a vicinity where any of the servants would see her whilst bypassing Laura Place.

Walking quickly with her head down, she'd skirted around the houses until reaching Sydney Place. Pausing to catch her breath and bolster her frayed nerves at her audacity, she'd started to walk towards Great Pulteney Street, inwardly trying to convince herself that she was doing the right thing.

It seemed her prayers had been answered when Giles had walked around the corner.

"I'm so glad to have bumped into you," Giles said. "I was trying to pluck up courage to come and call at Laura Place."

"My family are not at home today," Nancy said.

"Oh. Good. I think," Giles said ineloquently. "Miss Stock, I know I ask too much, but could we find somewhere to be private? I really need to speak without suffering interruptions."

"Of course. Whatever you wish," Nancy said. She had no idea how private Giles meant, but she was determined to spend every moment with him, whatever the cost to her reputation.

"Good. Let us find somewhere suitable," Giles said, emboldened now that he was away from his mother. He offered his arm to Nancy, and they walked together towards Weston. It was a fine day, so they took their time but tried

186

to keep to the quieter areas, not following the main route, which would undoubtably have them seen by someone with whom they were acquainted.

Eventually, Giles saw a small cluster of trees in a field that offered some shade. They walked to the copse, and Giles gallantly took off his frock coat, and although it was impeccably made of a fine blue wool from none other than Weston's, he sacrificed it to the ground in order that Nancy didn't have to sit on the grass.

Nancy tried to stem the nervousness she felt now that they were far away from anyone else. She'd never been so private with a man before and didn't really know what to say. She took her time straightening her skirts around her, so she looked respectable, even though she wasn't necessarily acting it. Being alone would condemn her in her family's eyes, let alone that of the wider society. She had to trust in fate that they wouldn't be discovered.

"I should have brought some refreshments, but I did not think I would be so fortunate as to see you alone," Giles stated. "I have missed you."

"And I you," Nancy said shyly.

"My mother was a monster with what she said. I don't want you to think my whole family feels as she does. Anthony is in favour of our union, if you are still willing for it to happen?"

"That is very kind of Lord Lever, but what if your mother tries to prevent us from getting married? She could cause all sorts of problems," Nancy said.

"Anthony is the head of the family, so his opinion matters the most," Giles assured her. "Do you think your father will approve of me?" Now it was his turn to be unsure of himself.

"He will. Of course he will, but… " Nancy faltered.

"My mother," Giles responded dully.

"It's just that he is so prejudiced against the aristocracy that I am not sure he would agree to my joining a family in which some of its members are so against a person of my kind. I feel from what she said that you would not be able to persuade her to think differently?" Nancy tried to explain her own parent's prejudices.

"I am willing to cut myself off from my mother. I have told her exactly that. You mean more to me than she does," Giles said gallantly.

"I would not want you to do that!" Nancy exclaimed. "You might come to despise me if there is a rift with your mother."

Giles took hold of Nancy's hands. "You are such a dear thing, my sweet Nancy. The fact that you wouldn't wish for me to be estranged from the person who has insulted you and your family shows at least one of the reasons why I love you so much. For I do, Nancy."

"And I love you," Nancy whispered, her cheeks aflame.

Giles squeezed the hands he was holding before cupping her cheek with one hand and slowly brushing his lips across hers. He was not the most experienced young man, but he could guide an innocent like Nancy into enjoying, yet not being overwhelmed by, her first kisses.

He removed her bonnet after a while and allowed himself to feel the tendrils of hair across his fingers while he kissed her some more. Encouraging her to touch him, he felt his heart quicken when she eventually became bold enough to wrap her arms around his neck.

Breaking their embrace, Giles rested his forehead against Nancy's. He was warmed inside when he saw how her pupils were dilated and her lips were rosy from being kissed thoroughly. He smiled into her eyes.

"I love you, and the sooner you become Mrs Giles Russell, the better," he said huskily.

Nancy smiled. "I wish we could marry soon."

Giles paused. "Would you forgive me for saying something I don't think you will like?" Nancy looked immediately alarmed at his words, but he touched her lips gently. "I am not going to do anything today other than kiss you. Please don't be worried."

"What is it you want to say?" Nancy asked, once reassured that she was not going to be persuaded into a situation that she might want but that was too far for her sensibilities to go.

"Could we please elope? We know we are perfectly matched, but I cannot risk not being able to convince your father. If we make a dash over the border, the decision has already been made, and I would spend the rest of my days making it up to your parents," Giles babbled.

Nancy pulled away a little, turning her head so Giles couldn't see the emotions flitting across her face.

"I have upset you," Giles eventually said. He'd held her hands whilst she was thinking over his proposal, but there hadn't been any reassuring squeeze from her.

Nancy turned towards Giles. "I am only upset that my family will not see me married," she explained with a wistful smile. "You are right though. I can't risk my father not accepting you as my suitor, and so yes, I think we should elope."

"Oh, Nancy! That is wonderful!" Giles flung his arms around his bride-to-be and pulled her into a warm embrace. "You have made me the happiest of men. Now we have to plan how and when."

"It will have to be soon. We'll be leaving Bath either tomorrow or the day after. Papa wants to return home as soon as he can," Nancy said.

"Tomorrow then," Giles decided.

"How will we manage it?" Nancy asked, wide-eyed at the thought of what they were going to undertake but not completely unaffected by the excitement of such a rash scheme.

"I will make-up some excuse that I need to use Anthony's carriage. I will have to ask him to forward me some blunt, which will be a little trickier. He is no fool, and he gave me some on my arrival in Bath," Giles said, trying to think of a story that would be convincing for his brother.

"I can provide what funds we need," Nancy said.

"What? No! It is my job to provide for you," Giles said.

"But it'll be your money once we are married," Nancy pointed out not unreasonably. "I should perhaps tell you what I should get if Papa does not change his mind about my dowry at our sudden marriage."

"I am marrying you for you, not your money," Giles interrupted. He flushed a little. "I know I have not much myself — just a small legacy from my father. I will inherit more if Anthony does not marry by the time he turns thirty, but he's in love with Mrs Price, so as long as he straightens out their misunderstanding, he will be married himself soon. It does mean though that I will not bring many funds with me," he explained.

"It honestly doesn't matter," Nancy smiled. "I did not know there was a chance of your inheriting your brother's portion. Is that usual?"

"No. It was just my father being peculiar," Giles admitted. "Mother has been a real termagant about it, to be honest. I am glad Anthony is looking to marry. Or he was. He has had his own setback."

"It sounds very complicated," Nancy said. "But we potentially have nothing to worry about. My dowry is five thousand a year."

"F-f-five thousand?" Giles spluttered.

"Do you love me a little bit more?" Nancy asked coyly.

"My good grief! I would have you surrounded by protectors if you were a daughter of mine," Giles said. He suddenly put his head in his hands, all his laughter gone. "Your father will be convinced I've married you for your money. I will be branded as a fortune hunter."

"But we shall know the truth, so it does not matter," Nancy assured him.

"Yes. You are right. The money has never mattered to me. Let's return home now. But will you be on Great Pulteney Street at eight of the clock tomorrow morning? I think we should get an early start."

"You wish to pick me up in such a public place?" Nancy asked shocked.

"Good point. Where shall we meet?" Giles asked.

"Can you arrange for my portmanteau to be collected this evening? I will pretend I am giving Mrs Price some of my dresses. No one will suspect anything untoward if I am with my family all evening," Nancy suggested.

"Not even your cousin?"

"No. She will believe me," Nancy assured him.

Chapter 19

I am annoyed.

Why can I not just ask the chit to marry me? I have a lot to offer someone who's background is in trade. I am not marrying her for money. Well, not her money anyway. What foolishness is stopping me from walking the dozen or so steps to her residence and proposing? It is a simple thing to do, yet it seems to be beyond me. It would be far simpler to marry Miss Carruthers. Why can I not make the offer?

This is so damned frustrating. I will not make a fool of myself by pining over someone who is repulsed by me. I will not. Her rejection was clear, despite what my grandfather has tried to convince me of.

Blast it.

I miss her despite her actions.

I long to see her. To make everything right, so she will tease me and laugh at me.

What the devil am I going to do? I cannot think straight. It doesn't make sense.

I wish I could see her.

*

Julia took a few deep breaths. She was not one to lose her temper with Miles, but his behaviour since the previous day had been questionable. She couldn't understand it.

Eventually after Miles shouted at her for the fifth time that morning, Julia had reached the end of her tether. "I don't appreciate being shouted at, young man," she scolded. "You will remain in your chamber until you are ready to act like a decent human being and speak civilly to me."

"I want a horse!" Miles demanded.

"We have been through this time and again. I refuse to try to explain one more time why we don't have a stable full of animals as you would wish. You are going to have to learn that we don't always get what we want," Julia said sharply.

"If you were Mr Prescott's lightskirt he would let me have as many horses as I want. I know I promised not to say anything but it is unfair! He wants to give me horses, and I want horses. It is you who is stopping it. Why will you not be his lightskirt?" Miles demanded.

Julia looked horrified. It took her a moment or two to be able to speak, but when she did, Miles knew that he'd gone too far. "Get out," Julia said quietly.

"Mama, I — " Miles started, not quite knowing how, but understanding he'd overstepped the mark with his normally placid parent.

"Get out!" Julia shouted. "I'm sick to death of being punished because of your selfish father! I don't ever want horses mentioned again! Every day I am argued with as if it were my fault we are as poor as we are. He overspent! He had such little regard for us that he did not care what happened to us! If he had lived we would have lost everything, and yet you will not stop talking about blasted horses! Go to your room and stay there until I say otherwise! I can't bear to be near you at the moment."

Miles ran out of the room in tears, sobbing loudly. Julia made a move to follow him, but she couldn't. She was too upset herself. Constantly feeling a failure was bad enough, but Miles' suggestion that she had let him down by not agreeing to Mr Prescott's scheme was too much.

Head in hands she sobbed.

Patience walked into the drawing room a little later and immediately rushed to her granddaughter. "What is it?

193

What has happened?" she asked wrapping Julia in an embrace.

Through sobs and hiccups, Julia explained what had happened with Miles. Her face was red through crying, and her eyes were swollen. Patience gently wiped the tears away while Julia told of the argument between her son and herself.

"I said such cruel things. I should not have uttered the words I did,"

"We all say things we don't mean. He will one day have to learn the impact on his life of Bruce's actions. Perhaps he is old enough to understand now?" Patience soothed.

"How can I make him understand?" Julia sobbed. "He is too young to realise the implications of his words about being a lightskirt. What if he repeats it to someone else? I will be a laughing stock, even to the staff. They must already be talking if Miles knows about the offer that man made."

"It is my fault," Patience said. "When Mr Prescott approached us in the street, I was intent on giving him a piece of my mind, but I was bird-witted to think I could get the better of a man like that. He is no slow-top in trying to get what he wants. He knew in speaking to Miles it would stir up the pepper pot."

"As usual we excuse bad behaviour as if it were caused by one of us," Julia said, finally drying her eyes and sitting a little straighter. "I did nothing to suggest I was something of a wanton doxy, and yet he presumed it was perfectly acceptable to make his offer."

"He is a rogue of the highest order, and I'm only sorry I did not see Lord Lever landing him a facer," Patience said. "I can report it certainly hit its mark, as the bruise he was sporting was a fine one indeed! I am surprised he left his lodging until it had faded."

194

"A man with so much gall would hardly hide when he could gain sympathy by concocting some sort of Canterbury tale to suit his purpose," Julia said with disgust.

"I am going to visit Gabriel this afternoon. I don't suppose you would like to accompany me?" Patience asked.

"No! Not at all. I could not face either of them," Julia responded immediately.

"They should be told why you reacted in the way you did. They would understand," Patience reasoned.

"I cannot prove to them completely that I was a fool, which is what they would think if I tried to explain the situation. Could you imagine their response if I said that, although I know his Lordship is nothing like Bruce, I reacted as if I were going to be struck as Bruce would have done? It sounds idiotic to me. I don't want to see mockery, or at best pity, in their eyes. It is better to leave without seeing them. They don't need to know about my past. It will not achieve anything, especially now," Julia said.

"I don't agree, but I cannot force you. I think it is time I make arrangements to leave tomorrow. I don't think there is anything more for us here. I am sorry it was not the break I had hoped it would be," Patience said, standing. "I will go to the Pump Room, and then after lunch, I will visit Gabriel. He has not been attending the Pump Room. I'm presuming it is because of what has happened rather than him not being well."

"Please send him my best wishes and tell him, tell them both if you can, that I am truly so very sorry," Julia said.

"I will but perhaps you will have a change of heart by the time I return for lunch. I will send some refreshments in on my way out. Stay here for a while. You look drained," Patience advised.

195

"I don't think Bath suits my constitution," Julia smiled wanly. "I seem to have cried an excessive amount since I arrived. I've never been such a watering pot."

"Only these last few days," Patience reminded her. "Until then, your bloom had returned."

Julia sighed when her grandmother left her. It was true; until Mr Prescott had made his outrageous offer, she'd been really enjoying her time in Bath. No. That wasn't true. She'd been enjoying her time with Anthony. The location had been irrelevant.

When had he become so important to her? She'd thought he was attractive when they'd first met, but she certainly hadn't liked him. Within a short period of time though, she'd started to suspect there was more to him than was on the surface, and it was probably then that she had begun to fall in love with him. For that's what she was: very deeply in love.

He'd offered for her when she was at her lowest. Without doubt it was a proposal made for her sake and not his. This from the man who was convinced he had no emotions.

He was the best of men.

And she'd rejected him in the way likely to hurt him the most. There was no way to make it better, and she would mourn that fact far into the future.

*

Patience entered the townhouse with a cheery hello. Carrying some delicious looking pastries, she walked into the drawing room. Julia was still seated, but Patience could see she'd straightened her hair and washed her face. Julia didn't exactly look happy, but she looked more composed.

"I thought we deserved a treat today at lunch. I even bought two of Miles' favourite. I am sure he will be ready to eat these, along with what cook has prepared."

"You spoil us," Julia said, but she stood and took the parcel from her grandmother.

"Until my dying breath, my dear," Patience said. "It was quite quiet in the Pump Room today. That is what set me on my shopping spree. I thought staying there for the sake of it was tedious. I think I have come to rely on Gabriel's nonsensical gabblings too much for my entertainment."

"He is very amusing," Julia admitted.

"And he knows it," Patience said.

"I'll take these through to the dining room and then go and make my peace with Miles. I expected him to creep downstairs before now, but there has not been a murmur. I must have really shocked him when I shouted. I have never done that before. Yet another reaction I have to be ashamed of."

"It is good to be a little afraid of our parents. As long as it is a healthy fear," Patience said with a chuckle. "I remember my own mother. When she stared at one of us in a certain way, she could guarantee our good behaviour, and yet she never laid a hand on us or raised her voice."

"As one who has been at the receiving end of one of your own glares, I can guess which parent you resemble," Julia said archly before leaving the room.

Patience stood in front of the mirror fixing her hair and feeling a little saddened that she'd be saying goodbye to Gabriel later that afternoon.

He'd sent a note around after the fracas at the Assembly Room, hoping that Julia was well and expressing his anger at what Mr Prescott had done. He'd hoped to see her soon, but there had been no firm arrangement in the letter. Her

197

answering note had offered thanks and little else. They were both in a strange situation, each protecting their own family, whilst hoping for a reconciliation.

Seeing him again on her arrival in Bath had brought back many happy memories for Patience and a lot of laughter. She'd forgotten how much he made her laugh. He had very quickly resumed his position as one of her favourite people. Yes. She would be sorry to say good-bye to him, for they'd very unlikely meet again.

Patience's melancholy thoughts were interrupted by the hasty entrance of Julia into the room.

"What is it?" Patience asked immediately.

"It's Miles. He is gone," Julia said, clinging to the doorframe for support.

"What do you mean, gone?" Patience asked, trying to stem the panic threatening to paralyse her.

"His room is empty. Nanny was packing the nursery up, ready for our departure, so she has not seen him for hours. He has taken his outerwear," Julia said, swallowing the bile threatening to rise in her throat at her racing mind as to what could have happened to her son.

"Where would he go? Let's think this through sensibly," Patience urged, trying to show no panic in front of Julia.

"I have no idea! He was upset. He could have been gone hours! I was too harsh with him! I have probably sent him running as far away as his legs could carry him," Julia said with a moan.

"Julia, stop," Patience said, gently but firmly. "Now is no time for recriminations. We need to concentrate on finding him. Let's set the staff to making a thorough search of the house, and then we can look farther afield."

Patience rang the bell and gave strict instructions to the footman. Immediately the house was filled with noise as every nook, cranny, and corner was searched for the missing boy.

It wasn't very long before the same footman entered the room and, with a shake of his head, expressed what Julia and Patience had already guessed.

"Search the garden and the surrounding streets," Patience instructed.

With a nod, the footman left the room once more.

Julia paced the room. "I can't just wait here," she said, coming to a stop.

"Where could he have gone?" Patience said. "There is no point running around Bath without a plan. That won't help anyone."

"You are right. He will be near a horse," Julia said in despair. "I cannot visit every stable. Oh! You don't think — no, surely not... "

"He does not know where he lives," Patience said quickly, immediately knowing to whom Julia was referring.

"I must check there first though," Julia said. "He promised him horses. He will have found him or at least set-out to find him."

"Julia, you cannot go there alone," Patience said, moving to her granddaughter.

"I must find Miles!" Julia said sharply.

"You go to Mr Prescott's abode alone and being his lightskirt will be the best you can hope for. Not even taking a servant would offer protection in this situation. He is a cad who would twist your visit to his advantage. Don't be eager to ruin your reputation in such a way," Patience said firmly.

"But Miles — " Julia snapped.

"Needs a respectable mother. You need to be accompanied. Now don't argue. We need help, and there is only one person who can give us assistance and protection," Patience said.

Julia took a deep breath. She didn't have to ask who Patience meant. "He might not be willing."

"We both know he will offer whatever help he can give. Go to him first. I shall stay here in case Miles is found by the servants. Now, hurry!" Patience urged.

Chapter 20

Anthony put up his hand to his coachman. He had not called for the vehicle, but Giles had some time ago in order to visit a friend, and yet here it was trundling down the widest street in Bath where he least expected to see it. Even more curious, the crest had been covered up.

The carriage was brought to a halt, and the coachman nodded to his master.

"James?" Anthony asked.

"Doing as young Mr Russell directed, M'Lud," came the answer.

Anthony raised his eyebrows and walked to the carriage door, opening it slightly, due to the curtains being drawn. He stopped when he saw the guilty expressions of his brother and Nancy.

"I take it your friend in Colerne was not available to visitors?" Anthony asked dryly.

"Trust it to be now of all times that you decide to learn the art of sarcasm," Giles responded.

Anthony issued an order to James before pulling the curtain back on the window. "I dread to ask, but what the devil is going on?"

Giles and Nancy looked at one another in panic before Giles sighed. "Unfortunately, he's the most intelligent of my siblings, so there is no point trying to concoct a falsehood. He would see through the deception immediately."

"I am overwhelmed by your flattery," Anthony said. "I am hoping that the thought that has sprung to my mind, isn't correct."

"If it involves a dash across country, you are on the right track," Giles admitted, blushing at the look of incredulity his brother was aiming in his direction.

"So, permanently depriving me of my carriage and coachman was not a consideration when you were making your plans?" Anthony asked.

"Well, no, in the scheme of things, it was not," Giles admitted. "To be fair, you would have got them back. Just not quite as quickly as you expected."

"Insolent pup," Anthony said. "I shall have to think of some retribution for your gall, but in the meantime, please explain why you feel the need to flee across the border."

Giles looked uncomfortable. Anthony had always seemed much older than the nine years that separated them, and he hated to appear young and foolish before him. "Mother made her position very clear about any ideas I might have in securing a marriage with Miss Stock. I couldn't risk Mother poisoning Mr Stock, bearing in mind he already has a low opinion of anyone from the *ton*."

"And running away with his daughter and potentially causing his family, and yours, a scandal is the way to endear yourself to your new family?" Anthony asked.

"If you put it like that, no," Giles said, a tad mulishly. "But what were we to do? Stand aside and watch Mother destroy our only chance of happiness?"

Anthony ignored the dramatic words and turned to Nancy. She was dressed as finely as she always was, but her cloak was of a drab wool. He supposed it was part of her disguise, but to him they looked like a pair of innocents, embarking on a misguided journey.

"Miss Stock, I must ask you the following questions, so please forgive my intrusion. I hope you will be honest in your replies," Anthony started. "Do you wish to marry my

202

brother? You have my assurance that there will be no recriminations if you don't. In fact I will offer you my protection until I return you to your family if that is the case."

"I am not going to harm her!" Giles snapped.

Anthony turned back to his brother. "Be quiet. I have finished with you for the moment."

Giles crossed his arms over his chest, annoyed that yet again because of a family member, he was no longer in charge of his destiny.

Anthony returned his attention to Nancy. "Well, Miss Stock? Have you been coerced, bullied, or persuaded into this present situation in which you find yourself?"

"No, my Lord," Nancy said, although her voice was shaky. Giles wasn't the only one to be intimidated by Anthony.

"You want to marry him then?"

"Very much," Nancy replied.

"That is something, I suppose," Anthony said. "And have you dreamed of a large wedding when you married? I have been told some young ladies plan what sort of a celebration they would like before even receiving a proposal."

Nancy flushed a deep red. "I have had the occasional discussion with my Mama about what would be nice."

"I suppose a dash to Scotland wasn't part of those plans?"

Looking down, Nancy seemed to colour even more. "N-no."

Anthony sighed. "Giles, take your chosen one home and speak to her parents. Ask them properly for her hand in marriage. You are personable. I am sure you will have them convinced of your suitability in a very short period of time. Don't alienate them from the get-go."

"But what about Mother? You know how she is when she does not get her own way."

"Mr Stock is a successful businessman. He will have dealt with all sorts of fools over the years. Fanny will just be another one to add to the list. If it's any consolation, she will probably never even see them. She was likely issuing idle threats to try to bend you to her will," Anthony said.

Giles looked doubtful. "It is a bit of a risk for me to take. She can be unpredictable."

"I would like to think my rank would give some credibility to my recommendations over anything Fanny might utter, either directly or indirectly," Anthony said. He turned once more to Nancy. "Tell your father I shall visit him soon to offer my welcome into the family if he should agree to the marriage between yourself and my brother. I will also bring my grandfather along, so I shan't make any blunders when promoting Giles as a suitable husband. You know how Gabriel can make anyone like him. I am sure between the two of you, Mr Stock will be completely convinced of my brother's suitability to be your husband."

Giles smiled. "Thank you, brother. I appreciate your support," he said.

"You're welcome. Especially if it means I will not have to fund your overspends anymore," Anthony said. "Miss Stock, I hope your pockets are deep because my brother is an expert at wasting money."

"Don't say that!" Giles exclaimed mortified.

Nancy laughed, realising Anthony wasn't being serious. "You are being teased, I feel," she said to Giles.

"Well, I hope so," Giles spluttered. "As a married man, I will have responsibilities. No more wasting a quarter's money at Brook's for me!"

204

"That is music to my ears, brother," Anthony said, with a ghost of a smile. "Now, I think it is time you returned Miss Stock to her family and started convincing them that you're the ideal candidate for their daughter. No more foolish schemes Giles. You say you are ready to take on the responsibility of being wed. Show everyone that is the case."

"We will not do anything rash, I promise," Giles said with a wide smile. "Thanks Anthony. You've been a great help."

"Good. Goodbye. Miss Stock, I shall look forward to when I can call you sister. I have long thought you perfect for my brother," Anthony said, once more making Nancy blush. He stepped back out of the carriage and shut the door. Looking up to James he nodded. "They are ready to return to Miss Stock's abode," he commanded.

"Yes, M'Lud," James responded, immediately starting to turn the carriage on the busy roadway.

Anthony stepped back, idly watching his vehicle as it progressed down the street, soon lost amongst the other horses and carriages entering and leaving the town by one of the main routes.

Before he'd turned away to continue on his walk, he noticed Julia far down the street. She was walking quickly and looked agitated. Anthony's first thought was that her discomfort was because she'd seen him, but then he realised he was being idiotic; she didn't appear to be noticing anything around her. Unsure of whether to go to her or not, he hesitated and remained standing, prepared to appear nonchalant if she ignored him and walked by.

Instead of disregarding him, Julia approached Anthony once she set eyes on him, her face a mask of worry and concern.

"Miles is missing," she said without preamble, the choked words telling Anthony everything he needed to know.

"Tell me everything," Anthony commanded gently. Now was not the time for going over what had gone between them.

"We argued, and I sent him to his chamber. He keeps going on and on about horses. My grandmother and Miles had seen Mr Prescott, and he had promised Miles a ride in his carriage and a chance at driving his horses, which obviously had Miles' head full of nonsense. I think he must have gone to Mr Prescott, only we don't know his address. I have no idea what he would do if Miles managed to find his residence. Grandmother said Mr Prescott was mocking about what had happened at the ball. He was completely unrepentant, even telling Miles he would have a stable full of horses if I agreed to his offer," Julia explained, babbling.

"He would be foolish to have taken Miles in such circumstances," Anthony said.

"It would be a perfect retribution for what happened the other night. He might think I would change my mind," Julia reasoned.

"Prescott is no coxcomb. He would not embroil himself in something so scandalous, which relies on a young boy arguing with his mother and then seeking him out. No. If Miles has tried to find him, the boy will have done it off his own back. I am more inclined to think he'll be found somewhere local," Anthony said. His mind was inwardly jumping from thought to thought, but outwardly he was his usual calm self.

"Do you think so?" Julia looked at Anthony with a pitiful look of hope and longing.

"Yes. His motivation is around horses, not Mr Prescott. Come. I have an idea," Anthony said. Taking hold of Julia's arm, he placed it on his own and guided her into his town house.

Once inside, he gave instructions that had Gabriel, the butler, and a few footmen gathered in the hallway. Explaining that Miles was missing, he gave instructions. "Mrs Price's staff are searching the area around her home. I want you," he indicated the butler and footmen "to make a search of Sydney Gardens. He loves it there and might have gone to explore it alone. Mr Bannerman, Mrs Price, and I will search the stables at the back of the house. If there is no luck there, we will spread our search to the other stables nearby. Once you have searched Sydney Gardens, join us. We all have a lot of ground to cover."

The group separated, and the party of three left the house through the garden at the rear and into the area that contained the stables for the grand houses. It was an area the gentry didn't usually frequent, but none of them noticed the surprised looks cast in their directions from the grooms and stable hands who were working there; they were too intent on the job in hand.

Gabriel split from Anthony and Julia to start searching at the opposite end of the stables.

"Check each stall," Anthony instructed. "He'll not want to be found by anyone in the stables. They would likely give him a box of his ears for being where he shouldn't be."

"I was a young boy once. I know the type of hiding place a boy would seek," Gabriel said tartly, but set-off at a brisk pace. Gone was his usual joviality; his fondness for Miles was great, and the thought of the boy being lost had him hurrying to the start of his search.

Julia had been silent throughout. Anthony was worried about her. Grabbing hold of her hand in an inappropriate open show of support, he squeezed her fingers gently. "We will find him," he said.

"He is all I have," Julia said quietly.

207

"And you will have him back soon," Anthony reassured her. Keeping hold of her hand, he walked into the end stable.

They searched each bay, upsetting a few of the horses along the way. The beasts were used to the finest treatment and having two strangers searching their stalls did not gain approval. There was a lot of annoyed neighing and braying, but although the stable hands grumbled at the disturbance, none would openly challenge a man who was clearly a member of the Quality.

After ten minutes a shout brought Julia and Anthony out of the stable they were searching. The bellow had come from Gabriel, who had Miles by his side.

Julia almost ran towards her son, but Anthony kept pace with her. He was concerned with how she might react because of the stress of the day.

Coming to a halt in front of her son, Julia knelt down, grabbing Miles by the shoulders and almost shook him. "What possessed you to run away? Do you know how much worry you have caused?" she shouted.

Miles flinched at the words, but answered his mother. "I wanted to see the horses. I did not want to upset you. I know you don't like them, but I long to be near them, Mama."

Julia sobbed and enfolded her son into an embrace. "Oh, Miles! I am so sorry! I thought I had lost you!"

Miles wrapped his arms around his mother's neck and tried to comfort his mother. "I am sorry, Mama. I promise I won't do it again. I just needed to be near the horses for once."

Anthony stepped forward and put his arm under Julia's elbow. "Come," he said gently. "Let us get you both home."

Julia lifted Miles off his feet and insisted on carrying him back to Henrietta Street. She wasn't prepared to release her son to anyone or let them carry him. She didn't notice the stains on her dress where her knees had touched the dirty ground of the stable floor, or the effect his muddy boots had on the light material. All that mattered was that Miles had been found and was safe.

The group walked slowly. Anthony sent out messages to his staff in Sydney Gardens and ahead to Patience. Eventually reaching their destination, they entered the drawing room where Patience was waiting.

Rushing over, Patience lifted Miles out of Julia's arms and embraced him, whilst covering his face with kisses. The behaviour soon had Miles giggling and wriggling to be freed from his emotional relation.

Anthony chose the time to have a word with Julia. He led her a little away from the others, standing in front of one of the two large windows that filled the room with light.

"Might I make a suggestion?" he asked.

Julia took hold of Anthony's hands. "Thank you."

Anthony smiled and squeezed Julia's fingers. "I did what anyone would have done."

"The way things were left — " Julia started.

"Now is not the time to go over such a thing," Anthony interrupted. "You are a good mother, but I think you have this aspect wrong."

"What do you mean?" Julia asked, stiffening a little.

"By keeping Miles away from horses, it's making them something he is even more desperate to get involved with," Anthony tried to explain.

"He has to realise that we cannot afford to house one," Julia said.

"Yes. From what he's said, he does understand, but until his father's death he was surrounded by the animals. It has been two huge changes in a very short period of time."

"So, you are telling me that he is being deprived?" Julia responded coolly.

"No. He is being given everything he needs, and he is happy. Anyone can see that. I just think that his lack of contact with horses is a bigger longing because there is no contact when there's no reason for it to be so severe," Anthony said.

Julia's expression looked as if she were about to tear a strip off Anthony, but then she sighed and turned away slightly. Looking out of the window, she spoke quietly. "I don't want him to become like Bruce."

"And your husband loved horses," Anthony responded.

"Yes. Above everything and everyone else," Julia responded.

"Then he was a fool," Anthony said.

Julia gave a wan smile. "Thank you. After the way I have treated you, I don't deserve that compliment, and it says everything about you that you offered it."

"Just because father and son shared a common interest does not guarantee anything else. Miles is a mixture of both of his parents," Anthony continued, once more not referring to anything that had occurred between them. "I would like to take Miles out for a ride with me on Belle."

"But — "

"Before you give a thousand and one reasons why I should not, trust me on this. If I take him out, he will have something to focus on other than longing. He will have new memories of riding on a horse that have nothing to do with his father," Anthony reasoned.

210

"Will that not make the situation worse? I can't rely on people to indulge my son in his need to be in contact with horses," Julia responded.

"No, you cannot. But I am sure occasionally there would be someone in his life who would be willing to either loan a horse, or you could hire one for the day. It wouldn't be the same as stabling one himself, but he would no longer have just the memories of spending time with his father and horses. In some respects his new memories would make the older ones just pleasant reminiscences rather than his whole focus," Anthony continued.

"What if it does not work?" Julia asked, still uncertain.

"Then you can curse me to the devil, and I will commit to paying for the hire of a horse every week for a year as my punishment," Anthony said with a twitch of his mouth.

Julia smiled, probably the first one since the ball. "I would certainly curse you, but there is no need for you to spend your money in such a way."

"As it is my money, I'll spend it how I please," Anthony said with false loftiness. "Have I your permission?"

"Yes."

"Good. You have made the right decision." Anthony turned back to face into the room. "Miles. I wish you to be ready tomorrow at nine of the clock."

"But we are to leave tomorrow," Miles said, looking at his mother and Patience.

"I think we can delay our departure a little," Julia said, looking at Patience for confirmation.

"Of course," Patience said, with a glance of curiosity towards Gabriel, who shrugged his shoulders almost imperceptibly.

"Excellent," Anthony continued. "I shall arrive with Belle, and we shall have a ride around the countryside for an hour or two."

"Really?" Miles almost squealed. "Mama?" he asked, disbelieving that she would agree to the scheme.

"Yes. Really," Julia said, her heart heavy at the pleasure on her son's face. It seemed Anthony could be proved right.

"Oh, Lord Lever! That would be ever so super! She's the finest horse!" Miles said, fit to burst at the offered treat.

"I will expect you to do exactly as I say. She is not used to anyone riding her apart from myself," Anthony cautioned.

"I will do anything you tell me to," Miles promised. "Do you hear that, Grandmama? I'm going to ride the best high-stepper in the whole of Bath!"

"You lucky boy," Patience said.

"We shall leave you be," Anthony said to Julia. "There is just one thing more, Miles. If there is any repeat of today's behaviour, my offer is withdrawn permanently."

"I won't run away again, I promise," Miles said solemnly.

"Good. I shall see you on the morrow."

Anthony and Gabriel left the house and returned to their own dwelling.

"That is a good thing you are doing for the child," Gabriel said as they walked.

"It is no hardship," Anthony said. "Although Belle will not appreciate the extra weight until she gets used to it."

"Don't underestimate what an impact your actions will have on a young, impressionable boy. I have a feeling you will receive complete adoration from him from now on. I hope you are prepared for hero worship."

"Let's see how the ride goes first, shall we?" Anthony asked dryly.

Chapter 21

Anthony's expectation of enjoying a quiet evening at home was to be disappointed. He was sitting in the drawing room with Gabriel and Fanny, who had deigned to join the men for their evening meal. The atmosphere had been tense with Fanny's presence, but they were still struggling through it when Giles entered the room.

It was the first time he had been seen since Anthony's conversation with him, but the smile on his face and the sparkle in his eyes gave Anthony the information he needed.

Standing, Anthony shook Giles's hand. "We are to wish you happy?" he asked, knowing there was no point in skirting the issue.

"Yes, you are, brother," Giles responded. Turning to his mother, he addressed her, gaining courage from Anthony's support. "Mama, today, I spoke with Mr Stock, and he has agreed to allow me to marry his daughter. Before you say anything, I have told him of your possible reaction and your objections," he continued. "In fact, I was brutally honest with him. It carried a great deal that Anthony favours the match and is willing to visit Mr Stock, along with Mr Bannerman. He said he would welcome you anytime you wish, brother. I also told him about my finances, and he believed me when I said I was willing for a smaller dowry to be settled on Miss Stock if it would help to convince him that I was not marrying her for her money."

"You young fool!" Fanny snapped. "You set him up to this!" she spat at Anthony.

"No. He did not," Giles said calmly. "In fact, it was you who first insisted that I get to know which young ladies

213

Anthony was spending time with. It was a risk you took in that I would fall in love myself when you were trying to prevent Anthony from doing so. But you didn't consider that because you were so wrapped up in stopping Anthony from marrying that it clouded your judgement. I should thank you, Mother, for I doubt I would have ever come to know Miss Stock so well if you had not encouraged me."

Fanny glared at her son. "She is the daughter of a 'cit'. You expect society to welcome her into their midst? You are a fool if you do."

"To be honest, Mother, I couldn't give a fig what society does or does not do. I am going to be married to the prettiest, nicest person I have ever had the privilege to meet, and we are going to be wealthy, but more importantly we are going to be welcomed by my brothers and everyone in her family. Nothing else matters," Giles said, for the first time truly standing up to his mother.

Anthony was impressed by the young man. It seemed as if he'd matured since the morning, and he was glad to see the change. He was pleased Giles was going after what he wanted. It would give Anthony something to dwell on during the night about what he wanted himself, but refocusing on Giles and Fanny, Anthony watched his stepmother visibly seethe.

Fanny turned to Anthony. "You've caused this!" she spat.

"Really?" Anthony drawled. "And how did I do that?"

"If you had just stayed in your damned hunting lodge until after your birthday, none of this would have happened," Fanny snapped.

"As always, I am sorry to disappoint you, but there was never any intention on my part to allow Giles to inherit."

"And yet it seems he will anyway," Fanny continued with glee. "There is only one month until your birthday."

"Only is a funny word. One could also say, there is a whole month until my birthday," Anthony said.

"I have heard about your public proposal. You were that desperate that you had to propose in a packed ballroom," Fanny said. "She obviously had the sense to turn you down as we've not seen her for days. She has more intelligence than I gave her credit for. Pray tell, who else is there to try to persuade to marry you if you cannot convince a penniless widow?"

"Of all the… " Gabriel started.

Anthony shook his head at his grandfather. "I think it is time for you to leave, Fanny. I don't see why any of us should put up with your bad behaviour for a moment longer. It is clear you have not enjoyed your stay in Bath. I shall make arrangements for your removal to Leicester first thing in the morning."

"Leicester? Why on earth would I go to Leicester?" Fanny asked distracted enough not to immediately react to the fact she was being turned out of her son's house.

"As I will be taking up residence with my wife at Lever Hall, there will no longer be a place for you there. I appreciate that you despise my company almost as much as I despise yours, so rather than giving you the Dower House, I shall hand over my hunting lodge to you. It is very comfortable. I made it so in order to offer a level of homeliness when escaping you," Anthony responded pleasantly, but firmly.

"How dare you speak to me with such a lack of respect!" Fanny screeched.

"I am giving you the same amount of respect that you've given me," Anthony said with unconcern. "Why should I continue to tolerate someone who dislikes me and has happily shown that dislike almost from the first day we met?

I have put up with enough. We all have. I will not permit Miss Stock or my own wife being subjected to your poison. You will not live on my estate any longer."

"I refuse to remain here to listen to your disrespectful words," Fanny said. She turned to Giles. "And you should be ashamed of yourself, not coming to my rescue when I am being spoken to so horribly."

"Everything he says is true, Mother. It is a fact that whomever we marry will not be welcomed by you, and I don't understand why. You could be surrounded by family who loves you, but instead you make it very difficult for us all," Giles said with more emotion than Anthony had shown, but he was determined to stand up to his mother. The motivation to protect his future wife was very strong in the smitten young man.

Fanny got up, and with a huff, stormed out of the room. Anthony pulled the bell at the side of the fireplace and instructed the butler to arrange for his stepmother to leave the following morning. He instructed that a carriage should be hired rather than using the family carriage.

"She will be furious about that," Giles responded when the butler had left the room.

"I have decided not to indulge her any longer," Anthony admitted. "Perhaps I should have opposed her attitude more forcefully years ago, but I never felt able to fully challenge her. I suppose I was still hoping to gain her approval in some form. Foolish really, as in reality, I did not have a hope."

"I am sorry, boy, that you were alone for so long," Gabriel said, moved by his grandson's words.

"It's not your fault. You had no control over any of it," Anthony pointed out.

"I should have fought more."

"My father would probably never have sought your help if that had happened. He could be extremely stubborn," Anthony admitted.

"Neither of my parents were easy to like. At least everyone remembers your mother as being a lovely lady. That must offer some comfort. I spend my time cringing with embarrassment with mother, and you have to admit that father was just a brute in the main," Giles admitted for the first time.

"Unfortunately there is no point longing for someone who can have no impact on our lives. I've realised pining for a dead mother does no good," Anthony responded, revealing a little of the anguish of his younger self.

"I wish we could spend some time with Wilfred. The three of us, just getting to know each other as real brothers without family prejudices causing problems," Giles said.

"If you have an extended stay at Lever Hall when you have completed your marriage trip, we could invite Wilfred down from school," Anthony offered. "It would be good to get to know him, especially as you have turned out better than I expected."

"Praise indeed from the head of the family!" Giles laughed, before becoming serious. "I should like that, and I am sure the Stock family would see it as further approval of our marriage, so thank you. Prepare yourself for a large wedding, though. Mrs Stock is planning a great event."

"I thought that might be the case," Anthony admitted. "I would keep out of the way if I were you."

"No. This husband-to-be is going to be involved in every decision that's made about our wedding," Giles said. "And with that in mind, I will bid you both goodnight. I have permission to go around to the Stocks whenever I wish, so I shall be gone early tomorrow. I will not be attending many events from now on. Unless they do, of course."

The two men wished Giles a goodnight. When the door closed at his exit, Gabriel turned to Anthony. "I'll give him a week before he is sick to death of hearing about the wedding preparations!"

Anthony laughed. "He will still have a place here if he does need to escape."

"How long do you intend staying in Bath?" Gabriel asked.

"Until Mrs Price leaves," Anthony admitted.

"They were supposed to be leaving tomorrow," Gabriel pointed out.

"That has been delayed now, thankfully. I am not taking young Miles out just to postpone their removal, but it will hopefully give me some time to speak to her," Anthony explained.

"I knew from the first she was the perfect one for you," Gabriel gloated.

Rolling his eyes, Anthony grimaced. "Don't get ahead of yourself. It seems like only hours ago that I intended asking Miss Carruthers to marry me."

"And why didn't you?"

"I don't know."

"I do," Gabriel said. "Your heart was not in it."

"Leave my heart out of this."

"I was not sure you had one, but now I think it belongs to Mrs Price."

"Sometimes, you betray your senility," Anthony said.

"You are just missish because you know I am right," Gabriel chuckled.

*

Anthony arrived at number ten Henrietta Street at nine of the clock, promptly. He suppressed a smile when he saw

Miles waiting at the open doorway with Julia in the background. Hearing the excited, "He's here!" as Miles tried to walk calmly through the doorway brought a laugh to his lips.

"Are you ready to do exactly as I say?" he asked, sounding stern.

"Oh yes, my Lord. I will be perfectly behaved," Miles promised.

"I now know what I need to do to get his full co-operation in future," Julia said, as she followed her son out of the doorway.

Anthony smiled at her. "If only you could ride something better than a mule, you would have such an effective weapon in your arsenal."

"I am a lost cause where that is concerned," Julia said.

Anthony had the distinct impression that there was some background to her words, but once more he wasn't in a position to question her about it. Instead he climbed back onto Belle and helped Miles sit up in front of him.

"Are we to travel at a gallop?" Miles asked.

"I doubt your ride would be very comfortable if we did," Anthony said. "We also have to be aware of the extra weight on Belle. She would not have an enjoyable ride either."

Miles stroked the horse's neck. "She is lovely. I wouldn't want to harm her."

"She is," Anthony said, looking at Julia in such a way that made her cheeks glow. "We will be back when I feel Belle has had enough. Don't worry if we are gone for a while."

Julia nodded and waved them out of sight. Returning into the house, she met Patience who was coming down the stairs.

"Has our hero of the moment taken Miles as promised?" Patience teased.

"He has, looking fine in his caped greatcoat, as one would expect," Julia said with a sigh.

"He is a splendid man," Patience pointed out.

"I know. I wish I were good enough for him," Julia responded.

"I refuse to react to that comment on the grounds that it is ridiculous," Patience said primly.

"You are very loyal to me, but in truth, I am not worthy of him," Julia argued.

"That is silly in the extreme, but more importantly, he does not think in that vein, or he wouldn't be putting himself out for the child. We know him well enough to realise that he is not a natural with children."

Julia smiled. "No. But I am so afraid of being mistaken in anyone I am attracted to, I'm constantly doubting myself. I was badly at fault in my choice with Bruce."

"That was the folly of youth and a scoundrel of a man. This time you have chosen to fall in love with a man who says whatever he is thinking. There are no hidden parts to him."

"That is true," Julia confessed. "I know deep down he is nothing like Bruce."

"Thank goodness! You are finally talking sense!" Patience responded.

Julia scowled at her grandmother, but received a laugh in return. If Julia was coming to her senses, Patience was prepared to put up with any number of glowers.

*

Anthony didn't say much as they rode through the outskirts of Bath. He was aware that Belle would be a little on edge because of the new situation, and he wanted to be able to react immediately if something made her skittish.

Miles was also quiet, seeming a little in awe of Anthony now that he was so close to him.

Eventually, when they had travelled onto the quieter lanes and roads, going deeper into the Somerset countryside, Anthony started asking the boy about his experience and knowledge of horses.

Miles answered every question eagerly, and Anthony was impressed that, although Miles had only been five when his father had died, he had already learned a lot about his favourite animal.

Becoming more confident with his new friend, Miles started to unknowingly give snippets of information about his history. "Papa used to argue with Mama about horses," he said guilelessly as they trotted along.

"Your mother said she is not a good horsewoman," Anthony admitted.

"Papa said she was hopeless," Miles admitted, failing to notice the slight stiffening in Anthony's body. "But it was the money he lost that would start him shouting at her."

"Oh?" Anthony felt a rascal in allowing the child to continue unchecked, but a part of him needed to know more about Julia.

"Mama said we had no money to spare, but Papa didn't like it when she said that. My nanny used to talk to the housemaid. They said my Papa was a rum one who almost liked to give his money away."

"They should not have spoken about your parents in front of you," Anthony said.

"I sometimes pretended to be asleep," Miles admitted. "I didn't like the shouting."

It was loud enough to reach the nursery, Anthony thought grimly. It didn't sound like a happy household. "I don't think anyone does. My father used to shout a lot."

221

"Did he?" Miles asked, twisting slightly to view Anthony's face as if to check that he was being truthful. "Were you frightened?"

"Sometimes," Anthony admitted. "But I was a lot bigger than you were."

"Nanny said Papa made Mama cry too often," Miles said. "She said he was too handy with his fists for a gentleman. 'Should be in the ring,' she used to say. I didn't know what she meant, though. It is funny. I don't really remember what Papa looked like, but I do remember the shouting."

Anthony felt pity for the boy. "Sometimes we remember more about the times when we are afraid," he said gently.

"I was not sad when Papa died," Miles admitted. "The shouting stopped, so it was nicer without Papa, but I have not told Mama that. I think it would make her cry, and she does not cry as much these days."

"You are a wise boy," Anthony said. And too young to have known violence and an unhappy home, he thought. Feeling some compassion and empathy for Miles, he was decidedly unnerved by the loathing he felt for Julia's husband. "Your mother would be upset to know what you remember."

"I thought so," Miles said sounding older than his years.

"It's good to talk man to man," Anthony stated. He had to be careful about raising the boy's expectations, but he wanted to offer some form of support. "If you have any concerns in the future, seek your tutor or a trusted servant who has been with the family for years. They will listen and offer help."

"I like talking to you and Mr Bannerman," Miles admitted.

"Have you told Mr Bannerman about the arguing?" Anthony asked. He would be having strong words with

Gabriel if he had known something so important and not divulged it.

"No. But he makes me laugh, especially when I worry about money."

"You worry about money?" Anthony asked incredulously.

"A little. I know Mama hasn't much, and I have heard her talking to Grandmama about working. I don't want Mama to leave us," Miles admitted.

Anthony reacted on instinct, he hugged Miles. It was the first embrace he'd given to anyone in his life. "She will not leave you. She just worries too much sometimes," he said gently.

"She does, but that makes me worry. I have dreams that she has gone away," Miles said. He'd rested his head back onto Anthony's chest as a reaction to Anthony's embrace.

Resting his chin on the child's head, Anthony was stunned at the level of feeling the boy had stirred within himself. Anthony had felt protective towards Julia, but that was linked to the attraction he felt. Towards Miles it was different. He could only imagine it was what a parent felt towards their child. It made him swallow. If he could convince Julia to marry him, he would have her in his life forever, and he would be able to provide a safe, loving home for her son.

It made him scared of failing but determined to try his damnedest to do his best for them both.

*

Julia had tried to stay away from the window of the drawing room, but she had walked the few steps from where she was trying to read a novel too many times to count.

"They will be fine," Patience said with a smile.

"I know. I just hope Miles behaves," Julia said.

223

"Have faith in your son," Patience berated her granddaughter.

"I do, but Lord Lever is unusual in his ways. Miles could offend without thinking, or Lord Lever could say something that would upset Miles," Julia responded.

"As they both love horses, I am expecting them to return as best of friends," Patience said.

Eventually, Julia saw the pair arrive home. Miles was beaming, and her shoulders sagged with relief as she smiled at them both through the window.

"Need not have worried?" Patience asked, putting down her needlework in expectation of the pair entering the room.

"It appears not," Julia said, turning away from the window.

Miles was the first to bound into the room, chattering away to Anthony before turning to his relations. "It was splendid!" he exclaimed. "Belle is the best horse ever! She never once complained of my weight."

"That's wonderful," Patience said. "What a grand horse!"

"Oh, she is! Lord Lever said, if you don't mind, Mama, we could go out again tomorrow?" Miles asked.

"I hope it does not clash with your plans about leaving?" Anthony asked. He had not shed his greatcoat, hat, or gloves, as he didn't intend to stay. He had a lot to consider, and he wouldn't think clearly whilst in Julia's company.

"We do need to leave Bath," Julia said. How was it that he seemed to fill the room even more with his outerwear on, she wondered.

"There is no hurry, child," Patience said.

"May I, Mama?" Miles asked.

"Yes, of course," Julia said.

Miles whooped and went to leave the room, excited to tell anyone who was willing to listen. As he was leaving the room, he turned to Anthony and solemnly bowed. "Thank you, my Lord, for giving me the best treat ever, and I especially enjoyed our man-to-man time."

Anthony bowed in return. "I enjoyed it too, Master Price."

Miles beamed before leaving the room. Patience smiled at Julia, proud of the way Miles had behaved.

"Mrs Price, if you have no objection, I would like to bring another horse around with me tomorrow. I will lead the boy all the way, but he is very confident and has a good riding position," Anthony stated. "I have not mentioned it to him in case you object to it."

"He has been in the saddle almost since the day he was born," Patience said, giving Julia a look.

"It has been such a long time since he has ridden," Julia said. "And Bath is so busy. The horse could be startled."

"I could lead it until we leave the town and only then put him in the saddle," Anthony persuaded.

"That would be acceptable to you?" Julia asked. "I know I am being a little over-protective."

"Of course I'd be willing to do that. I am not going to ridicule the concerns of his mother. Your worries are valid but can be overcome easily," Anthony said gently. "Thank you for allowing me another day's riding with him. He is a pleasant young man. I was surprised but pleased we got on so well."

"Man to man, apparently," Julia said with a wry smile.

"Don't knock the connection between two gentlemen of the town," Anthony responded archly before saying his farewells and leaving the ladies.

225

Chapter 22

Anthony might struggle with identifying emotions correctly, but he was under no doubt that the smile on Miles' face when he saw Anthony the following morning was one of utter delight. Anthony led the horse he had arranged for Miles.

Miles had been waiting once more at the doorway and stepped forward with Julia. "Is that horse for me to ride?" Miles asked, barely daring to believe his good fortune.

"Once we leave Bath behind, yes," Anthony said.

"Oh my goodness, Mama! I am going to ride on my own!"

"I will be holding a leading reign all the time," Anthony cautioned.

Miles nodded. "I have not ridden alone since Papa died, so I am glad you will be helping me."

Anthony laughed and looked at Julia. "That went easier than I expected," he said.

Julia smiled in return. "He's a sensible boy." She helped Miles climb in front of Anthony, and the slightly strange configuration moved off. Turning away, she saw Patience had come to the front door.

"It is a kind thing his Lordship is doing," Patience said.

"It is," Julia acknowledged.

"A single young man does not usually go out of his way to pander to a young boy."

"Lord Lever is slightly different. I think he would always respond to a child's plight," Julia defended Anthony.

"Are you still determined to fail to acknowledge that he is smitten with you and that is driving his actions?" Patience asked.

"Grandmama, I think you are reading too much into a kind gesture," Julia said. She couldn't speak openly about Anthony because she would betray her feelings to the relation who knew her well. Anthony had stirred longings in her that she'd never expected to feel again — that she'd not felt since the first few months of meeting Bruce. Before his true nature was revealed.

Even though her affections were engaged, she could not allow anything to happen. The way she'd reacted to Anthony had been unfair and unjust. Not all men were like Bruce; she knew that, but if her instinct was to shy away from physical contact, it was not a good start for any relationship, especially one with Anthony's background.

*

Anthony was to get a great deal of pleasure from his adventure with Miles. Once they'd joined the quieter roads, they'd stopped, and Miles had been placed on the steady mount.

"I've already been out on Belle, to let her rid herself of some steam," Anthony explained. "I have been assured that Chester, here, is as docile a creature as we are likely to find in any stables, which makes him perfect for now."

"It must be wonderful being able to let fly over the hills," Miles said wistfully.

"Let us go one step at a time, shall we?" Anthony suggested dryly.

They'd travelled along the lanes with Miles doing most of the chattering, but it wasn't the babble that would bore a man like Anthony. For such a young child, he was quite mature. He certainly could talk about horses for as long as Anthony would wish.

Eventually, Anthony decided that it was time to return to Bath.

"I don't suppose I could ride Chester all the way home, could I?" Miles asked.

"We will see how he copes on the outskirts of town. If I see or feel any sign of skittishness, we stop and you join me," Anthony replied firmly.

"Of course," Miles answered.

They travelled at a slow and steady pace, but the horse was true to the character that had been described. He was calm and docile even when walking along the busy roads of Bath with Miles on his back.

Arriving home, Miles jumped down deftly onto the pavement. "That was the best day out ever!" he exclaimed to Anthony. "Thank you, Lord Lever."

"You are welcome." Dismounting himself, he was a little surprised to see Patience hurrying down the path towards them.

"Hello! Are you to join us for tea, Lord Lever?" Patience said.

"I should return home," Anthony said.

"Oh, that is a shame," Patience said.

Anthony decided to take the woman into his confidence a little. "Mrs Hancock, could you ensure your granddaughter will be at home this afternoon?"

"Yes, of course," Patience looked delighted at Anthony's request.

"Thank you. I shall return, say, three of the clock?" Anthony asked.

"We shall be here. You have my promise of discretion," Patience said.

"I thought I would."

Anthony turned to remount his horse. "Lord Lever?" Patience halted his progress.

"Yes?"

"What happened the other night wasn't any reflection on your character," Patience said hurriedly, wanting to say so much more, but unable to do so in the time they had.

"I appreciate your saying that," Anthony admitted.

"Julia's history — "

"Is complicated," Anthony interrupted. "I realise it is, even if I don't understand fully."

Patience waved off the young lord, hoping beyond hope that the afternoon would sort out the doubts Julia still had for Anthony.

*

Arriving at number ten Henrietta Street at three in the afternoon, Anthony was surprisingly nervous. If his plans for the afternoon didn't go as he hoped, he could think of nothing else that would bring them to the conclusion he wanted and to which he hoped Julia wasn't averse.

He was led into the drawing room. Although now in his frock coat and not his great coat, he'd opted to keep hold of his gloves, hat, and cane. He bowed to the two ladies as he entered the room.

"Good afternoon, Lord Lever. This is an unlooked-for pleasure. We thought you had abandoned us this morning when you did not stay for refreshments," Patience said pleasantly.

"I had some business to attend to. Am I too presumptuous in asking that you would accompany me on a small picnic, Mrs Price?" Anthony asked.

Julia's expression was one of slight panic, and she looked as if she were going to respond in the negative, but Patience, anticipating her granddaughter's reaction, responded first.

"Oh, my dear Julia, what excellent timing his Lordship has. It was only moments ago you were expressing the

229

desire to be out of doors and now you have the chance to do so. And away from the bustle of the town. A picnic. You will enjoy that, and it will give me the opportunity to visit Mr Bannerman, for I haven't seen him for these last few days," Patience responded sweetly.

"That is a fortunate coincidence," Anthony said. "My Grandfather would welcome your company. He is a little at a loss now that my stepmother has left us. He has no one to curse," Anthony responded.

"Your stepmother has left Bath? Has your brother?" Julia asked, curiosity forcing the questions.

"No. Giles remains with me. He's to wed, which I shall tell you all about whilst we travel," Anthony said.

Julia wasn't against going out with Anthony; in fact she liked the idea far more than she should. It was a credit to him that he would suffer being near her in the first place after what had passed between them, but she was under no doubt that the conversation that was needed would be difficult for herself.

She took a little time to dress for the outdoors, wearing her dark blue pelisse and matching bonnet, over a paler blue day dress. As always, her clothing was old, but she didn't feel too shabby, having picked out the best of her daywear.

Coming down stairs, she smiled at Anthony who was waiting for her at the bottom of the steps. He offered his arm and started towards the open doorway. "Mrs Hancock sends her goodbyes. I think she was very eager to see my grandfather," Anthony said. He'd actually received a warm embrace from Patience as she left the house, but he wasn't about to divulge that to Julia; it would only make her feel under pressure, and he wanted her to enjoy her day.

"She will be impatient to catch-up on what has been happening. She will be sorry that she didn't know sooner about your brother," Julia admitted. "Although, I have to admit, I am curious myself. Mr Russell expressed no hurry to marry when I first conversed with him. What has happened to change his mind so suddenly?"

Anthony handed Julia into his carriage, and after the door had been closed and they were comfortably seated opposite each other, he smiled at Julia. "As my grandfather would say, he has fallen completely head over heels in love. I've seen a big change in him in these last few days, even to the point that he has been standing up to his mother."

"You had better tell me more," Julia responded.

Talking about Giles and the happenings at Anthony's house meant the pair could relax with each other. Julia wasn't afraid that the conversation would suddenly turn towards herself and what had happened between them, although it would need to be addressed at some stage. For the moment, she could revert to normal and tease Anthony.

When they arrived at a suitable location, already chosen by Anthony, the large picnic box was unloaded, and a small table and chairs were set-out near the hilltop. The view showed Bath to its full advantage; the warm day meant that the sky was not filled with smoke from the thousands of coal fires in the town. Instead, the sun seemed to glint off the limestone buildings, making the day seem even brighter.

When the footman had set everything out, Anthony nodded to him. "I shall call if we need anything," he said, dismissing the servant and waiting for his retreat back to the coach, which was just out of sight. He smiled at Julia. "I hope you are hungry. I did say the food was for two people, but I feel we could feed many more."

Julia's eyes travelled over the pies, tartlets, meat platter, cheeses, breads, jellies, and meringues that filled every inch of the table. "I don't think we would eat for days if we finished this off."

"I think we should tuck in. We could be here some time," Anthony said, cutting a large slice of game pie.

Both enjoyed the leisurely meal. Chatting occasionally, it was a comfortable time for them.

After Julia had commented for the second time about the view, Anthony smiled at her. "I remember you said you would like to fly away from everything the time we watched the balloon flight. When I discovered this little area one day whilst out riding on Belle, I thought of you immediately. It is as if we're watching over what is going on but are far enough away for the events down there not to affect us. I wondered if it would be enough of an escape for you."

Julia paused before responding. His sentiments touched her. "It does feel as if there is nothing that could reach us here," she admitted.

"Nothing can. Especially not our pasts," Anthony said, watching Julia closely.

She looked away quickly, but placed her fork on her plate, what little remained of her appetite immediately disappeared.

"You know so much about my background," Anthony said gently. "Instances that I have never confessed to anyone else, even to my grandfather. These last weeks you have been my confidante. Yet I know so little of you."

Still not looking at him, Julia smiled bitterly. "There is little of value to know."

"Whoever led you to believe that sentiment was a fool and a liar."

"That's very kind of you to say, but as you have pointed out, you don't really know me."

"I would like to get to know you, to show you that we are not all selfish rogues of the highest order," Anthony said gently. She was like a frightened animal; he was afraid she would bolt and then he would have lost her completely.

"And yet, I classed you the same as him," Julia said bitterly. "Even though I know you are not. When it came down to it, I reacted towards you as I did him."

"That was his doing and not yours."

"You were angry with me, just as he would have been."

Anthony felt his anger bubble at her words, but knew she was trying to put him off. Her fear would push him away, rather than allow her to risk trusting him. He moved slowly until he reached her hands, which were clasped tightly on her lap. Covering both of hers with his one hand, he squeezed gently. "Trust me."

Julia looked at him then, her eyes full of fear and anguish. "I do. I should not have reacted in the way I did. I apologise. It said more about me than it did about you."

"You reacted in the way you were used to your husband acting," Anthony said. "How often did he beat you?"

Julia paused, but then sighed. There was no point in lying or trying to hide the truth; she knew he suspected how her marriage had been from the few comments he'd made. "Regularly. Whenever anything didn't go to plan, and things all too often went awry," Julia admitted. She had looked down at the hands in her lap. Moving her left hand, she gripped the top of Anthony's as if she needed to cling to him for support.

"And no one stopped him?" Anthony had to fight to keep his voice even. His insides were in turmoil.

"I tried at first," Julia admitted. "But that was before I knew if he was challenged it made the matter worse. Grandmama also tried, but one time he threatened to

233

banish her from the house, and she stopped arguing against him. He took pleasure from then on in taunting her, trying to push her so that he could separate us."

"The blaggard!" Anthony ground out.

"I was not a good wife," Julia said.

"How so?" Anthony didn't want to dismiss her statements for she obviously believed them.

"I only produced one child. He started to say I was barren, but I had lost one after I had fallen down the stairs. After that I didn't become pregnant again."

"Fallen?"

Julia smiled sadly. "With a little help."

"Good God, he could have killed you!"

"Yes. From that day on, as I lay in bed losing our child, I wished him dead," Julia admitted. "I could not tell anyone the truth, but I think everyone knew what had happened without anyone voicing their suspicions. Now I am a complete hypocrite in that I tell Miles two wrongs don't make a right. Yet what type of wife am I who wishes her husband dead?"

"Someone who wants to live?"

"Perhaps. But it does not make it the right thing to have done. Then it seemed my prayers had been answered for he died. I didn't mourn Bruce. How terrible is it to admit that? I felt relief when I was told he was dead. Relief it was over. Relief I could one day return to who I was before I met him. Maybe that change will happen, but it has not yet."

"I don't think you give yourself enough credit," Anthony said. "Miles is a well-adjusted child. He is well-mannered and intelligent. I am suspecting his attributes are down to your influence, rather than your husband's."

"Bruce went to hit him once," Julia admitted. "Not even Grandmama knows that."

234

"What happened?"

"We were in his study. He had started ranting about some issue or other, and Miles disagreed with something he had said. It was the innocent logic of a child. He was only four at the time. Bruce flew into an almighty rage, but I managed to get between them. I had grabbed a letter opener and threatened him. He laughed at me, but I think he thought I would actually attack him, so for the first and only time, he backed down. He never went near Miles again," Julia admitted.

"At least you did not have that fear."

"I meant, he did nothing with Miles. There was no contact. He ignored him completely."

"That surprises me, the way Miles talks about his father."

"A lot of his memories are ones that I have suggested to him. There were many hours of horse-riding as soon as he could walk. But once the incident happened, it was the grooms who indulged Miles, not his father," Julia explained. "But I don't want my son's memories to be bad ones. There is no benefit to it."

"No. I suppose not. Are you in touch with your husband's family?"

"Not at all. They blamed me for selling the horses, even though they knew the amount of debt that had been left. I think they wanted some of the animals because Bruce could certainly choose good horseflesh, I'll give him that. A pity they did not want to pay, just wanted them as gifts. Unfortunately, that was not an option with creditors knocking on the door. His family didn't take too kindly to my handing over the animals to be sold to pay off some of our debts."

"It must have been hell."

"It wasn't pleasant, but it was not all bad, surprisingly enough, for there was also a calmness I felt. I was no longer living in fear of being beaten almost every day. Not many would admit feeling solace when their husband suffered a fall when hunting and died as a result."

"There are probably more people for whom the death of a spouse is the means to a release from a tortuous marriage than we will ever know. No one admits it, but just think about the marriages that were arranged to join families or fortunes. In many cases those cannot have had a good start," Anthony reasoned.

"Yet mine was supposedly based on love," Julia pointed out.

"That he abused. I am sorry you suffered so. At least now you can be happier."

Julia turned away at Anthony's words.

"What is it?"

"Sometimes I feel as if everything is an act. As if I will never return to that carefree young woman I once was," Julia admitted. "I'm ashamed to admit it, but I was jealous of Miss Stock and Miss Carruthers. Not because of their beauty, albeit they are very pretty. It is their innocence, their wide-eyed anticipation of the future being perfect. Even though they probably consider themselves ladies of the world and worldly-wise."

Anthony chuckled. "Yes. I expect they do. But you are wrong to long to be who you once were. You will never be her again. You're a mother now, which will have changed you. You have seen some of life that you should not have, and you have had to deal with the trauma of losing everything. All those affect a person, but it does not mean to say that you will never be happy again," Anthony reasoned.

"As much as I'm loath to sound like a pathetic creature, I am not sure I would know what happiness is," Julia admitted.

"That makes two of us," Anthony said. "I am self-aware enough to know most emotions have passed me by for one reason or another."

Julia smiled at him. "For one who states he cannot feel anything, you respond to the trials and troubles of those around you. It is as if you cannot help reacting to our needs."

"Probably because I don't understand how to deal with my own turmoil. It is easier to focus on the others I care about. Although it is a recent development to be honest. These last few weeks have been a revelation; before then I didn't realise I cared about anyone. But today is not about me. I have talked enough about myself on many occasions. I want to know about you."

"I think you know everything," Julia said with a shrug.

"Oh, not at all," Anthony insisted. He stood and held out his hands to Julia.

Without hesitation she took them. "What are you up to now?" she asked, standing.

He faced her, holding her hands. He smiled mischievously. "I am going to fire questions at you, and I want you to answer me quickly. No thinking about your answers. You are often cautious, too considerate of others, and I want to know your true opinion on some important issues. Shall we start?"

"I am not sure I'm ready for this."

"Of course, you are," Anthony said, lifting one of her hands to his lips and kissing it. "Favourite colour?"

"Red."

"Good choice. Tea or hot chocolate?"

"Tea!"

"Of course. A lady of distinction. Jam or marmalade?"

"Jam."

"Especially strawberry, I hope. Favourite fruit?"

"Pear."

"Not apples? Favourite dance?"

"Roger de Coverley."

"Hmm. Favourite composer?"

"Handel."

"Excellent. Blonde hair or dark?"

Julia faltered a little. "Dark."

"That is good to know. Picnic or horse ride?"

Julia laughed. "Picnic."

"I knew that," Anthony said smugly. "Blue eyes or grey?"

"I don't think, I — "

"You are thinking about it," Anthony cautioned.

"Are you surprised?" Julia asked primly.

"Blue eyes or grey?"

"Grey," Julia sighed.

"I prefer brown myself," Anthony smiled and leaned a little closer. "Especially on a wife."

Julia blushed but forced herself to say what needed to be said. "I know you had informed Mr Prescott that we were engaged, but I don't hold you to a proposal made under those circumstances. You were very good that night. In fact, absolutely wonderful with how you protected me and went above and beyond what you should have done."

"I reacted poorly when you recoiled from me."

"I am sorry," Julia said. "I should have trusted you. I *do* trust you. But I reacted as if I did not. It was inexcusable."

"You were upset. I realise that now. I have to come to understand that things aren't necessarily as clear cut as I think they should be. It is something I am trying to keep in mind when I get frustrated, but it can be a struggle," Anthony admitted. "I was angry when I left you, but it was at the situation more than anything. To you it might have seemed as if my actions had a purpose, but in reality, I could not protect you as I wanted to."

"I'm not your responsibility. If my conduct caused Mr Prescott to behave inappropriately, it should not have been your duty to rescue me from that situation," Julia explained.

"I would like you to be my responsibility," Anthony admitted.

"I think we should return home," Julia said.

"You are running away from me."

"I suppose I am," she admitted. "You don't deserve to be further mistreated by me. Once more, I am sorry."

"Stop apologising. I will not keep you here any longer than you want to, but I don't think you are as unaffected by me as I feared. I would even go as far as to say you might actually like me," Anthony said.

"Are you teasing me, my Lord?"

"I think I might be."

"How things change," Julia said dryly.

"They do indeed. And I hope to change your mind about us," Anthony continued.

"Us? Is there an us?" Julia asked.

"I want there to be," Anthony admitted. "I'm going to work my damnedest to convince you that there should be an 'us'. If it takes me years to do it, I will."

"But your father's will," Julia pointed out.

Anthony leaned forward and kissed Julia gently on the lips. He was encouraged that she didn't pull away. "I have discovered that there are some things more important than money," he said gently. "I am not about to force you into a situation you are not comfortable with because of a vindictive clause in a will. If I thought you had no feelings towards me, I would leave you be. Call me vain or presumptuous, but I think you might like me as much as I like you. Because of that, I am going to win you over Mrs Price, but at your pace, not mine. Now come, I shall return you home."

They walked arm in arm to the waiting coach. The footmen sprang into action, collecting the remains of their picnic. Anthony handed Julia into the carriage, and instead of sitting opposite her, he sat next to her. He did not sit too close, but close enough to thread his fingers through hers and hold her hand the whole way home.

Chapter 23

"You said what?" Gabriel exclaimed, his breakfast fork clattering to the table, egg catapulting across the pristine tablecloth unnoticed.

"She has been through the roughest of times. I am not putting pressure on her to do something that at the moment she wouldn't be comfortable with," Anthony defended his actions.

"But your birthday is approaching!"

"I am aware of that," Anthony said with a sigh. "I have thought about this long and hard. Giles has made it clear that he is not comfortable with running the estate. I shall ask if we can live in the Dower House, and I will work for him. With a roof over our heads, the portion that is mine whether or not I marry, will be more than enough to live off. I'm not quite a pauper. Some inheritance is entailed to me."

"I realise that. And you will have my wealth, for what it is, when I die," Gabriel said.

"I would rather have you around," Anthony said honestly.

Gabriel blinked at the words. For Anthony, they were almost gushing. The simple, straightforward way they been uttered meant a lot to Gabriel. "I am glad to hear it, but one day it will happen."

"Until then, I am quite happy to be able to provide a good home and life for Mrs Price and even a horse or two for young Miles," Anthony smiled.

Gabriel leaned back in his chair. "Well I'll be," he said.

"What?"

"It has happened, hasn't it?"

"What has?" Anthony was suspicious.

"You have gone and fallen head over heels in love. I wished that you would, but I never expected that it would cost you your heritage," Gabriel said, half in wonder, half saddened.

"I have no idea what you are talking about," Anthony said dismissively. "All I know is that I cannot face being married to anyone else."

"Don't you see that is the biggest clue that you are smitten? Only she will do," Gabriel explained. "I knew she would be perfect from the moment I saw her."

Anthony rolled his eyes. "Don't start claiming credit for my wishing to marry her. It is nonsense. If we had continued the way we started, she would have hated me, and I would have thought she was a harridan."

"That was only your poor social skills causing problems. Once you were motivated, you tempered many of your foibles," Gabriel said with a smile.

Pausing for a few moments, Anthony considered Gabriel's words. "If that's the case, surely that is wrong? I would have thought we needed to be our true selves with the person we marry."

"Marriage is all about compromise. It can be nothing else when living with another," Gabriel explained with confidence. "But you will have a relationship with your wife like no other. You will tell her things that you wouldn't trust with another."

"I already have," Anthony admitted.

"In that case, she is definitely the one for you, and I am genuinely thrilled, my boy. I just wish it were not costing you so much," Gabriel said.

"I will gain far more than I lose," Anthony assured him.

With those words Gabriel was content. His grandson was in love, and as long as he had someone who adored him in return, Gabriel could be happy. Anthony would not be alone.

*

Julia had spent a sleepless night wrapped in a large warm blanket and sitting on the window seat in her bedchamber. She'd gazed out into the dark night, going over and over her feelings — what she should do and what she wanted to do.

How different she felt from when they'd first met. She'd hung back when Patience had approached Gabriel, not because of who she was being introduced to but because meeting new people meant trying harder to be happier, to seem undamaged. It had taken a lot of effort, and she didn't always have the energy for it.

But these last few weeks had caused a change in her. She'd wanted to spend time with Anthony; had looked for him at every event, every assembly. Dressing to look her best and spending time over her appearance had been two aspects of her life she'd ignored whilst with Bruce, wishing only to blend into the background so no one would notice her, especially her husband. Now it was different. She looked forward to dressing up, to appear at her best, especially when she was to see Anthony.

He was a good man. What he'd said to her must have cost him some inner qualms, but he had put her above his future. Some would say he was foolish, idiotish, even, but to her it was such a sacrifice, it touched her deeply.

Miles adored him. It wasn't the only thing to consider, but it helped. Who was she trying to fool? *She* adored him!

Her problem wasn't around Anthony; it was more to do with herself. Could she love freely once more? Abandon her insecurities and learned behaviour? She would have to if she were to give herself to him. She couldn't agree to the

243

marriage on any other terms; it wasn't fair to Anthony to do so.

Patience found Julia in the same position on the window seat but fast asleep in the morning, after being notified by the maid who had entered the room in order to light the fire. Seeing the young woman in such an unusual position, she'd backed quietly out of the room and sought out the mistress.

Patience crossed the room, and joining her granddaughter on the window seat, she gently woke Julia.

Julia smiled and stretched awkwardly when she awoke. "Oh, dear, I think I'm going to regret my sleeping position. I am terribly stiff," she said with a grimace.

"I think you should remain in bed for a while. Those dark eyes would suggest you have not had much rest," Patience said gently.

"Keeping me away from the callers, so I won't frighten them off?" Julia grimaced.

"Certainly, you could scare off the most hardened of visitors," Patience joked before becoming serious. "Have you come to any decision?"

"I change my mind so many times, I am not sure I even remember what I am supposed to be deciding on," Julia groaned.

"Whether you are going to marry a decent, handsome, rich man or not, even though he clearly loves you," Patience pointed out with a smile.

"He hasn't said that."

"His actions do."

"Seems so simple does it not?" Julia asked rhetorically.

"It can be if you let it. I think it is time for you to stop worrying about what could go wrong and enjoy everything that is right about him. Now, come; back to bed with you, my sweet."

Julia allowed herself to be guided to her bed, and although she didn't believe she would sleep again, she snuggled into the soft mattress. She was breathing the steady rhythm of a deep slumber before Patience had left the room.

*

Julia walked through the pathways in Sydney Gardens with Miles skipping along at her side. She'd slept far longer than she'd liked to have done and was left with a dull headache as a result. Needing to go outside, she'd brought Miles out for a walk they both enjoyed.

Feeling a little separate from the other promenaders, she continued to mull over Anthony's intentions.

Roused from her musings by Miles' shout of welcome, she could have groaned to see Anthony and Gabriel walking towards her. Blushing furiously, she managed to smile. It was ridiculous. She knew she would have to face him, but she wished her heart didn't beat quite so fast and her cheeks alight with flame when she did. It put her to such a disadvantage.

They exchanged their good afternoons, and Gabriel immediately turned to Miles. "I believe they have a new flavour of ice in the hotel. Do you think we could escape these two and go try some? My grandson says he doesn't like ices," he said.

"Really?" Miles looked at Anthony in astonishment.

"Just not today," Anthony said, appreciating what his grandfather was trying to do.

"Oh. May I, Mama?" Miles asked Julia.

"Of course," Julia said. "I would like to try it too."

"We will bring you some back," Gabriel said quickly.

Julia shot him a look, but it was met with an innocent smile. "Very well," she said, accepting defeat.

As they watched Miles and Gabriel's retreat to the hotel, Anthony looked a little uncomfortable. "I don't wish you to remain here, if you are not happy to. My grandfather is unsubtle most of the time, but when it is to do with me, he is especially so."

"I now know why he gets on with my grandmother. She is the same where I am concerned," Julia responded. "It is fine. Truly. It's just that I act like a foolish chit when I am around you."

"This is a recent thing," Anthony pointed out. "You were more like a fish-wife at the start of our acquaintance."

Julia half-spluttered, half-laughed. "Honesty is not always the best policy, my Lord."

"It is when it brings a smile to your lips," Anthony said. "Shall we sit? Or shall we disappear into the labyrinth and make them search for us?"

"I think sitting is best," Julia said.

They sat on the nearest empty bench, one of them looking slightly uncomfortable, one appearing hopeful but hesitant.

"Have you managed to think of what I said yesterday?" Anthony asked tentatively.

"I have thought of little else," Julia admitted.

"I am not sure if that is a good thing," Anthony responded, which brought another smile to Julia's lips.

"I am glad I am not the only one who's confused."

"I see it as a very simple question," Anthony probed. "It is whether or not you can bear to see me every day for the rest of your life, even though I am bound to make so many faux pas that you'll be cursing me to the devil regularly."

Julia smiled. "And this is you selling yourself to me?"

"I am nothing, if not honest," Anthony shrugged, trying to appear nonchalant.

"Whatever the consequences."

"Sometimes we have to go after what we want. What we need. I need you, and I think you need me," Anthony said quietly. He was desperate to touch her but couldn't. They were in far too public a place.

"You deserve someone better than me."

"But I don't think anyone would love me as much as you do."

Julia glanced at Anthony. "I love you?"

"I hope that was a statement and not a question," Anthony responded with a devilish smile that was tinged with a little uncertainty.

Julia laughed. "You are incorrigible."

"With you I can be everything."

"For someone who states he has trouble expressing himself, you are doing a fine job of being very eloquent," Julia admitted.

"Does this mean, I am convincing you?"

"The problem I have — no, *one* of the problems I have is this: If we marry soon, it could appear I've only married you for your money now that you have said you will wait for it," Julia said.

"God save me from complicated women!" Anthony groaned, putting his head into his hands.

"My Lord, sit up! You are drawing attention to yourself!" Julia hissed, mortified at the curious looks they were attracting.

"At the moment, that's the least of my worries," Anthony admitted. "I have to convince the woman I love to marry me when all she does is put up one problem after another to try to stop us being as happy as any other couple has ever been. I love you, Julia. Is that not enough?"

"It is just that there are so many hurdles to overcome. You need to understand what we have to face," Julia said.

Anthony turned to Julia, and taking her hands in his, he looked into her eyes with such intensity that Julia couldn't have moved if she'd wanted to, despite their being in the open an creating a spectacle of themselves. "I never loved anyone else, until I met you. I didn't *feel* until I met you. I am not expecting an easy life. I am prepared for trials and tribulations, but that doesn't stop me wanting you. If your way of saying no is to place reason after reason as to why we should not be together, just say you don't want to marry me. It won't hurt any less, but at least I will know where I stand."

"I am so afraid I won't be good enough for you," Julia took a breath in order to admit her biggest fear. "But more than that, I don't know if I can have further children. After the loss — "

"It does not matter," Anthony replied, squeezing her hands. "We already have a son, and with your consent, and his, I will officially adopt Miles, so he legally becomes mine. He will not get the entailed property, but he will be our son in all other aspects of our family life."

Julia squeezed Anthony's hands. "Your father was a fool for not seeing the kind of person you are," she said, moved deeply by his words.

"I used to think I took after my father, but my grandfather has recently said I take after my mother. I'm not sure how unbiased he is being, but I do realise I am different than my father. When I accepted that, it felt as if a weight had been lifted. I will never know what my mother saw in him, but I am thankful I can claim a connection to her."

"She must have been a lovely woman."

"I believe she was."

Julia took a breath. "I think you'll need to get a special licence, my Lord."

Anthony looked at her for a moment. "Are you sure?"

"Completely. I have always been sure of loving you once I came to know you, but I just did not know whether you deserved to have someone as damaged as I inflicted on you. But I have suddenly realised, I can't bear the thought of not being with you for the rest of my life. I just cannot save you from myself. Call me selfish, but I am afraid I need to be with you," Julia admitted.

Anthony let out a breath of relief. "Thank goodness for that. So, we are to marry? You're not going to change your mind?"

"Yes, we are to wed. Soon. I need a rich husband," Julia responded, archly.

"Only the best for my wife. For she is to have some difficulties to put up with," Anthony said.

"Oh?" Julia was immediately wary.

"Yes. You see, I have this overwhelming urge to show everyone, whether stranger or friend, exactly what I feel about my wife-to-be," Anthony said, before pulling Julia towards him and kissing her in the most shockingly public way.

Julia had placed her hands on his chest in an effort to push him away, but when Anthony moaned slightly when their lips touched, her hands slid around his neck instead. Pulling him to her, she kissed in a way she'd never kissed before.

It would be reported later in the Upper Assembly Rooms that Lord Lever and Mrs Price had behaved in the most indecorous way possible. Shocked looks would be shown when told that Lord Lever, in addition to brazenly kissing Mrs Price, had lifted his future wife onto his knee, as if she were some doxy. And she'd responded equally as hoydenish by laughing and running her hands through his hair.

*

Julia and Anthony were eventually interrupted by the arrival of Gabriel and Miles. Anthony clung to Julia when she tried to wriggle off his knee.

"Oh, no, you don't. I am keeping hold of you now I have you," Anthony said, with a gentle kiss.

Bruce had sometimes forced Julia to do things she hadn't wanted to, and she had a dislike of being held against her will, but somehow with Anthony's arms wrapped around her waist, all she felt was an overwhelming feeling of being secure and protected. She leaned back into him with a sigh.

"Mama?" Miles asked in confusion.

"I think your Mama and my grandson are to get married. Soon," Gabriel said with a wide smile.

"In a matter of days," Anthony confirmed. "Do you mind, Miles? You will have me as your new Papa."

Miles' eyes grew round at the news as he looked between Julia and Anthony. Just as everyone was beginning to suspect the child wasn't pleased, he broke the silence. "Does this mean I get to have my own horse?"

"Miles!" Julia chastised.

Anthony laughed. "It's a reasonable question," he said to Julia. "I think one horse to start with, but eventually I expect you will need more."

Miles flung his arms around Julia and Anthony. "Excellent! This is the best day ever!"

Epilogue

I am happy.

That is a bold statement from someone who had no idea what happiness felt like until very recently.

It is true what they say in that you don't miss something until it's gone. I did not realise how much of my insides were a dead void. A whole lot of nothingness swirling about the empty space. When the change began to happen, I was panicked and felt unprepared for it. There was some comfort in emptiness and only uncertainty with new sensations. I could not have stopped the change though — Julia started it with her teasing and compassion. It was probably within only hours of knowing her that she had started to effect the change in me.

The day that I married Julia was definitely the happiest of my life. She walked down the aisle with Patience and Miles on each side whilst I stood at the alter flanked by Giles and Gabriel. There were only the Stock and Carruthers families in attendance. Just our good, true friends. The ton would probably despair at my associating myself with 'cits', but they have accepted me for who I am, faults and all. Which is more than the aristocracy ever did.

I know what it's like to feel a frisson of anticipation before I open my eyes of a morning, knowing she is going to be there, wrapped in my embrace, for I cannot bear to be away from her for even a single night. She smiles when I utter gushing nonsense; I warn her before I say the words that she should cover her ears and sing until I spout the words I just can't hold back. Instead, she smiles with such tenderness, it makes my heart flip and increases the amount of words I feel compelled to say.

She promises to give me lines on my face. Laughter lines. I think she might achieve her aim. She says it is because I look younger than she, my complexion being line free. She ignores the deep grooves that years of constant frowning have left behind. Hearing myself laugh was strange and still is, especially when I laugh at silliness, usually involving Miles.

He spends more time with us than he does above stairs. I cannot shut a child away as I was. Julia says he will be spoiled, but I cannot separate a child from the family as was my upbringing. I am not perfectly comfortable all the time with interacting with everyone, but I will not force loneliness or separation on another human being.

Gabriel lives with us now. I see him watching me with a mixture of love and wistfulness. I am glad he is able to share his twilight years with a more communicative me. He still rails at me, but we have quieter moments in which he tells me about my mother and grandmother. I'd never asked him before in any detail, but now I want to know about my family, my history.

It is not all easy. I see Julia's expression sometimes when we are in company or when Giles or Wilfred visit. It is usually as a result of me saying something. She tries to explain that not expressing exactly what I feel is not being duplicitous but considerate of others. It's harder than it seems, but I am getting better at it. Most of the time.

Patience also lives with us. Gabriel threatens to marry her one of these days, but she warns him she will refuse. I have no idea whether or not each is funning with the other, but they seem content with their relationship as it is. I think marrying might spoil the genuine affection and respect they share, but I cannot pretend to know for certain.

Giles has settled with Nancy and is happy. They make a handsome couple and no doubt will have a large brood of children. Nancy tends to seek me out on the few occasions when we are in aristocratic circles. I don't think she'll ever feel completely comfortable in that environment, as I never did, so we stick together and try to ease the tension for the other. Giles is of an easy nature and is content to spend more time with those from Nancy's background, considerate of what makes his wife happy. He is not under my shadow in those circles — not disregarded as just a second son. He has grown as a result, and our relationship has been better since his visit to Bath. I hadn't wanted him there initially, but now I will be forever grateful he accompanied his mother.

Fanny tried to inflict her will on Wilfred, but he is of a more stubborn, forceful nature than Giles and refused to allow her to dictate to him what he should do. She had wanted to take him out of school and go abroad for a year or two with him. Wilfred completely rebelled and sought my support, which I was happy to supply. Being head of the family does hold some sway. A suggestion that Fanny might like to travel abroad with a companion has seen her settle in Switzerland, leaving the hunting lodge I'd offered to be her residence. I hear she repines of how her family has been polluted by the 'cits' in society. A pity she cannot see what joy those connected to her now feel. At least her bitterness does not affect my brothers or myself anymore.

I had thought my life was complete since my wedding, but this morning things changed once more. I didn't think my insides had room for more emotion, and it appeared they did not when Julia told me I was to be a father to another child other than Miles. Upon hearing that a new addition to the family will arrive in the autumn, my eyes filled with tears. I have never cried.

Julia wrapped me in an embrace, kissing my cheek and whispering. "I hope those are happy tears."

As I clung to her, I laughed and cried. I didn't know there was such a thing as happy tears. I now know there is.

I cannot believe I was afraid to know what it was to experience emotions. I had no idea what I was missing.

Yes. I am perfectly happy and determined to be a good, loving father to my children, for I hope there will be many.

I am no longer alone, and it is wonderful.

I feel, and it is liberating.

I love my wife and know she loves me.

I am truly happy.

The End.

About this book.

There were two real motivations that led me to start this story. The first was that most of us feel like outsiders sometimes. We all have masks we wear to hide what we're feeling, even when we are with those who love us the most. Hiding from emotions can be easier than facing or expressing them.

The other motivation was about how some people don't seem to fit in to social situations. I'm married to a man who — let's say, is very often socially awkward — and sometimes I mentally end up with my head in my hands as he speaks the truth. He should be congratulated for 'saying it as it is' but he's got into trouble over the years (particularly in his workplace!) for being brutally honest, and at home, either myself or our children can be heard saying 'why did you just say that????'

We are all expected to fit into what is considered socially normal, but the older I get, the more I can be heard saying 'embrace your weirdness'. It is what makes us individual and interesting after all. Unfortunately, society hasn't changed vastly over the last few hundred years. I read so many books and biographies about the Regency era in which people didn't quite fit there as well.

I wanted a story in which we, as readers, are privy to some of the inner turmoil from which a person can suffer. Both my characters are flawed, but one has been from the neglect he received he received and one from the environment she found herself in after marriage and finding out the true nature of her husband. The paths they were on could have continued to hurt themselves individually, but

255

people are amazing, and the ability to love can overcome any difficulties we've faced in the past.

I hope you've enjoyed Anthony and Julia's story. I think they deserved a complete happy ending. Don't you?

About the Author

I have had the fortune to live a dream. I've always wanted to write, but life got in the way as it so often does until a few years ago. Then a change in circumstance enabled me to do what I loved: sit down to write. Now writing has taken over my life, holidays being based around research, so much so that no matter where we go, my long-suffering husband says, 'And what connection to the Regency period has this building/town/garden got?'

That dream became a little more surreal when in 2018, I became an Amazon StorytellerUK Finalist with Lord Livesey's Bluestocking. A Regency Romance in the top five of an all-genre competition! It was a truly wonderful experience, I didn't expect to win, but I had a ball at the awards ceremony.

I do appreciate it when readers get in touch, especially if they love the characters as much as I do. Those first few weeks after release is a trying time; I desperately want everyone to love my characters that take months and months of work to bring to life.

If you enjoy the books please would you take the time to write a review on Amazon? Reviews are vital for an author who is just starting out, although I admit to bad ones being crushing. Selfishly I want readers to love my stories!

I can be contacted for any comments you may have, via my website:

www.audreyharrison.co.uk

or

www.facebook.com/AudreyHarrisonAuthor

Please sign-up for email/newsletter – only sent out when there is something to say!

www.audreyharrison.co.uk

You'll receive a free copy of The Unwilling Earl in mobi format for signing-up as a thank you!

Novels by Audrey Harrison
Regency Romances – newest release first

The Drummond Series:
Lady Lou the Highwayman – The Drummond Series 1
Saving Captain Drummond – The Drummond Series 2
Lord Livesey's Bluestocking (Amazon Storyteller Finalist 2018)
Return to the Regency – A Regency Time-travel novel
My Foundlings:-
The Foundling Duke – The Foundlings Book 1
The Foundling Lady – The Foundlings Book 2
Mr Bailey's Lady
The Spy Series:-
My Lord the Spy
My Earl the Spy
The Captain's Wallflower
The Four Sisters' Series:-
Rosalind – Book 1
Annabelle – Book 2
Grace – Book 3
Eleanor – Book 4
The Inconvenient Trilogy:-
The Inconvenient Ward – Book 1
The Inconvenient Wife – Book 2
The Inconvenient Companion – Book 3
The Complicated Earl
The Unwilling Earl (Novella)

Other Eras
A Very Modern Lord
Years Apart

About the Proofreader

Joan Kelley fell in love with words at about 8 months of age and has been using them and correcting them ever since. She's had a 20-year career in U.S. Army public affairs spent mostly writing: speeches for Army generals, safety publications and videos, and has had one awesome book published, *Every Day a New Adventure: Caregivers Look at Alzheimer's Disease*, a really riveting and compelling look at five patients, including her own mother. It is available through Publishamerica.com. She also edits books because she loves correcting other people's use of language. What's to say? She's good at it. She lives in a small town near Atlanta, Georgia, in the American South with one long-haired cat to whom she is allergic and her grandson to whom she is not. If you need her, you may reach her at oh1kelley@gmail.com.

50759104R00156

Made in the USA
Middletown, DE
27 June 2019